What readers are saying about
the Bloodstone Bird

"Brilliant. Absolutely magical!"
Gareth, aged 12

"This book is almost impossible to put down!"
Mia, aged 10

"A stunning array of mystery, danger and fantasy.
Not one to be missed."
George, aged 14

"A brilliant fantasy set in two worlds...
A very exciting book."
Luke, aged 12

"I give it a 10/10."
Thomas, aged 9

"A good mix of fantasy and real life."
Vicky, aged 14

The Bloodstone Bird

Inbali Iserles studied at the universities of Sussex and Cambridge and now practises as a lawyer in the City of London. Her passion for globetrotting has taken her from the depths of the Amazon Rainforest to the bubbling geysers of Iceland. Inbali lives in London with four degus – exotic rodents adopted from the RSPCA.

Her first book, *The Tygrine Cat*, won the 2008 Calderdale Children's Book of the Year Award. A chance discovery on a London street set in motion the story of her second novel, *The Bloodstone Bird*. "Nothing is what it seems," says Inbali. "While the city may look dull, adventure looms around every corner, down gloomy alleyways and even below your feet. Riddles can open secret doors – magical gateways to tropical worlds…"

You can find out more about Inbali at:
www.inbaliiserles.com

By the same author

The Tygrine Cat

the Bloodstone Bird

INBALI ISERLES

WALKER
BOOKS

This is a work of fiction. Names, characters, places and incidents are
either the product of the author's imagination or, if real, used fictitiously.

First published 2008 by Walker Books Ltd
87 Vauxhall Walk, London SE11 5HJ

2 4 6 8 10 9 7 5 3 1

Text © 2008 Inbali Iserles
Cover illustration © 2008 Phil Schramm

This book has been typeset in Weiss

Printed and bound in Great Britain by Clays Ltd, St Ives plc

British Library Cataloguing in Publication Data:
a catalogue record for this book is available from the British Library

ISBN 978-1-4063-0404-6

www.walker.co.uk

For Talinka

— Dangerous Secrets —

"In the beginning, Aqarti was a lush paradise surrounded by endless sea. It should have been the best of lands, but no one got along. The birds hated the beasts; the beasts despised the birds. Waves crashed angrily against the shore and the fish grew restless."

The old woman stopped to clear her throat. Family members sat around her on woven mats. Jonto played panpipes, filling the hut with pulsing notes. His sister, Manah, tapped a beat on a drum. Others sang quietly.

Spirals of incense rose like purple cobras. Candles flickered among blossom and bright red feathers. The light inside the hut was hazy, despite the midday heat; shutters protected the family from the glare of the outside world.

The old woman smiled. "The creatures met to decide what to do about the bitterness between them, but this just led to squabbles. 'You must stop fighting among yourselves and find harmony,' urged the wind."

"Only harmony will bring happiness!" exclaimed a young boy, repeating a phrase of the story that he, like the others, had heard many times. He clapped his hands together.

The child's mother glanced towards the door. "Hush now!" she scolded. "Remember we must keep our voices low. We do not wish anyone to hear us..."

Outside the jungle hummed with insects. Creeping foliage stirred in the breeze. High in the tree canopy, birdsong possessed the sky, drowning out sounds from the hut below. Yet the faintest melody of pipes lingered in the heat.

The old woman repeated the child's words. "Only harmony will bring happiness."

"Only harmony will bring happiness," echoed her family.

"No one really knew who, or what, this 'harmony' was," said the old woman. "No one really thought about it in their haste to find it. The strongest animals were assembled to go in search of harmony. First came Bryda, a terrifying panther. She shot through the jungle, flashing her eyes and baring her teeth. But soon she had run so hard that she had reached the shore. 'I cannot swim,' Bryda admitted. 'I can go no further.'

"So Sivan, the razor shark, was sent to hunt for harmony. He swam out beyond the coral sea and the other creatures cheered. He dived deep into the ocean until the water grew cold and airless, and not even a string of seaweed could be seen for miles around. 'There is no one here,' Sivan admitted. And so he returned home."

"Then Great Aruva went to look for harmony!" cried the child.

"I am just coming to that," said his grandmother. "Although she was not known as Great Aruva then – only Aruva." The old woman smiled, reaching the point in her story that they all liked best. "The animals were about to give up. With so much hatred between them, some already prepared for war. No one thought there was any point in looking any more. No one, that is, except the bird Aruva. She flew upwards through rainbows and into the clouds, dodging lightning, hailstorms and tropical typhoons. She flew until she reached the very limits of the sky, up to the land of the sun. 'You dare to approach me? What brings you here?' erupted the sun. 'I seek harmony,' said Aruva bravely, 'I seek the key to happiness on Aqarti.' The sun was moved that the bird sought such a noble gift…"

Manah frowned. Her fingers relaxed against the drum. Had she heard something move outside, between the twisted vines? The rustle of leaves; the gentlest of footfalls?

The old woman continued. "'I will confide in you a secret,' the sun told Aruva, 'but first you will have to fly into my very heart, into my eternal fires. And if you do, I fear you will die—'"

The flimsy door to the hut shattered and guards burst in, black figures against blinding light.

"Stop in the name of the Keeper!" bellowed a guard. Somebody screamed. People were yelling, darting towards the door. A toddler tripped over a candle and in moments flames had clawed across the woven mats and were writhing up the wall. The child wailed and cowered in the shadows.

"Come with me." Jonto beckoned, dropping the panpipes and reaching out his hand. Two guards grabbed him and yanked him back.

"Jonto!" shrieked Manah. Flames leapt to her right, the crack and hiss of burning wood mingling with cries of terror. A dark figure was rushing towards her, a guard, his hands outstretched. His bare foot snapped one of the bright red feathers.

"Get out of here, Manah!" shouted Jonto. "Find help!"

Manah spun round and bolted out of the rear door, into the jungle's endless labyrinths. She turned back, horrified. The hut was ablaze, a ball of fire rising under two great suns.

— Stuff the World —

At 7.27 a.m. the van pulled up outside 13 Gully Lane. It was a typical winter morning in London – dark, dreary, with a biting wind.

As the delivery man trudged towards the shop, he noticed that security shutters covered the windows. The yellowed CLOSED sign on the door could have been straight out of another era – from a time before cars, computers and telephones. Peering between the slats, the man caught his breath. Two small black eyes returned his gaze, unblinking. Startled, he stepped back. Above the door, the words "Stuff the World" were painted on a wooden board in old-fashioned lettering. He jabbed the buzzer with a stumpy finger.

In the flat behind the shop, Sash was making his sandwiches: thick slabs of salty, white cheese on dark bread. "Dad, there's someone at the door!"

Perhaps his father was lost in his reading. Or was he even in? Sash started down the windowless corridor that led to the study. He was forbidden from entering. "Private," his father called it. Private, nothing to do with Sash, nothing to concern himself with. Standing in the darkness, he strained his ears. Silence. A strip of hazy light glowed beneath the door. "Dad?"

The buzzer sounded again and Sash hurried into the shop.

When the front door creaked open, the delivery man hesitated. A tall, black-haired boy stood on the doorstep, looking down at him. "Yes?" said the boy, unsmiling. He blinked, brown eyes beneath dark lashes.

"Special delivery," replied the man, holding out a clipboard, a parcel cradled under his arm. He glanced inside the shop. A grizzly bear reared over the door, paws studded with barbed claws, snarling yellow fangs. The man gasped, even though he knew that the bear was no longer alive. He took a deep breath as his eyes roved to a pair of dusty otters that pounced at a trout, eternally watched by a silent raven. Suspended from the ceiling swooped a falcon, talons splayed to catch its prey. Two penguins waddled past a curious badger, under the shadow of a mounted stag's head. And could that be a real lion shaking its mane near the till at the back of the shop?

Sash signed for the parcel obediently. But as he reached out to take it, the man drew back.

"What is this place?"

Sash sighed. He had lived alone with his father behind the shop for a year. During that time, he had come to recognize the mixture of disgust and fascination on the faces of passers-by. People always reacted the same way. At least no one at school knew what his father did for a living.

"It's a taxidermy shop," said Sash.

"Stuffed animals?"

"Yes."

"What's in the parcel?" The man still cradled it protectively. He was staring into the shop, neck craned and lips slightly parted. Perhaps he had noticed the monkeys playing on a shelf, or the python that slunk towards them hungrily.

A hint of a smile crossed Sash's face. He wanted to say: "Pigs' tails. Pigs' tails, bats' ears and rats' feet." That would give the man something to think about. "Don't know," he said instead. It was the truth. But the truth was never as satisfying. Disappointed, the man shoved the parcel at Sash and returned to his van.

At 7.36 a.m. Sash went to wash the plate he had left on the dining table. The sink was full of soapy water. He glimpsed some objects gathered at the bottom. Reaching in, he lifted out a glass eye the size and weight of a marble. The eye stared at Sash, who replaced it in the sink. He rinsed the plate and stacked it against a couple of glass beakers and a set of surgical scalpels.

The kitchen doubled as his father's workshop. Half the dining table was occupied by a wooden mount, sheets of plywood, galvanized wire, a large branch broken from a horse chestnut tree and a bottle of cheap nail varnish. The subject of the work was nowhere to be seen – it was probably in one of two vast freezers that dominated the room. But Sash knew it was a bird. He could spot the telltale signs (a wooden mount, a perch cut from a branch).

It was more than that. His father rarely stuffed anything but birds these days unless by special request. In the shop, animals of all shapes and sizes greeted the rare visitors but in the flat behind it, birds cluttered the walls and populated every corner and cranny. Sash no longer noticed their feathery forms as he moved through the rooms: pheasants pecking for scraps within bell jars, mounted quails, kestrels and peacocks; whatever his father could find on his sourcing expeditions. The finest specimens adorned the mantelpiece in the cluttered living room, awaiting guests who never arrived: a toucan with an enormous beak, a pair of brightly coloured macaws. Even the bathroom was inhabited by a family of ducks and a gloomy barn owl. Only Sash's tiny bedroom was free of birds and their small glass eyes.

Sash struggled for a moment with his red and black school tie. He searched for his rucksack. It was slung over a chair on which a pelt from a weasel dangled. The weasel was one of his father's recent orders, requested by a man in Orpington who bred them. Strange pets, thought Sash. He lifted the rucksack carefully so as not to disturb the pelt and wandered down the corridor to his father's study; knocked. Silence. The strip of light beneath the door had vanished. Sash frowned, withdrawing to the kitchen.

By 7.43 a.m. he was on the street outside Stuff the World, locking the door. Gully Lane housed a string of small shops with flats hidden behind them or above them off street level. There was a rug shop, a pawnbroker's, a charity shop and the place on the corner that sold fried chicken. They were all still dark and deserted: shutters closed, blinds drawn.

Sash should have left twelve minutes ago. For a moment he considered taking the bus but there were roadworks on Highgate Road and the number 46 was on diversion. It would take him an hour to get to school by bus – too long. He would miss half of Latin and be sure to pick up a detention.

Sash tugged up the hood of his parka. He had a long walk ahead of him and it was starting to rain.

— East Heath College —

Sash hastened through the gates of East Heath College, an imposing Gothic building that looked more like a church than a school. Turrets pointed above the atrium, each bearing the school's crest: an eagle over a bridge.

East Heath College was nothing like the state school that Sash had gone to in Peterborough. At the time his father, Max Baranovski, was working for various museums and occasionally prepared stuffed animals for private sale, but with only limited success. Stuff the World was intended to change their fortunes. It had all happened so suddenly. Sash was midway through his first term of year seven when his father announced that they were moving to London. By the time that Sash was enrolled at East Heath College, his classmates had already got to know each other. He had been an outsider from the start.

Sash had been a student at the school for almost a year, but he still felt out of place as he entered the deserted atrium. Paintings of former High Masters glared down at him. "Education is a serious matter," they seemed to say. Sash paused to catch his breath beneath a wooden plaque bearing names of Heatheans who'd fallen in war. Most recently in the Gulf and Afghanistan, several in the Falklands, many in the First and Second World Wars. Other battles appeared in faded paint, older, more mysterious: the Boer War, the Crimean. Sash threw his parka on a hook, straightened his tie and went into his classroom.

Mr Mills was reciting a Latin poem in his nasal voice and didn't pause as Sash entered, although his pale eyes flicked cat-like across the room.

With relief, Sash sank into his seat at the back of the class. Perhaps Mr Mills hadn't noticed.

No such luck. "How good of you to join us, Mr Baranovski. And only seven minutes late."

"Sorry, sir," murmured Sash.

His classmates turned to look at him.

Sash bit his lip and shrank into his chair. He stared at his desk. Someone had etched a caricature of the teacher with a compass. The beaky nose was surprisingly accurate.

With a smirk, the teacher enquired: "*Quare Vergilius 'fatis' cantat?*"

Sash glanced up. He hated Latin, would never get the hang of it. He had begged his father to let him sit out the class.

"Don't you want the benefits of a classical education?" his father had demanded.

Not really, Sash had thought. But there was no point trying to reason with Max Baranovski.

"Do you have any idea how much I'm paying for you to attend this school?"

Actually, Sash did know. His father had mentioned the fees more than once. "I didn't ask to go there! I'd be fine at a comp."

"My only son! I want what's best for you. I want you to have all the advantages that I never had. What I wouldn't have done at your age to have gone to a school like that!"

"I know..." Sash had been keen to avoid another lecture on the hardships of growing up in a poor Russian village on the outskirts of Moscow.

"If you sit out the class you'll be a laughing stock," his father had warned him.

Mr Mills was standing in front of the whiteboard. He leant his hand against it and tapped his fingers with exaggerated impatience.

Sash replied to the teacher in faltering Latin.

The classroom exploded.

"For heaven's sake, Baranovski, if you can't keep up you will be excluded," snapped Mr Mills.

Sash felt his cheeks redden. His father had forced him to take Latin and now he was a laughing stock anyway. Not that this was new. The students here seemed to delight in mocking him: too tall, too quiet, too common. It had been different at his school in Peterborough. If someone didn't like you there, they'd corner you in the corridor. Fights were frequent. People soon learned that Sash Baranovski gave as good as he got. That didn't stop his father from wringing his hands in despair when Sash came home with a black eye or swollen lip. "This boy has a temper," his report card confirmed. Another reason to move to London, Max Baranovski had said.

Sash watched the clock above the whiteboard. It felt as though time was spinning backwards. He noticed Verity Tattersall whispering with her friend Camilla Asquith. Verity Tattersall: blonde, pretty, clever and (from what Sash had overheard) impossibly rich.

Verity caught him looking at her and scowled disapprovingly.

"Nice one, Baron Oiksky," sneered a short, stocky boy, who sat several desks away, James Goodwin-Black. Grandson of former Minister of Trade, Sir Charles Goodwin-Black. Someone else burped loudly and others laughed.

Sash focused on his desk. His right hand gripped his left, the knuckles white, waiting for the attention to pass. Maybe he could talk to his father about leaving East Heath College. If Max was in a good mood tonight Sash could bring up the idea of attending the local comprehensive. He didn't care how rough it was or how many students there were to a class; the more the better – it was easier to lose yourself in a crowd. The thought comforted Sash, although he knew in reality he wouldn't say anything. His father would ask him how his day had been and he'd say, "Fine."

"Did you learn anything?" his father would enquire and Sash would nod. Max never asked what, and Sash never volunteered.

At lunch Sash sat outside by the playing fields, hunched within his parka, eating the sandwiches he had made that morning. He stayed away from the noisy canteen with its sloppy lasagnes and sickly rice puddings. Outside the air was clearer and Sash could eat in peace. He hardly noticed the boys practising rugby on the damp grass, only half hearing their war cries as they charged towards the ball. Sash had avoided team sports at his previous school and Mr Healy, Head of Games at East Heath College, had granted him permission to run rather than play rugby or cricket. He loved long-distance running, never finding it boring or lonely.

A gaggle of girls led by Verity Tattersall passed on their way to the atrium.

"Tell us more about Costa Rica!"

"It must have been amazing!"

"You are *so* tanned!"

"Am I really?" replied Verity. "Oh, it was so wonderful. I surfed the whole time. It's the best surf in the universe! And we stayed on the most beautiful beach! Did I tell you that our hotel had three swimming pools?"

They ignored Sash as they drifted past him. He threw the remainder of his sandwich to a waiting pigeon and headed inside.

The first class after lunch was Maths, Sash's favourite. He enjoyed solving problems and he liked his teacher, a young woman called Miss Freeman who wasn't stuffy and didn't talk down to the students like the others. He entered the empty classroom before the bell to read through his homework.

"Can I talk to you a moment? It's important."

Sash looked up with a start. He hadn't heard anyone come in behind him. He turned in his chair to see Verity and the girls who had been with her outside. A short distance away stood James Goodwin-Black with Angus Slaughter, a ruddy-cheeked boy with freckles and carrot-red hair. Sash tensed.

Verity had spoken.

"What is it?" he asked uncertainly.

Verity smiled at him. She had an unusually pretty face and Sash relaxed a little and almost forgot that James was there. They had been in the same class for a year and Sash couldn't remember her ever having addressed him.

"Well, people have been asking… Why is it that you have a girl's name?"

The others burst out laughing. Sash felt a jolt in his stomach, as though she had jabbed him with one of his father's taxidermy scalpels. He swallowed and stared back blankly. He'd heard it before of course, but somehow coming from Verity it felt worse.

James high-fived Angus. Two of the girls giggled but Verity continued to watch Sash, waiting for him to respond. Her face remained composed, even pleasant.

"It's short for Aleksandr," offered Sash weakly. "It's Russian."

"Are you Russian?" asked Lucy, a snub-nosed girl.

"My dad is."

"Where's your mother from?" said Angus.

"She... She's English."

"So what does that make you?" asked Verity.

"I know what it makes him," sneered James. He and Angus stepped closer to Sash's desk. They loomed above him. Behind them, Sash noticed three other boys enter the classroom and approach curiously.

Don't get angry, he thought. Don't get angry, don't look at them and don't say anything. They'll get bored. He focused on the desk. Today was turning out to be worse than normal. Sash was used to being ignored. Being ignored was far preferable to this kind of attention. If only he hadn't been late for Mr Mills's class. If only the delivery man hadn't called. If only his father had signed for the parcel. Where had he been, anyway? There had definitely been light under the study door. There one minute, gone the next...

Taking his cue from James, Angus joined in. *"Baron Oiksky,*

Goodwin-Black is talking to you! Hasn't your English mother taught you any manners?"

James drank noisily from a can of Coke, making unpleasant sucking sounds.

Sash shut his eyes. He was going to ignore the comment about his mother. If he rose to it, more would follow. All the same, he could feel his muscles tensing.

"He's not from round here, is he, Slaughter? Do you suppose he knows about the drains?"

"Well, I'm not sure that he does. Maybe we should tell him?"

"Maybe we should. They run right beneath the school, you see, and they're deep as anything! Isn't that right, Slaughter?"

Sash hated the way they referred to each other by surname. There was something unnerving about it. James and the other boys had closed in around him. Verity and her friends hung back, watching a short distance away and whispering behind their hands. Sash felt an acid taste in his throat. His hands formed fists beneath the desk. He remembered his report card from Peterborough: "This boy has a temper." No: he wasn't going to rise to it. He wasn't going to get into a fight.

"Didn't someone drown down there?" offered Angus.

"That's right, Slaughter. A careless caretaker fell into the drainage system and was never seen again. Wouldn't want to end up there, Baron Olksky."

Sash had heard about the caretaker. The man had been an ogre. He had worked at the school years ago and was said to have drowned in the drains. Sash doubted it was true. He'd probably had enough of this place and taken the first train out, he thought: that's what I'd do if I could.

"Are you paying attention, Oik?" said James. "We're trying to help you!"

"Goodwin-Black's giving you top advice," Angus put in. "You should watch your back. I'm not saying that you'll come to harm but … you know … accidents happen." He leant over Sash's desk.

James took his cue. "You might find yourself in trouble, just like that careless caretaker. Doesn't do to be careless. Whoops!" James tipped his Coke over Sash's homework.

Sash snapped, leaping from his desk, the chair legs screeching. He was a good head taller than James and in moments he had thrown him up against the wall.

"Calm down! I was only fooling around!" James bleated.

The others watched, frozen. Sash let go. James stumbled, backed away.

Sash returned to his homework. It was ruined. He had worked on it for hours. For a second or two, he wanted to howl with rage. He took a deep breath, swallowed, picked up the sodden papers by the corner and threw them in the bin, just as Miss Freeman entered the classroom.

She took in Sash's harrowed appearance, the disordered desk and the group of students near by, James smoothing back his ruffled hair. "What's going on?" she asked.

Silence.

"Sash, are you OK?"

"Yes," he replied, eyes downcast, moving back towards his desk. He couldn't bear the look of concern on her face. His thoughts leapt furiously to his father. Dad made me come to this stupid school; he made me take Latin; he made me late. *I hate him.*

Miss Freeman glanced in the bin. "What did you throw away just now?"

"Nothing, miss."

The teacher opened her mouth to say something but at that moment the bell sounded and the room was flooded with students.

I'm never coming back to this school, thought Sash. I don't care what anyone says. I'll run away. I'll get a job. I'll do *anything*.

After class, students gathered noisily in the atrium, tossing school bags, play fighting and joking. Sash moved invisibly between them. He spotted James and Angus bearing down on a small year seven boy, forcing him to empty his pockets. Obediently, the boy held out a Snickers bar.

"Bloody hell. Haven't you got a phone or something?" Angus complained.

The boy shook his head, putting the Snickers back in his pocket,

"Not so fast!" James swiped it and tore off the wrapper. "Next time you'd better be carrying more than chocolate," he said with contempt, stuffing the Snickers in his mouth. Spotting Sash, he smiled menacingly, chocolate and peanut caking his teeth.

Sash looked away. He knew that his outburst would not go unpunished. He had humiliated James and he would pay for it. Let them try, thought Sash angrily. For a moment, he lost himself in a delicious thought: a world without classmates who called each other by surname. A world without the school bell; without teachers; without Latin. A world without rules.

It was 4.15 p.m. and already London was growing dark. Sash started the long journey from East Heath Road to Gully Lane. Taking a shortcut through Pond Rise, he glanced at handsome Victorian houses that rose enticingly beyond manicured front gardens. He thought of sofas that weren't frayed at the edges, of central heating that didn't pack up at the first sign of frost. He could only imagine the lavish sitting rooms and endless bedrooms, the hi-tech sound systems, DVD players, PlayStations and plasma screens. Living somewhere like that must be like living in a dream.

As he reached the corner of Pond Rise, Sash noticed a girl in a red and black striped scarf – East Heath College colours. She meandered down a tree-lined drive past two silver Mercedes, which glittered in the fading light. A smiling blonde woman threw open the front door, one hand lost

28

inside an oven glove. Sash thought he could smell freshly baked biscuits cooling in the kitchen: a hint of cinnamon, a trace of nutmeg.

As though sensing his eyes on her, the girl paused on the doorstep, turning to gaze in Sash's direction. Verity Tattersall. The scalpel-jolt he had felt when Verity laughed at him suddenly returned. He set his jaw. He would never trust that girl. Not as long as he lived.

— Fish and Chips —

As Hampstead turned to Gospel Oak, detached Victorian houses gave way to terraces and council developments. Sash made his way down Highgate Road into Kentish Town. At the junction of Highgate Road and Fortess Road, four lanes of traffic funnelled into two. Armies of cyclists wove between grumbling cars. Gridlocked and impatient, the cars inched forward, their fumes lapping at Sash's feet in murky gusts.

A group of students from the local comprehensive had gathered at the corner of Gully Lane, outside the shop selling fried chicken. Sash watched as they chatted amiably. He cursed his unzipped parka – if they turned now they would see his blazer and stripy tie. Any move to conceal them would invite attention. He stared at the ground, willing the students to ignore him. He almost succeeded. They seemed too absorbed in themselves to notice Sash. But just as he had passed them, someone muttered something. Sash heard the word "posh" but not the rest, followed by a high-pitched cackle. He hurried along the street, pausing before Stuff the World. He didn't want to be seen entering. Cautiously, he glanced back. A boy was entertaining the others with an impression from a film he'd seen. Sash was already forgotten.

Inside the shop, Max Baranovski was preparing a stuffed squirrel for the post. He held it carefully between narrow fingers and smoothed down the fur on its forehead with a toothbrush. A woman's voice soared from the old tape player at the back of the shop, singing an aria from an opera. Max liked to listen to classical music as he worked. Despite practising an art that was often messy and involved the use of chemicals, he was immaculately dressed in his ironed white shirt and navy tie. Wire spectacles balanced on the tip of his nose. "See this. The trick is not to over-preen. The taxidermist always wants the perfect specimen, but nature is imperfect. Fur is sometimes ruffled, twitching and shifting in response to muscle tension beneath the skin." He looked up. "My boy, how was school?"

"Fine."

Max held up the squirrel for his son's inspection.

"Pretty good," said Sash.

"Pretty good?" Max raised his bushy eyebrows. "Have you ever seen a more convincing animal?"

Sash had seen a live squirrel on his way home, swaying

on the branch of a tree and watching him mischievously. Of course, it wouldn't do to say so. "It's very realistic."

"Yes. And it's not just *any* squirrel either: it is *this* squirrel, this squirrel alone. An old one, long in the tooth you might say. That is the secret of great taxidermy. Referencing. Do you think I made it up as I went along? Or simply checked a photograph of a young squirrel in a book? If someone built a model from a photograph of me as a boy, would it look like me today? No. I set out half a dozen photographs of this species, adult females, all of them, each in different poses. Reference everything, that's the only way." He put down the squirrel and examined it critically.

"No two animals are the same," said Sash.

Suddenly, unexpectedly, Max smiled. "My clever son!" he exclaimed. "Let's do something nice for dinner. You work so hard at school, you deserve a treat."

Sash bit his lip. The mention of East Heath College brought his problems flooding back. "Dad, about school…"

The opera singer hit a high note. The old tape player crackled grudgingly.

"Ah!" Max clicked his fingers. "We'll pick up some fish and chips and have a TV dinner! There's a documentary on migratory birds tonight. How does that sound?"

Sash smiled with what energy he could muster. His father was in a good mood and he didn't want to spoil it. He made his way towards the door at the back of the shop that led to their flat. As he passed his father, Max patted him on the back. "That's my boy!" he said warmly.

Sash sloped into the kitchen. He set down his rucksack on a chair and leant against the table a moment, wondering what he should do about school. Of course, there was nothing to be done, it was a fact of life. He peered down the darkened corridor towards his father's study. What *does* he do in there? Why aren't I allowed in? wondered Sash. On a whim, he hurried down the corridor before he allowed himself to think of the consequences. His hand closed decisively over the door handle.

"I need some meths!" called Max. Sash recoiled, heart thumping, diving back into the kitchen just as his father burst in through the shop. "Did you hear me? I need some methylated spirits, you will go to the shop and get some?"

Sash nodded, but didn't trust his voice.

Max frowned. "What are you up to?" His eyes darted towards the darkened corridor and back at his son suspiciously.

Sash stared at the peeling linoleum. He could feel his father's eyes boring into him. For a moment, Sash felt the urge to ask him about the study – to demand to see it, even. Why all the secrecy? He stole a glance at his father. Max's bushy black eyebrows knitted over his eyes. The moment passed and Sash looked away.

"Here." Max pressed a ten-pound note into Sash's hand. "Get a big bottle. And pick up the fish and chips on your way back. Haddock for me, plenty of vinegar."

* * *

Sash and Max watched the documentary in silence, plates balanced on laps. Max didn't like anything to interrupt his viewing. Sitting forward on the battered armchair, he ate his meal with a knife and fork. On the mantelpiece, the toucan and macaws stared on endlessly. Between them rested two photographs. The first was a five-year-old Sash, smiling shyly at the camera. The second was a young woman in a small, silver frame, never looked at nor talked about: Susanna Drake from Hampshire, several weeks before she married a young Russian student called Maxim Baranovski.

Two Victorian prints of tropical birds stared down from the wall in their dark, wooden frames. Max had found the prints at a car boot sale. They were oddly technical, as if they had once formed part of a reference book on bird species, and they bore Latin names, printed beneath the images in block capitals: TROGON MEXICANUS; TROGON TEMNURUS. Next to them was a ceremonial mask covered in feathers that a friend had sent Max from Papua New Guinea.

Sash picked at his chips despondently, mulling over his day. James had been humiliated in front of their classmates and was almost certain to seek revenge. He might have forgotten by tomorrow, of course, but Sash knew that was unlikely. He had been teased by James before but he had managed to keep his temper. Now that he'd lost it, things were bound to get worse. He would just have to put up with it.

On the television screen, dozens of green bee-eaters flew

34

in formation across the Jordan Valley and into the heart of the Negev Desert. Surfing the air currents they brought noise and colour to the arid land. A single bird darted ahead, leading with instinctive assurance. Towards the rear the formation frayed. Sash noticed a solitary bird drift apart from the flock to hover alone over the desert. Do they ever get lost? he wondered.

The gap between the bird and its flock expanded rapidly. Soon the others were far ahead. Sash blinked at the screen. The stray bird had fluttered into a bank of cloud. Sash sat up. Soggy chips scattered around his feet.

"For heaven's sake!" snapped Max. "Can't you do anything right?"

Sash scooped the ruined chips onto his plate. He glared at his father. He wanted to say something cutting, to stamp his feet, to shout. But Max had already turned back to the television and was watching intently.

Pushing his plate away, Sash said nothing.

— A Wish in the Night —

Dark bodies flitted between the tall trees of the jungle, diving over Manah's head. Not birds: bats. Gasping for breath, she knelt on the damp ground. Shivers of red sky glistered between black branches. Gazing up at them, Manah found the moon.

She had been running for hours, fleeing the guards. When she blinked, she still saw the hut devoured by flames and thought of her brother, Jonto, and the others she had left behind. She tried to stay calm, to plan her next move. Breathing more evenly, she squinted at the ground, clearing away stray twigs and throwing them aside. She tugged up her hood and reached inside the folds of her dress where she had tucked a handful of flowers and some gorpi berries. The flowers had wilted and the berries were squishy, but it was better than nothing. She placed them in front of her, except for some loose petals, which she rubbed gently between her fingertips.

Shutting her eyes and inhaling the sweet smell of the crushed petals, Manah started to sing. She sang to Great Aruva, the bird that discovered the secret of harmony and split the sun in two.

"Deliver us a warrior," she sang. "Let him be tall and strong; let him be noble and wise. Bring him to me, I will help him: he will stop the Keeper – he will return to us the land we used to know." She pictured her brother, Jonto, and her voice quivered. But she didn't cry. There was no time for tears. Great Aruva would find the warrior, she told herself. She would send him. She would—

Manah sucked in her breath. She had heard something – *someone* – creeping through the undergrowth. She reached for her dagger.

— Old School Rules —

Sash's first class the next day was Physics, where he resolved to keep a low profile. He was both relieved and unnerved to find the students oddly subdued. Even James and Angus said nothing, staring ahead indifferently as Sash took his seat.

Dr Clifton was pacing the room, clutching a marker pen.

"As you will remember, last week we spoke about tides. Lucy, would you like to remind the class what a 'tide' is?"

Snub-nosed Lucy sat up in her chair. "A tide is the rise or fall in sea level caused by the moon or the sun."

"Marvellous," said the teacher. "Yes, the periodic rise and fall of large bodies of water with respect to the land, caused by the sun and moon, by their gravitational pull. This week, we're going to talk about eclipses so I hope you've done your homework!" He went to the whiteboard and started drawing circular objects in formation: the earth, the moon and the sun. "An eclipse occurs when one celestial body moves into the shadow of another. In a full lunar eclipse, the moon seems to disappear – to vanish from the night sky. Would anyone like to explain how an eclipse of the moon comes about?"

"Clouds?" offered Piers, a portly boy who for reasons unknown always sat near the door.

"Not clouds. Remember what I told you – an eclipse occurs when the object, the celestial body, falls under the shadow of another celestial body. So the moon is in shadow, that's why it seems to disappear."

"From a comet?"

"A nice idea, Duncan, but no."

Sash knew the answer. A lunar eclipse took place when the moon fell under the shadow of the earth. But the last thing he wanted was to draw attention to himself, so, as usual, he sat in silence.

Verity raised her hand.

"Yes?"

Her cut-glass voice rang through the classroom. "The moon seems to disappear because it's in the earth's shadow."

"Excellent, Verity," said Dr Clifton.

Sash took a quick look in her direction. She was leaning forward, blonde hair tumbling down her back, smiling sweetly at the teacher.

"And a solar eclipse?" the teacher enquired.

"That's the same thing, only the sun is in the earth's shadow rather than the moon," replied Verity with self-satisfaction.

That's wrong, thought Sash.

"And what light would be falling on the earth to cast the shadow?" asked Dr Clifton.

For the briefest moment, Verity's face closed into a scowl but she quickly regained her composure.

The teacher turned and paced between the desks. "Would anyone else like to have a go? Mr Slaughter?"

Angus had been scribbling something on his notebook – something unrelated to astronomy, Sash presumed.

"W-what's that?" Angus stuttered.

"Not 'what', 'pardon'," corrected Dr Clifton. "I was asking you whether you could explain a solar eclipse."

"It's when the sun disappears in the middle of the day," offered Angus.

Several of his classmates tittered.

"When the sun *appears* to disappear. And we already know that, Angus. I was venturing to establish whether you understood *why* a solar eclipse comes about."

"Sorry, sir..."

"How about you, Sash?"

Sash hesitated, glancing at James who pulled an ugly face. "It's ... it's when the moon gets between the sun and the earth. It sort of looks like the sun's been wiped out for a few minutes, until the moon's passed and the sun appears behind it. It's not really an eclipse though, not in the proper sense." His voice felt disconnected from his body, as though someone else was speaking. He cleared his throat.

"No? And why's that?"

Sash stole a look at the teacher. Dr Clifton was rolling back and forth from the heels to the balls of his feet, smiling expectantly.

"I guess..." Sash swallowed. His throat was dry. "I guess you could say that an eclipse of the sun is an optical illusion that happens when the object nearest to us on earth, the moon, seems much larger than it is and completely hides the more distant object, the sun, which is obviously much larger in reality. The shadow over the earth is still that of the moon, not the sun. I don't see how the sun could have a shadow..." It was the most that Sash had ever said in class. He bit his lip, feeling heady and breathless.

"Yes, a perfect explanation," declared Dr Clifton, clapping his hands together and nodding enthusiastically. He started to wander again between the chairs, smiling broadly to reveal smoke-yellowed teeth.

Sash sighed and relaxed into his seat.

Verity blinked at him curiously, as though seeing him for the first time.

"Filthy know-it-all," muttered James under his breath. "We're going to get you, creep."

"James, did you have something to add?" asked the teacher, still smiling and nodding absently.

"No, sir," James replied.

A growing menace developed during double French and lingered through Geography. Sash caught James and Angus exchanging looks, whispering and pointing in his direction. He examined door handles carefully before turning them, held onto his rucksack protectively and never let his notebooks out of his sight. And yet Sash had the feeling that a plan against him was hatching and that despite his vigilance he would be unable to stop it.

After lunch, Sash made his way to the changing rooms for Games. Other boys snickered as he entered. Sash ignored them and pulled on his running gear. Shaking away the cold, he jogged out of the changing rooms and headed across the playing fields towards the track. He passed the girls' hockey team and was intercepted by one of the sports instructors, Mr Greene, a hairy, thickly built man who reminded Sash of a gorilla.

"Good of you to volunteer for rugger today, Baranovski. Grab some spare boots and join us for the warm ups. Hurry!" he added as Sash blinked at him, confused.

"I ... I run," offered Sash. From the corner of his eye, he could see James and some other boys watching and sneering.

"Not today. Don't be dozy, Baranovski. Slaughter's hurt his ankle and we're one man down. Competing against St Paul's in a few weeks, need to keep in training. Slaughter tells me you stepped into the breach. Good of you."

Sash glanced at Angus Slaughter, who was sitting on a nearby bench. Angus pointed to his ankle and shrugged.

"But I don't know the rules," said Sash.

"The laws," Mr Greene corrected. "Pretty straightforward object: score as many points as possible! You'll pick up the rest soon enough."

"I can't play rugby," Sash protested weakly.

"Nonsense! Anyway, we won't go into a full game, just work on the finer points: tackles, line-out and the scrum, to be precise. As you'll be aware, Mr Slaughter's our top lock, winning balls in the line-out. That'll be your job today. You're pretty tall, you can jump. You're on the narrow side, but you'll do. Just try not to hurt yourself." Mr Greene gave Sash a friendly smack on the shoulder.

Sash stood still, shaking his head. There must have been a misunderstanding. "But Mr Healy said..."

"I know about your running arrangement but taking part this once won't kill you. Do you good to show some team spirit. Chop, chop, Baranovski, and wipe that gormless look off your face. We're losing training time. Throw on some boots and let's get cracking!"

So that was their plan, Sash realized grimly. He went into the changing rooms and dug out a pair of old rugby boots from the shoe bin. They were too small and pinched his toes but they were the best he could find. With a sense of dread he returned to the pitch where the teacher was already leading the boys in a series of jumping jacks.

After the warm up, Mr Greene blew the whistle and the boys took their places. "Between the props, over there, Baranovski!" he yelled, directing Sash to Angus's usual position.

James smirked. "Old school rules," he whispered. "Can you take it like a man?"

Mr Greene blew the whistle again and before Sash knew what was happening, Colin Williams, an enormous boy with bulldozer shoulders, was bounding straight at him with the ball in hand, others in pursuit.

"Tackle him!" shouted Mr Greene.

Sash stiffened and stretched out his arms.

"This is for Goodwin-Black," spat Colin as he drove his shoulder into Sash's chest. Sash yelped and gave way.

"Stop him!" cried Mr Greene, oblivious to the injury.

Sash spun round only to smack into another boy.

"Clumsy idiot!"

"Sorry," Sash murmured. He wanted the action to wash past him.

But Mr Greene had blown the whistle. "Knock on."

"Scrum!" yelled James delightedly. He gripped Sash's legs with sweaty hands and other boys huddled round. Sash was trapped between them, amid anonymous arms and legs in a shifting, grunting mass of boys. As Mr Greene blew the whistle again, Sash felt himself sinking under James's weight.

"Baranovski, try to hook the ball with your foot!" instructed the teacher.

They scrummed down again, but this time the front rows collapsed in an untidy heap, taking Sash and the other locks with them. Sash felt a knee sink into his ribs. It was no accident.

The whistle blew again. "Penalty!" yelled Mr Greene, indicating that Sash's team had possession.

"Catch!" someone shouted and the ball flew in Sash's direction. He grabbed for it and went down, others piling on top of him, boots digging into his shins and elbows in his back.

"Release the ball!" barked Mr Greene and Sash let go of it immediately. Others grappled to ruck it backwards with their boots, trampling over him.

"Careful!" shouted Mr Greene. "Play the ball, not the man!" But he didn't stop play. He had been distracted by Angus, who had hobbled over to him and was talking in inaudible tones, pointing towards the changing rooms.

A moment later someone thumped Sash on the back of the head so hard that he lurched face-down, taking in a mouthful of mud. Scrambling to his feet, he noticed Angus wink at James and stalk back towards the changing rooms. He wasn't limping.

An hour and a half later Sash stumbled across the playing

45

fields, filthy and exhausted. A hockey game was in session. Mrs Abbot was shrieking instructions at the girls: "Olive, tackle her! *For heaven's sake tackle!* Come *on*, Camilla's wide open!"

Sash shuffled past them without looking up. Bruises were rising along his back and a cut under his chin was bleeding. His muscles throbbed; by tomorrow he would scarcely be able to walk.

Near the entrance to the girls' changing rooms, Sash saw Verity pacing in her hockey kit, clutching a mobile phone.

"No, Mummy, please don't… You have to try again, you just have to," she whimpered. "I'll do anything, I'll help, please let me help… How can you say that? It has everything to do with me! Couldn't you just think about it, please, Mummy?" As Sash approached, she looked up and their eyes met for a moment. Verity's were puffy and red-ringed. "I've got to go," she whispered into the phone before snapping it shut and disappearing into the changing rooms.

Sash showered only after the other boys had finished. It meant he would be late for History and he'd probably collect a detention or some extra homework, but it was better than spending any more time with them. He buttoned his shirt and pulled on his tie. Reaching for his blazer, Sash noticed a strip of frayed fabric. Someone had torn off the school badge in haste, leaving a yawning hole. Sash gripped the blazer, knuckles white, dizzy with rage. Angus, it had to have been, he was the only boy to have sat out Games. The thought of History with the same classmates was suddenly unbearable. His mood black, Sash scrunched the blazer into his rucksack, threw on his parka and started the long walk home.

Max Baranovski was rearranging the window display when Sash appeared.

"You're early."

"Last class was cancelled," Sash lied, moving quickly past his father towards the flat beyond the shop. He was halfway through the door when his father called after him.

"Stop!"

Sash halted in the doorway. "What?"

"'What?'" echoed Max. "Come back here."

Reluctantly, Sash turned round.

"Your face, what happened?"

"Rugby happened."

"Where's your blazer?"

Sash started, touched his chest. With a surge of frustration, he realized that his parka was again unzipped, revealing only his shirt and tie. His father was like a hawk. He missed nothing.

"It's... I left it at school."

"You are telling me the truth, Aleksandr?"

Involuntarily, Sash looked at his rucksack.

Max narrowed his eyes, black brows furrowing over them. "Show me."

Sash sighed and placed the rucksack on the counter next to the till. His father would find out anyway, he would root out the truth sooner or later. Sash was too tired to conjure excuses.

"Mind the canary!"

"I see it." Sash lifted the stuffed yellow bird and placed it on a nearby shelf next to a chameleon – a lizard that, in life, could change its colour to hide itself from predators. Sash wished for a moment that he was a chameleon as he returned to his rucksack, unzipped it and drew out the crumpled blazer.

Max seized the blazer and held it to the light, taking in the torn fabric. Turning it over, he gasped at the tattered lining. "What on earth did you do to it?" he bellowed.

"It got torn."

"I can see that! You've been in a fight again, haven't you? I send you to one of the best schools in London and still you think with your fists!" Max's dark eyes drilled into his son, furious and implacable. "Why, Aleksandr? Why can't you control your temper?"

"I wasn't in a fight."

"Oh really? So how do you explain this?" Max shook the blazer under Sash's nose.

Sash shrugged.

"You careless, selfish boy! Have you any idea how expensive your uniform is? Do you know how much I pay for your school fees? It's not as though you have a scholarship, is it? That bursary from the school does next to nothing. It all comes out of my pocket. Do I look like a rich man to you? Do you think you can ruin your clothes and I'll just buy you more?"

"No," mumbled Sash, eyes downcast.

"I despair of you! Useless boy! Haven't you a single word to say for yourself?"

Sash set his jaw. This is your fault, he thought. If you didn't send me to that stupid school I'd be OK. I was managing in Peterborough, I was getting on just fine. Now everything's wrong, and it'll always be wrong! He shook his head and bit his lip.

Max sighed. His voice softened. "I'm worried about you, Sasha. What's going on?"

"I've told you not to call me that! It's a girl's name!" he hissed, swallowing an acid taste in his throat. "'Sash' is bad enough. Just leave me alone! Everything's fine. *Everything's just perfect.*"

"Don't take that tone with me, boy!" snapped Max, his anger flaring again. "Go on, get out of my sight!"

Sash grabbed his rucksack and headed for the flat, shuddering as the door slammed behind him. A crumpled note fluttered from the open rucksack to the floor – an invitation for his father to attend East Heath College parents' evening. It had languished in Sash's rucksack for days, forgotten. He tossed the note onto the dining table and stood still for several seconds, at a loss. His eyes filled with tears that he furiously rubbed away. *Useless boy.* That's what his father had called him. *It's not as though you have a scholarship, is it?* Good enough to pass the entrance exam but not good enough to merit financial assistance. *Can't you do anything right?*

Sash punched the dining table, which groaned beneath his fist. His cheeks burned red and he felt as though he would explode. Thoughts raged through him: I'm not good enough for Dad and never have been... He doesn't listen... He's not normal, he's weird, not like the other dads... It's like he's from another planet! He spends all day stuffing animals or hiding away in that study of his... Sash caught his breath and jerked his head towards the darkened corridor. That study of his... The glass eyes of Max's numerous stuffed birds drove into him, seemed to question him, his father's army of silent spies.

But why can't I go in there? thought Sash defiantly. I'm practically an adult! He treats me like a baby. I'm sick of it! With resolve, Sash hurried down the corridor to his father's study and threw open the door.

The curtains were closed and it took several seconds for his eyes to adapt to the dull light that seemed to dust the room in a fine coat of charcoal. Before him was a desk cluttered with notebooks, pamphlets and magazines. Underneath them, Sash glimpsed the corner of Max's laptop and behind it a printer stacked with paper. Next to the laptop was a chipped mug crammed with biros, pencils and assorted feathers. Above the desk, a wall calendar called "Birds of the World" had been annotated with Max's spidery handwriting. Next to some dates, Max had written the letter "B", next to others, "C" and by the remainder, "H". The "Bs" were circled with red pen. In the boxes next to certain dates (all past, Sash noticed), Max had scribbled further comments, sometimes in Russian Cyrillic script and sometimes in English: "swell", "непроходимый" and "rapid". He knew to pronounce the Russian word "ner-poho-dimyi" but he wasn't sure what it meant.

To the right of the desk was a shelf piled with dog-eared magazines and a brochure advertising boating holidays. Sash noted this with surprise – since when had his father been interested in boating? Next to the brochure, a jar that once held gherkins had been filled with a clear liquid, perhaps formaldehyde, and something resembling a knot of white fabric was floating inside it. Sash reached for the jar to take a closer look. With revulsion, he realized that the floating object was a gosling, only a day or two old. It was naked but for a few stumpy feathers at the base of its wings and a tuft of down on its forehead. An unknown term in its watery prison had drained the baby goose of colour. The beak seemed misshapen and smiled at Sash ghoulishly. The swirling liquid in the jar caused the gosling to sway, as if dancing to some unknown music.

Sash shoved the jar back onto the shelf. Can't Dad just

be normal? he thought with a wave of despair. Can't he be a postman, a lawyer, a bus driver, or work behind the counter of a bank?

His eyes roved across the room. In the far corner sat an oak trunk with a rusted metal lock. On top of it, Sash spied a leather-bound book. It looked ancient. From the doorway, he could just make out the title: *Waterways* by someone called Arundel Sanderson. Next to the book was a large torch and what appeared to be a compass.

Sash took a step towards the trunk but paused as the floorboards beneath him sighed. Carefully, he shifted the pressure onto his back foot and glanced over his shoulder. No sign of his father. Turning back to the desk, his eyes fell on a map. Sash lifted it carefully. The print was tiny and he had to strain to read it. Some of the place names were unfamiliar: Falcon, Frith's Illicit Sewer, Tyburn Road. Even so, Sash was in no doubt as to the location: with its snaking central river and the open spaces of Parliament Hill, Regent's Park and Battersea, it could only be London. A diagonal line had been drawn across the page from Hampstead in north London down to Blackfriars Bridge in the City. What was his father doing with this strange map?

Sash's attention shifted to an open notebook on the desk. Several lines of verse were written in English in Max's hand. In the margin, he had attempted a series of calculations that looked like algebra, equations culminating in a large question mark. The verse must have been copied word for word, as Max usually wrote in a combination of Russian Cyrillic and English when making his own notes, mainly Russian. Without thinking, Sash reached for a sheet of paper from the printer, grabbed a pencil from the chipped mug and scrawled down the verse.

Moments later he was in his room, heart racing, still shocked by what he had done. He had broken his father's cardinal rule and betrayed his trust. Sash felt guilty. But beyond the guilt, excitement quivered through his blood.

Sixty seconds in his father's study had raised more questions than it had answered. Sash sat on his bed and read through the verse:

On London's north–south river, long forgotten
When earth and suns align, with moon betwixt
Until again the moon's dark intervention:
Hidden from the world a doorway opens
Here you'll find the bird of flames descending from the sun
It heals all hurts and friendship binds with song.

Sash stayed in his room for most of that evening rereading the verse and wondering what it meant. He had the feeling that he had started on a journey, the end of which was far from known. What was the significance of the calendar with its odd annotations? Why had Max drawn a line across an old map of London? What did he do alone in the study for hours on end?

At nine o'clock Sash ventured out of his room in search of food, slinking past a mounted albatross that watched him from its perch. On his way to the kitchen, he paused at the foot of the darkened corridor. The door to Max's study was slightly ajar. A moment later it clicked shut.

Sash didn't see his father till morning.

— Folklore and Flame Bird —

The next day at school Sash found it easier to ignore his classmates' snide remarks. He had more important things on his mind. He was busy thinking about the mystery at the heart of his father's study. Even a message from his History teacher demanding to know why he'd missed her class had failed to unnerve him.

Sash had a break at eleven o'clock and hastened to one of the computer terminals in the school library. Glancing around to make sure that no one was watching, he removed the sheet of paper with the verse copied from his father's study. He went to an internet search engine and typed in "bird of flames".

Numerous hits appeared on the screen, several linking to phoenix legends, more still to wildlife organizations, others describing a species of flamingo, nature programmes and

55

computer games. Sash read several of the linked webpages carefully, looking for clues. *But what sort of clues?* None of the hits seemed relevant to the strange goings on in his father's study. One took Sash to a Russian fable about a firebird that was both a blessing and a curse to its captor.

Although Russian, like his father, the fable did not seem to bear any relationship to the bird of flames verse. Still, Sash scrolled down the screen, a dryness forming at the back of his throat. Somehow, he knew this story. He closed his eyes. He was five years old and his mother had just been taken to hospital. He was sitting up in bed, arms crossed, refusing to go to sleep. He didn't understand where his mother had gone and wanted her to come home to read him a story.

His father had stroked him gently on the head. "Come now, Mamma will be fine. I will tell you a tale to help you sleep, a tale from my old home, and when you wake up you will see her face…"

Sash heard a creaking sound. He turned to see the librarian wheeling a trolley full of books towards some shelves. Otherwise, the library remained deserted. Sash returned to the search engine, pushing away old memories. At the top left-hand corner of the screen, he read that he was viewing results one to ten of about 595,000.

He sighed. This was hopeless. He deleted the words "bird of flames" from the search engine and stared at the screen a moment. Then he reread the last two lines of the verse.

Here you'll find a bird of flames descending from the sun
It heals all hurts and friendship binds with song.

Next to these words, he scribbled: "But where? How do I find out?" He bit his lip and added: "What sort of bird? Special." Returning to the screen, Sash retyped the words "bird of flames" and added "friendship", but the numerous search results were seemingly irrelevant: a link to a laundry company, commentary on an Australian football club and an internet shopping site.

How do these searches work? he wondered. He selected the ADVANCED SEARCH link and requested an exact phrase search for "bird of flames friendship", which returned no hits. Then he searched for the exact phrase "bird of flames" together with the term "friendship" (in any order). The search revealed a smaller number of hits. The first appeared to be in Chinese with no available translation. The second was from a website, www.polynesia-myths.com, from an article called "Little Known Myths of Polynesia":

The myth surrounding a "bird of flames" may have originated in French Polynesia, although a similar story is documented in the journals of Captain Cook during his brief visit to Easter Island (or Rapa Nui) in 1744.

The story recounts the struggle to find happiness on a small island. The animals of the island bickered and thus the land teetered on the verge of battle. The bird of flames discovered the secret song

of happiness, which it learned from the sun, thus averting the threat
of war. This magical bird is said to have existed in an undiscovered
land, sometimes referred to as "the garden of the sun". Proponents of
the myth believe that the bird must be sought and its magical powers
used to bring an end to war.

The commentary had been written by a university student in Aberdeen. The sentences were complicated and Sash wasn't sure that he understood it all. He reread the passage, frowning.

The third link was only a footnote to an article published six years earlier in something called the California Institute of Animal Behaviour's Avian Review:

Some have even attributed magical powers to birds of paradise,
suggesting a relationship between them and the legendary bird
of flames, which learned the secret of harmony from the sun,
and whose exquisite song bound enemies together in everlasting
friendship.

Sash scrolled up to the main article. It was a technical review of birds of paradise from Papua New Guinea and revealed no more about the mysterious bird of flames. But the footnote had to be relevant.

Sash reread the last line of the verse:

It heals all hurts and friendship binds with song

The line was consistent with the story that the bird was returning from the sun, having learned the secret of harmony or, according to the first article, happiness, and that it used this knowledge to bind the residents of its island together in friendship. For a moment Sash considered his father's fascination with birds. How many specimens occupied their small flat? Thirty? Fifty? Perhaps more. Then there were the documentaries, the subscriptions to bird-watching magazines and ornithological societies.

He heard a girl's voice not far behind him. "Was that your mum on the phone? What did she want?" Sash had been so absorbed in his thoughts that he'd failed to hear Camilla and Verity enter the library.

"My mum?" said Verity

"Wasn't it your mum on the phone?" asked Camilla.

"Oh yes, nothing really."

"She's been calling you a lot recently. Listen, Verity, is everything OK? You seem a little…"

"I'm great, honestly. Everything is fine." Verity smiled brightly.

The girls were approaching the computers. Sash jabbed the icon that took him to the East Heath College homepage. He grabbed his rucksack and hurried past them as Camilla found a nearby terminal.

Verity took a seat in front of the computer that Sash had vacated. A piece of paper was propped against the keyboard. She lifted it and scanned the verse that Sash had copied from his father's notebook.

Verity wheeled round in her seat in time to see Sash swing through the library doors and disappear into the corridor. Slowly, she turned back to the computer. After a few moments she pressed the BACK button; back; back; back to the article on the bird of flames. Poised on the edge of her chair, she reread the verse, pausing over the final line. She glanced at Camilla, who was busy emailing her cousin in Florida. Discreetly, Verity folded the piece of paper and tucked it into her History textbook.

— The Riddle —

The next Saturday afternoon, Sash entered the taxidermy shop to find his father seated at the till, spectacles poised on the end of his nose, needle and thread in hand. The sound of violins floated from the old tape player.

"Look at this, look what your father has done for you!" Max picked up Sash's school blazer, which had been resting next to the till. He presented it to Sash, who examined it appreciatively. His father had mended the torn stitching and patched up the lining. But for the absent school badge, it was as good as new.

"Thanks, Dad," said Sash, genuinely grateful.

Max smiled awkwardly. "I'm sorry about the other day, I mean, I'm sorry I lost my temper. Clothes get torn, it's not the end of the world."

61

"It's fine." With a pang of guilt, Sash thought about his secret visit to the study. He even considered owning up and asking his father outright what he was doing. But they were friends again now, why ruin it? What Sash had done could not be undone – a confession might ease his conscience but it wouldn't turn back the clock. Sash glanced at the stuffed falcon that swooped from the ceiling. It glowered at him, almost as if it knew of his deceit. Silently, it seemed to shriek: "You entered your father's study! *You entered your father's study!*"

Sash bit his lip, thinking of forbidden doorways. His mind leapt to the fourth line of the verse. Something about a doorway, a doorway hidden from the world. Suddenly, he had to reread that line. Standing beneath the falcon, Sash was again aware of being changed by his visit to the study. He could feel it now, that energy. It surged through his arms and tingled his fingertips. No going back, he said to himself. Not now.

The door to the shop rattled and an elderly woman wearing a plum-coloured dress and colourful beads stepped inside, clutching a walking stick. It was their neighbour, Gertrude Trench, who lived next door above a shop selling Persian rugs.

"Good day, Max!" she hooted as she closed the shop door behind her.

"Gertrude, how wonderful to see you, do take a seat!" replied Max in his best attempt at a cultured accent, grappling to straighten his already straight tie. He raised his eyebrows at Sash, who hurried to remove a stuffed badger from a wooden chair, patted down the velvet cushion and offered it to the visitor.

"Thank you, dear Aleksandr. How awfully tall you've become. I swear you grow three inches every time my back is turned!" She pointed a knobbly, accusing finger at Sash, who blushed. Her mist of copper hair scarcely reached his shoulders. Coughing throatily, she plopped down onto the chair and lit a brown cigarillo.

"I'll make some tea." Max turned to the electric kettle, which balanced on a shelf at the back of the shop.

"Please don't go to any trouble!" protested his visitor.

"No trouble at all!" Max turned to Sash. "Gertrude will be looking after you during my trip to Iceland. You'll behave yourself, won't you, boy?" Max's thick black brows knitted over his eyes. There was a dangerous edge to his voice.

"Yes," assured Sash, nervously rolling from foot to foot. He had forgotten about his father's plans to source wildlife specimens in Iceland's frozen tundra.

"Good." Max motioned towards a stuffed dachshund puppy curled by his feet in eternal slumber. "That little dog needs wrapping, it's going out by special delivery later."

"Sure," said Sash. He scooped it up gently. Heading through to the flat, he nudged the door behind him but it didn't click shut. He heard Gertrude Trench mention his name, and paused a moment behind the door.

"Aleksandr's so tall and handsome!" she crooned.

"I wish he'd stop growing! I buy him clothes and they're instantly too small for him," grumbled Max.

"Nonsense. You should be pleased! Such a good-looking boy. I wouldn't tell him that, of course, he'd die of embarrassment. I know what boys are like!"

"He takes after his mother," replied Max. "He has her eyes."

"But, my dear, the boy has *your* eyes," the old woman said. "The darkest brown eyes I have ever seen."

"Really?" Max seemed to hesitate. "Yes, brown eyes. I was thinking for a moment they were blue. What a strange thing to do."

"Sometimes the mind plays tricks. You still think of her, of course. Perhaps we see what we want to see." Her tone changed abruptly. "Ah, tea. How splendid!"

Sash clicked the door shut. He didn't hear what his father said next.

"I worry about him." Max shook his head. "He's so isolated. He had a couple of friends in Peterborough who'd come over after school. No one visits him now. And he's secretive too. It's my fault, I'm too hard on him..."

"It's only because you care so much," the old woman said. "Aleksandr must know that, deep down."

Sash placed the dachshund on the dining table and wandered into his room. Delving through his rucksack, he searched for the page with the verse. He unzipped each pocket and shook out his notebooks but it was nowhere to be seen. With growing unease, Sash backed into the kitchen, pushing aside bottles of spirits, wooden models, photographs of animals and a horse's skull. He stacked pots and pans and sorted through bills that had mounted on the dining table. He even peered into the bread bin. Moving quickly now, Sash dashed into the living room and started sweeping through it, trying to be methodical.

Where is it? he thought worriedly, kneeling on the carpet and raising one of the padded sofa cushions. Peeling off a torn stamp that was stuck to the underside of the cushion, Sash heard his father talking in his affected accent. There was another voice too. Not the wheezy shrilling of Gertrude Trench. A clear, friendly, youthful patter.

His father called out from the kitchen. "Sash, you have a friend here to see you!"

Sash froze, sofa cushion raised above his head. He didn't have any friends.

A moment later, Verity Tattersall stepped into the living room, neatly brushing back her loose blonde hair.

Sash's heart stopped and his jaw drooped helplessly. A twinging sensation caught him between the ribs.

"Lost something?" asked Verity. She turned to look at the mantelpiece, taking in the toucan with its oversized beak, the fading photographs and the colourful macaws. Her eyes trailed over the aging brown furniture, the peeling wallpaper and garish floral-print curtains. They came to rest on a pile of taxidermy magazines. She plucked one from the heap and began leafing through it. "'An alternative to wrapping the game bird in newspaper is to slip it head first into a lady's stocking. It is important to get it to a freezer as soon as possible and it is advisable to keep an icebox handy,'" Verity read aloud, assuming an informative BBC voice. "'Before doing this, be sure to wipe off any spots of blood with a gentle downward motion from the top of the feathers. Dried blood is difficult to remove...' Fascinating stuff."

Sash sprang to his feet so quickly that he staggered, almost toppling onto the sofa. Somehow Verity had found his address. She had seen the shop. She had seen his father. She had seen the kitchen with the dachshund puppy on the table, with the numerous birds. She may have noticed the horse's skull and the array of scalpels piled against the draining board. The horror of Sash's unfolding future flashed before his eyes. Come Monday, *everyone* would know. School was already bad. It was about to become hell on earth.

"What are you doing here?" he gasped.

Verity spared him only a fleeting glance as she set down the taxidermy magazine. Reaching inside her bag she pulled out a piece of paper, which she unfolded carefully and held up for Sash to see.

His eyes fell upon the first line:

On London's north–south river, long forgotten

Sash paled. For a moment he thought of grabbing back the page, but it would make no difference now.

"What do you want?" he asked weakly.

"Where did you get that poem from?"

"Keep your voice down, will you?" Sash shot a nervous look at the living room door.

Verity pushed it shut. Leaning against the door, she smiled. "This 'bird of flames'," she continued in a loud voice.

"Shhh!" Sash stole another glance at the door.

"Why the secrecy?" Verity replied.

"Must you tell the whole world?"

"The whole world?" Verity nodded slowly, as though it was all falling into place. "Oh, I see. You pinched the poem from your dad, didn't you? He got it somehow, something to do with his ... job... He doesn't know you've seen it."

"That's none of your business."

Verity smiled evenly, undaunted by the sharpness of his tone. "So what are you up to? Are you trying to find out about the bird in the poem?" She examined his face.

"I don't know what you're talking about!" Sash hissed. He felt red blotches rise on his cheeks and turned away. He tried to control his voice – to sound natural. "I'm not doing anything. Neither's my dad. We don't care about the stupid bird."

"'The stupid bird,'" Verity echoed. "That sounds like you know exactly what I'm talking about. And why would you mention your dad, unless, of course, he's involved?" She stared at Sash. Then she squinted at the page with the verse, reading aloud Sash's notes: "'But where? How do I find out? What sort of bird? Special...'"

Sash's flush deepened. He shook his head. "I didn't mean anything by that... I just..."

Verity nodded. "I get it! Your dad's been researching the bird, hasn't he? The bird of flames? And you think there's something in it. So you're looking into it too, aren't you, trying to get to the bottom of it before he does, without him finding out?"

"No!" snapped Sash. But secretly he couldn't help but be impressed by Verity's cunning. He considered her questions. He supposed it was true, his father probably was investigating the bird. Perhaps that's what Sash was also doing, although he hadn't really thought about it that way. Maybe this strange bird existed in a faraway land. Maybe Max was trying to find it. He occasionally went on sourcing trips abroad, mysterious journeys to far-flung places like Siberia or the Malay Peninsula. He never took Sash with him. What if these trips were really aimed at tracking down the bird of flames? Given his father's obsession with birds in all their forms, Sash thought this was possible.

He took a deep breath. "No," he repeated more quietly.

"Then why were you googling 'bird of flames'? What do you know about it?"

"How did you know I was googling—" Sash caught himself. "What's it to you? I don't know anything about a bird.

So you can just get out of here and forget you ever saw that … that poem, or whatever."

Verity tilted her head, still watching him. "Oh well," she sighed. "If you don't know anything about it, perhaps I'll just ask your dad…" She spun towards the door and closed her fingers round the knob.

"Don't do that!" Sash threw up his hands in a gesture of defeat. "OK, so maybe I am trying to find out about the bird… What does it matter?"

Verity released the doorknob and turned to Sash, bright-eyed. "I can help you," she said.

"You can't help," spluttered Sash. "I don't need your help."

Verity rolled her eyes. "Oh really? I assume you realize that the poem you pocketed is a riddle? Do you even under-stand the first line?"

"The river dividing north and south London is the Thames, everyone knows that," growled Sash defensively.

"It doesn't say that the river *divides* north and south London. Obviously, the river *runs* from north to south."

"Don't be stupid, there aren't any rivers running north to south."

Verity beamed triumphantly. "Actually, there are several. I think you'll be rather interested in one of them. It runs all the way from Hampstead Heath to Blackfriars Bridge, almost a straight line through the heart of London."

Sash opened his mouth to protest but suddenly he remembered the curious map in his father's study with the diagonal line running from north London to the Thames. "I've never seen this river," he said, but his tone had softened. Doubt was creeping in.

"Of course you haven't," replied Verity. "You can't see it, not without X-ray vision at any rate."

"Oh, I get it, it's an *invisible* river."

"Sarcasm doesn't suit you, Sash."

His cheeks reddened. It was the first time she had ever addressed him by name. "So what do you mean?"

"I mean that the river in your poem is obviously the Fleet, and that's been buried underground for two hundred years."

— The Art of Taxidermy —

"Was there any more to the riddle than you wrote here?" asked Verity, indicating the piece of paper with the verse.

"Not that I saw," said Sash. "My dad must have copied it from something else. If it was in his own words he'd have written in Cyrillic, you know, the letters you use to write Russian, or a mixture of Cyrillic and English. But he'd written it all in English, so it must have been copied." Sash wasn't sure why he had confided this detail. He was annoyed with himself.

"That probably explains the error in the second line."

"What error?"

"It says, 'When earth and suns align.' It should be 'sun' not 'suns'."

"I suppose so." Given the state of Max's written English,

Sash was surprised that there weren't more mistakes, but he didn't say so.

"It's all a sort of address, isn't it? I mean, it tells the location of the bird of flames. Your dad hasn't found it yet, has he? I mean, I think you'd know if he had. Do you think you can find it first?"

"That's none of your business!"

"OK, OK, chill out, will you?" Verity's eyes wandered again to the stuffed birds on the mantelpiece. "He's got a thing about birds, hasn't he? Maybe he thinks this one can improve his lot."

"There's nothing wrong with his 'lot', as you put it!"

"Of course not, I didn't mean..." Verity tailed off. She wandered over to the photographs. "Don't you look cute?" she said, peering at the one of Sash aged five. She turned to the black and white image of Sash's mother.

Sash started towards her, reaching out his hand protectively. He didn't want Verity to look at that photograph: it was private. Suddenly, the door opened and Max appeared, a tray of orange squash and wafers balanced on one hand. Sash noticed Verity fold the page with the riddle into her bag, although her eyes fixed steadily on his father.

"Sash, haven't you even offered your friend a drink?" asked Max.

"She wasn't thirsty," returned Sash.

"Did you ask?" Max turned to Verity and presented the tray.

"Thank you very much," she replied politely, taking a glass of squash and a wafer.

"Do take a seat," said Max. "Sorry, my son has no manners!"

"Dad!"

"Now, now, Sash, have a wafer and pipe down."

Verity giggled and the three of them sat, Max taking his usual place in the armchair.

"Shouldn't you be minding the shop?" asked Sash irritably.

"In a minute," replied his father.

"I was just looking at the black and white picture on the mantelpiece," said Verity, addressing Max and ignoring Sash.

"Ah yes, my wife, Susanna, Sash's mother," Max replied.

"She's very pretty."

"Dear girl, how kind of you to say so. She passed away when Sash was very young. We do miss her. Always such a calming influence. We men need that sometimes." He chuckled. "Mind you, she was never on time for anything. Very laid back, you might call it. Used to raise my blood pressure!"

Sash blinked at him, shocked at his father's easy familiarity with Verity. Had his mother really been a calming influence or was Max just saying that? Sash had lost her too young to remember. He thought about himself a moment. He wasn't calm. Quiet, yes. Not calm. But he was bad at timekeeping.

Not like Max, who was always punctual. Glancing at his father, Sash wondered which of his parents he took after more.

"I hadn't realized, I'm sorry." Verity nodded sympathetically and took a small bite of her wafer. She gestured at the macaws. "Did you work on these yourself?"

"Yes, I did," said Max. "Everything you see in the shop and back here as well."

"No, really?"

"Yes, they are all my creatures, I don't buy in my stock."

"Even the lion? But how did you…?"

"Zoos. Sometimes it is possible to obtain specimens from zoos, those that have died from disease or old age."

"How incredible!"

"Oh yes. I never kill for my pieces, never. There are some who'd disagree with me but I do not believe that the object of the taxidermist is to play God. Ours is an ancient, almost forgotten art – to record the natural world around us, to preserve it for generations. We are not here to take life, no, in a more immediate sense we actually restore it."

Sitting in silence at the end of the sofa, Sash looked on in amazement. He had never heard his father talk this way.

Max's eyes grew glassy as he nodded towards the toucan with the large beak. "That bird was found on a ranch in Brazil by one of my friends who was sourcing rare specimens. My friend froze it and had it shipped to England, not easy with all the red tape. When I got the toucan, it was more than a little worse for wear, but I worked on it for hours. Once it lay lifeless on a dirt track in Brazil. And here you see it, returned to its former glory, its beautiful feathers glossy, its eyes open. Now it will live for ever."

Sash frowned uneasily at his father, who gazed at the toucan unblinking. "Verity needs to go home," he interrupted.

"Of course," replied Max, seeming to snap out of his trance. "You will come again, won't you?"

Verity smiled. "That would be lovely."

"Good. Sash will walk you home."

Sash was about to object but he caught Verity's eye. She winked and nodded towards her bag, where he'd seen her hide the verse. Knowing that he was beaten, he led Verity through the shop and out onto the street.

A wind was rising on Gully Lane. Shivering, Verity wrapped her scarf round her neck and buttoned up her coat. "You needn't look so sorry for yourself, I'm helping you, remember?"

"Are you really? And I suppose you'll keep the poem to yourself?"

"Of course I will! I won't show anyone. That would ruin the fun. And don't worry, your" – Verity waved her hands, indicating Stuff the World – "unconventional arrangement here won't be shared either."

Sash narrowed his eyes. "What's in it for you?"

"I told you, I just want to help. I like a challenge." Verity glanced at her collar, flicking off a tuft of lint.

"I can't imagine you'd help *anyone* just for the fun of it," said Sash.

Verity threw him a mock-injured look. "What a terrible thing to say."

Sash shrugged. He wasn't going to apologize. He started pacing down the road, long-legged strides that meant Verity had to hurry to keep up. They walked in silence past the shop selling fried chicken at the corner of Gully Lane and soon found themselves on Kentish Town Road. Eventually, Sash spoke. "So how do you know about this river? The Fleet, was it?"

"My uncle's a water engineer. Well meaning but quite a bore. Always rabbiting on about sewage or whatever. He loves nothing more than to talk about underground rivers. Not that I've taken the slightest bit of interest. Not till I saw your riddle… I've done some reading – East Heath College has a surprisingly good library. I'll show you. Meet me there at eight o'clock Monday morning."

"Eight in the morning? Do you realize how early—"

Verity tutted impatiently, stopping on the pavement with her hands on her hips. "Do you want to find out about the bird or don't you? I'll see you then." With that, Sash was dismissed.

"Aren't I walking you?" He stood by, reluctant to leave her, having promised his father he'd see her home safely. It was growing dark.

Verity raised one eyebrow, a skill she'd evidently honed.

The gesture spoke more clearly than any words could: "Does it look like I walk?" she seemed to say. From the corner of her eye, she must have seen the approaching taxi. A moment later she had hopped inside and was speeding away up Highgate Road.

— Outsider —

It was happening already. In the citadel at the heart of the jungle, guards were tearing down ancient carvings, destroying the cone-shaped building that Manah loved so much. It would only get worse. Soon there would be little trace of Aqarti before the Keeper – of Great Aruva and the spirit animals. She turned away, appalled.

She had thought that they would catch her as she knelt to sing between the high trees. That had been a false alarm – a stray animal roaming the darkness. And here she was at the outskirts of the citadel, placing herself in even greater danger. Tiro had warned her against coming here. "Stay in the highlands," he had told her, "it is not safe for our kind down there." But she had to see it – she had to see the Bloodstone Bird. And how could she stay away from the citadel when she knew that Jonto and the others would be there, imprisoned in the Keeper's dungeon? If they were still alive… Manah stepped lightly behind a fern.

It was hard to survive in the lowlands outside the villages. She had eaten more gorpi berries in the last few days than she cared to remember. She had a sudden craving for coconut, a longing for its sweet milk. Islanders were banned from Rising Beach with its coconut palms – the Keeper's warning symbol was everywhere. But what did Manah care about the Keeper's rules? She was a rebel now, an outsider. You could do what you liked as a rebel, thought Manah – provided you were not caught.

— Long-Forgotten River —

When Sash threw open the doors of East Heath College library, he doubted that Verity would be there. He half expected to find himself the butt of an elaborate joke. Surely it was only a matter of time until everyone knew about Stuff the World?

Verity was seated in the corner beyond the computer terminals, books scattered around her. She frowned impatiently as Sash arrived. "It's eight-fifteen. Can't you be punctual for heaven's sake?"

Yawning, Sash threw down his rucksack and found a chair.

"What do you actually know about the city you live in?" asked Verity.

Sash didn't like these sorts of questions. His father came out with them occasionally. They tended to lead to

80

demonstrations of Sash's foolishness and the questioner's intelligence. "Not much," he replied.

"The Fleet used to be famous. It was the river that ran through the centre of London, back when it was basically the City, you know, the financial district or 'Square Mile'—"

"I know what the City is," Sash snapped. Verity had a way of talking that seemed to imply he was stupid.

"Of course," she said quickly. "I thought you should have a copy of the riddle." She handed him a page with the bird of flame verse written on it in her own neat hand. "Listen, this is important. The Fleet flowed down Ludgate Circus and touched Fleet Street – that's where my dad works. Here, look at this." Verity shoved an open book towards him.

Bleary-eyed, Sash picked up the book and started to read.

The River Fleet is the best known of London's subterranean rivers. It is also the most important in terms of London's development, serving as the city's main artery since Roman occupation around AD 50. The Fleet rises at Highgate and Hampstead Ponds in Kenwood, perhaps the only point where the once-great river can still be seen today. From there, it travels through Camden Town to King's Cross (once known as Brill to Battle Bridge). On it flows through Clerks' Well, or Clerkenwell, where its freshwater pools were celebrated for endowing bathers with good health.

The valley of the Fleet towards Ludgate Circus was once as wide as 200 metres, practically a ravine, and was a popular route for boats into the city. It was on the Fleet Valley that Fleet Prison was erected in 1197, primarily to hold debtors and bankrupts. The prison was destroyed during the Great Fire of London (and later rebuilt), when flames leapt from bank to bank.

Despite the early hour and Verity's presence, Sash couldn't help but be fascinated by what he read. *Two hundred metres.* As a runner, Sash understood what that meant. It was an enormous width – how could so much water be funnelled underground and forgotten? It was puzzling and somehow sad to think that a river once flowed through the centre of London, had done so long before the city's earliest formation some 2,000 years ago, and now that river was buried for ever. He looked up to find Verity watching him expectantly.

"Fleet Street's named after the river, lots of local land-marks are. And there's a Fleet Road in Hampstead," she offered. "I checked the definition of 'Fleet'. It's an Anglo-Saxon word meaning tidal inlet or stream, capable of floating boats. The northern route of the River Fleet would have been pretty narrow in comparison with the Fleet Valley. It says here that the north Fleet would have ranged between four and twenty metres wide at flood in the early nineteenth century. An anchor was dredged up south of Hampstead, so I suppose boats must have travelled up here too." Verity pointed at some commentary in another book she had been reading.

Sash frowned. Mention of boats had triggered his memory.

He had seen a reference to boating somewhere recently, somewhere unexpected. But where? "It says in this book that flames leapt from one bank to another in the Fire of London. The whole area must have been wrecked," he said. It was hard to imagine destruction on that scale.

"Yes, but if you read on you'll see that after the fire, Sir Christopher Wren, the architect who designed St Paul's Cathedral, remodelled the banks of the Fleet. It was supposed to look a little like Venice. It must have been beautiful. Have you ever been to Venice?"

Sash ignored the question. He doubted whether Verity cared if he'd been to Venice, in fact, she could have reasonably guessed that he hadn't. "So why was the river buried underground?" he asked instead.

"In a word: stench." Verity smiled wickedly. "Tanneries sprang up along the river's route. I assume you know what a tannery is, given your dad's ... vocation? Places where they dry animal skins for leather."

"I know what tanneries are," Sash growled.

"OK, touchy! They used to have live animal markets around the Fleet too, and butchers, and all sorts of revolting waste was chucked in. Eventually it was little more than an open sewer. Friars on its banks complained that they couldn't smell their incense over the pong." Verity crinkled her nose. "So they started to build over the river. The Fleet Valley in the south was buried in the first part of the eighteenth century, and the north followed in time."

"That's all fine, but what makes you so sure that the poem is about the Fleet?"

"Long-forgotten river..."

"Why not one of the other underground rivers?" Sash glanced at the book on the desk in front of him. "How about the Tyburn?"

"It's possible, I suppose, but it seems unlikely. 'On London's north–south river.' Well, it depends on what you consider to be London. Look at this, it shows the course of all the underground rivers."

Verity passed Sash a complicated map that appeared at the back of one of the books. The Tyburn flowed west of the Fleet through Regent's Park and Green Park.

"The Tyburn runs north to south through London," said Sash.

Verity sighed, as if he was an obstinate child, wilfully refusing to get the point. "Maybe now, but not four hundred years ago. Remember that what we call 'London' used to be only the City of London, the area around Ludgate Circus and Blackfriars, with a string of surrounding villages, and pastures, and even woods. These days Moorfields is all tower blocks full of lawyers and bankers but back then it really was fields! The Tyburn wouldn't have flowed through London proper, it would have run to the west, through the City of Westminster, which wasn't part of London till later."

"What makes you think the poem about the bird of flames was written four hundred years ago?"

"Maybe not that long ago but it isn't modern, is it? 'Betwixt' for example – sounds sort of Shakespearean, doesn't it?"

"'Betwixt'? I guess it does sound old-fashioned," agreed Sash. "But the poem can't be that old, or, if it is, it's not about the Fleet."

"Why not?" demanded Verity.

"Because it mentions London's long-forgotten river – meaning long-buried river, according to you – and if that architect redesigned the banks of the Fleet after the 1666 fire, it can't have been buried, let alone *long*-buried, at that time. If the southern part was only covered two hundred years ago, even two hundred and fifty years ago, that means the poem couldn't have been written much before the nine-teenth century. And I'm guessing central London was far bigger than the City by that time."

Verity glared at Sash. She raked her fingers through her hair. "You're right, aren't you? Yes ... of course that's true," she admitted testily. "I was *sure* it was the Fleet. It made so much sense... But it *could* be the Tyburn, I suppose. It could be any number of underground rivers. How will we ever know?"

Sash was surprised by Verity's response: by the degree of her disappointment. For a moment he thought she might cry. Awkwardly, he looked down at the table. His eyes trailed over the map. According to the blue lines snaking from the Thames on either side, there were more than half a dozen underground rivers in London: the Westbourne that flowed from Kilburn through Hyde Park, Counter's Creek that ran through the King's Road in Chelsea, the Effra that reached south from the Thames through Brockwell Park and Brixton. Others too, of varying size and length. Sash's eyes retraced the path of the Fleet. Aside from minor diversions and a fork north of Camden, its journey from Hampstead to Blackfriars was a line that ran at a slight angle through central London. It wasn't straight and smooth like the ruler-drawn diagonal line on the map Sash had seen in his father's study but it seemed to cover roughly the same area.

"This is just the worst setback," moaned Verity. "I was so sure. Now we'll never find the bird."

Sash felt a pang of pity for her, forgetting for a moment her cruelty in front of the other students and his promise to himself never to trust her. He spoke without looking up. "I found something, something that belongs to my dad. I went into his private study. He doesn't know that I did. I guess you already worked that out. Anyway, there was a calendar on the wall. He'd written letters on it at different days of the year. And there was a map of London too, with a line drawn from Hampstead to Blackfriars."

"Hampstead to Blackfriars?" gasped Verity.

"It was on his desk, next to the poem. I left it where it was."

"I told you!" she cried in a voice so self-righteous that Sash was instantly sorry he'd confided in her.

"I could have got it wrong."

"You didn't get it wrong! You know what you saw. You saw the route of the Fleet. I can't explain the calendar, though. Sounds like you need to take a second look, with my help."

"No way! I'm already going to be in enough trouble as it is." As he spoke, Sash was gazing at the map of London's underground rivers.

"Does your dad ever go away? On taxidermy jaunts or whatever."

Sash clicked his tongue irritably. "Actually he's off over half-term. And, yes, it is to do with taxidermy. If you must know, he's going to Iceland to source specimens. And it makes no difference because I'm not going into his study again, and you're definitely not going in there."

"We won't get caught," reasoned Verity.

"Forget it, OK?" His dark eyes flashed at her. He frowned, eyes darting back to the map. Had he just seen what he thought he'd seen? East Heath Road in tiny print. Yes, it was true: the Fleet seemed to travel directly beneath the street on which their school was built. Suddenly feeling light-headed, Sash trailed his eyes down to Kentish Town, north of Camden Town station and St Pancras Way. His head was bursting with confused thoughts and unanswered questions: why does Dad want me to go to this school so much? It was the only one he put me forward for when we moved to north London, the only school he talked about. Why the move to London anyway? It couldn't have been for business,

business is terrible. Why that odd location for the shop, tucked away from the world on Gully Lane?

This is crazy, it's ridiculous, thought Sash. His fingers gripped the map, held it closer. "But it can't be..." he murmured. Shaking his head slowly, finally absorbing the truth that had been staring him in the face, Sash wondered if it was possible that Max had picked the location of their home, and his school, according to the route of a river that had been buried underground for two hundred years. No one, not even Sash's father, would do something like that lightly.

Sash rubbed his eyes, bewildered. Dad really does believe that the bird can be found on the river's path, he realized with amazement. *He really believes in the bird of flames!*

Both on Saturday and this morning, Verity had speculated that Sash's father was hunting for an exotic bird, that Sash was looking for it too, and half-heartedly he'd acknowledged that this was possible. But he hadn't really believed it. Not until this moment. Now it was obvious to Sash that his father was trying to unravel a great mystery: the riddle of the verse, the riddle that would lead him to the bird. But he hadn't managed it yet; Verity was right in this too. That was the only plausible explanation for Max's secrecy, for the papers and strange calculations. What if Sash could solve the riddle first? Wouldn't his father be pleased? Wouldn't it prove to Max that his son was good for something after all?

Sash became aware that Verity was watching him with a curious expression.

"You're right," he said. "It's the Fleet. There's some kind of doorway on the river, a doorway to the land of the bird of flames. My dad must have been searching for it for ages." Even as the words escaped his lips, Sash realized how insane they sounded. Another land? A land that was reached by an underground river?

"You're pretty sure all of a sudden," replied Verity, one eyebrow raised.

Sash nodded slowly and returned to the map. Winding through north London was the passage of the Fleet. Just south of Kentish Town Road, it hooked onto a tiny street before heading down towards King's Cross. The street was Gully Lane, home of Stuff the World and a silent gallery of birds.

Just before the bell for class sounded, Verity replaced the books on their shelves and left to meet her friend Camilla. The message to Sash was clear: outside class, she would help him solve the mystery, but during school time nothing had changed. Sash absorbed this fact without surprise but couldn't help feeling a sense of rejection. Don't get involved, don't get attached, that's what he told himself, if you do, people will let you down.

When Sash passed Verity in the atrium during lunch she completely ignored him, laughing with a group of girls. From the corner of his eye, he saw James and Angus approach the girls to whisper in Verity's ear. Angus was clutching something, some sort of metal tool, perhaps a screwdriver. He raised it for Verity's inspection. The group sniggered briefly among themselves.

At the bell, Sash went into Maths with unpleasant memories of his confrontation with James the previous week. He found his desk at the back of the room as Verity and Camilla strolled in, taking their places near the window. Just as Sash was poised to sit, Verity spun round and frowned, mouthing, "No!" and shaking her head very slightly. Before Sash could respond, Verity had turned back and was chatting with Camilla about a recent shopping trip.

"I couldn't decide between the red or the blue, so Mum said we might as well get both."

"Good move!" Camilla nodded approvingly.

Sash paused, his hand resting on the back of the chair. Had Verity really mouthed, "No!" or had he imagined it? As he was pondering this, James entered the room and stole a glance in Sash's direction. There was an odd look on his face, a sort of half-formed smirk. That was enough for Sash: he moved away. Students were pouring in and it was hard to find a free desk. Unwillingly, Sash sat down next to James in the seat normally occupied by Angus.

"Move it, Baron Oiksky, that's Slaughter's seat!" snarled James.

Miss Freeman appeared behind him. "Seats are not allocated in this room, James, as well you know."

"But... But, miss, Slaughter always sits here."

Other students turned in their chairs, watching the exchange with interest.

"I assume he will be able to read the whiteboard from anywhere in the room. Don't worry, James, Angus won't be disadvantaged."

"But we work on the joint problems together," whined James.

"That might explain why both of you get so many of the answers wrong. Today you can work with Sash. As he's rather a whizz at maths, I look forward to seeing a marked improvement." Miss Freeman paced towards the front of the room. "Right, everyone, let's run through the register."

Sash noticed that most people, when they lost their temper, narrowed their eyes so that their pupils became dark raisins between clenched flesh. For instance, when his father was angry his eyes clamped almost shut, hidden beneath furious dark brows. James was different: his eyes bulged, popped three-dimensionally from his head, almost as though they would burst out at any moment. Sash distracted himself by watching the door.

Angus strolled in just as his name was called on the register. "Yes, miss," he replied, sauntering towards his desk. He saw Sash and stopped in his tracks.

The class silently took in the scene.

"Grab that seat at the back, and try not to be late in future," said Miss Freeman tetchily.

Angus opened and closed his mouth, carp-like. "I can't sit there," he managed at last.

"Why on earth not? Frankly, Angus, I'm getting fed up of this. Can't you and James be separated for more than five minutes?"

The class roared with laughter and Angus's face, which was already prone to ruddiness, grew scarlet from neck to forehead. He approached the vacant chair slowly, as if wading through treacle. He stood behind it, tapped the back and dragged it out from under the desk. Still he failed to sit down.

"Now, Angus!" snapped Miss Freeman.

Angus put his hand on the seat and pressed. The chair collapsed with a crack and thud.

"You knew that was going to happen!" stormed Miss Freeman.

"No, I didn't, miss, honest!" Angus threw his hands in the air in a gesture of innocence.

"Damaging school property is a very serious matter, not to mention the harm it could have caused a fellow student!"

"But, miss, I didn't do anything!"

"I want to see you after class, we can discuss it further then. For now, go and ask Mr McNaulty next door if you can borrow a chair."

Angus scowled and left the room.

"Sash, do you know anything about this?" asked Miss Freeman.

"No," he said.

The teacher was eyeing him suspiciously. He could tell that she didn't believe him. After a moment her lips curled into a small smile. "Very well," she sighed.

From the corner of his eye, Sash could see James, who was practically gnashing his teeth, and Verity, who had covered her mouth with her hand and was whispering to Camilla in apparent surprise.

— Inside the Trunk —

At precisely 5.30 p.m. the following Saturday afternoon, Max reversed the OPEN sign on the shop door and turned to his son.

"Now, boy, Gertrude is expecting you. She's made up the guest room. Remember to be helpful, always collect the dishes and do the washing up, don't wait to be told. And run any errands she asks you to. She doesn't walk very easily and may want you to pop to Tesco or to fetch her prescriptions."

"But, Dad, can't I just stay here? I'm old enough to take care of myself." He jiggled his door keys. "Look, I can just come and go, why trouble anyone?"

Max frowned, his thick brows furrowing. "Certainly not. You want people to think I'm an unfit father? I only wish I hadn't planned to leave now, during your half-term, but

I wasn't to know... It's the best time of year in Iceland for spotting any number of winter animals."

"It'll be freezing."

"Like I said, that's the best time to go. It's only for a week. I'll be back on Saturday evening. In good time for your school's event the following week."

"Oh, that." Sash had noticed that the mottled invitation to attend East Heath College parents' evening had found itself a spot on the fridge next to a flyer from the Guild of Taxidermists advertising their annual conference.

"I'm looking forward to it," said Max with a sudden, friendly chuckle. "Do you think I'll have a chance to look around the school?"

Sash didn't reply. He watched his father knowingly. Max's enthusiasm for the parents' evening probably had more to do with the Fleet's route than a desire to talk to his son's teachers.

Max ushered Sash out of the shop, clutching his battered suitcase. "Don't lose those keys, boy," he warned. "I need you to check on the shop every day, just to make sure that everything is in order."

"Sure," said Sash. He carried a large bag too, although he was only going as far as the flat above the neighbouring rug shop.

Max locked the door to Stuff the World and turned to pat Sash on the back. "Be good."

"I will," said Sash. He watched his father disappear down

Gully Lane towards the Underground station. Max stooped when he walked and seemed older than his forty-five years, as though the disappointments of life had sapped him of energy. Sash felt a creeping sadness and turned away. He rang the bell to Gertrude Trench's flat. He rang again. Shivering out on the street, Sash stepped back and tried to peer up through the windows. The net curtains were closed.

After five minutes of waiting in the street, Sash gave up and returned to Stuff the World. He would try again in half an hour. He stood for a while in the taxidermy shop, watching the sky blacken and storm clouds drift and regroup. He tried several times to get hold of Gertrude Trench, both by phone and by ringing the doorbell, but no one answered. By 6.30 p.m. Sash was starting to feel uneasy.

At 6.40 p.m. the phone rang.

"Aleksandr, this is Gertrude," wheezed a voice at the end of the line. "I'm awfully sorry but I had a little fall at the chemist this afternoon, terribly clumsy of me, they've taken me to casualty, a lot of fuss over nothing really. No, no, don't come in, I'm absolutely fine."

Sash remembered his father's words about doing the right thing. Out of the money Max had left him to contribute to meals at Gertrude Trench's house, Sash allowed himself five pounds to buy a bunch of flowers from the petrol station on the high street. He hopped on the number 46 bus to the Royal Free Hospital in Hampstead, where the old woman had been admitted. The route was still on diversion but Sash wasn't in any hurry, and he couldn't face walking in such grim weather.

Gertrude Trench was delighted by Sash's visit and his handful of yellow carnations. She told him that she had bruised her hip and would be in hospital overnight for observation. In time she would probably need a hip replacement but you could wait months for those. Her son was arriving from Ipswich the next morning to take her home with him for a few weeks while she got back on her feet.

"I have to get out of here, I could murder a smoke and the beasts won't let me!" sighed the old woman.

Sash nodded sympathetically.

"You must come to Ipswich too. I've spoken to my son, it's quite all right."

"Thanks, but there's no need, I'm going to stay with a friend." It was a lie but Sash desperately wanted to avoid a week with an unknown family. He wasn't used to lying, had never been much good at it, but since his secret visit to the study it didn't seem so hard.

"A friend?" Gertrude Trench seemed confused. "No, dear, you must come with me."

"I think it's best for you to rest without the worry," replied Sash. He thought quickly. "I'm going to stay with Verity." He smiled to himself. The lie had just shifted from silly to preposterous. The idea of staying at Verity's beautiful house was impossible to imagine.

"Oh yes, dear, that charming girl who came to visit you

the other day! What a very nice young lady," the old woman gushed.

Sash wished he could raise an eyebrow the way Verity did. Now would be a good time. "Nice" was the last word he would use to describe Verity Tattersall. "She lives near here actually, on Pond Rise."

"How splendid! What a lovely part of town."

A nurse had entered the ward and was fussing about with plastic bottles. "Time for your meds," she said. She looked at Sash quizzically, perhaps trying to work out whether he was her patient's grandson and if not, what he was doing there. "Sorry, visiting time is over."

"OK then, see you when you're back from Ipswich," said Sash. He started towards the door.

"Wait!" exclaimed Gertrude Trench, "I promised your father!"

"I'll be fine at Verity's."

"Could I have her parents' number?"

"Visiting time is over," repeated the nurse. She handed the old woman a collection of colourful pills, together with a paper cup of water.

"But…" Gertrude Trench began to protest but gave way to a bout of coughing.

"I hope you feel better soon," said Sash as he dived out of the ward. He hastened down the corridor, narrowly avoiding a man being pushed in a wheelchair. As he edged into a crowded lift he banished distant thoughts: of his mother who went to hospital when he was five years old and never returned.

Outside the street was deserted, it was raining heavily and the downpour had imposed a curfew on the city. Sash didn't have an umbrella and even the short walk to the bus stop left him soaked to the skin. He didn't care. A wonderful feeling of excitement was crackling through him.

For seven days he was free.

Sash was home by 8.40 p.m. He sat on the sofa eating a huge bowl of pasta topped with half a packet of grated cheddar while watching a severe weather warning: gale force winds, risk of hail, black ice. He channel-hopped to an action movie. A man in a black polo neck and tight-fitting jeans was diving across a busy restaurant, firing a sub-machine gun. Miraculously, the man managed to shoot down his fast-approaching assassins, each heavily armed, without hitting any of the diners or being shot himself. Sash's father would never approve, would no doubt insist that they watched the documentary about the snowy egret that had already started on *BBC2*. But his father wasn't home.

The buzzer made Sash jump. Who would be calling round at this time of the evening with a storm raging outside? With a rush of disappointment, he realized that Gertrude Trench might not have been so easily hoodwinked and could have sent her son to get him. He dragged himself through the flat and out into the shop.

Verity stood on the doorstep beneath a colourful umbrella.

"Don't hurry yourself or anything," she grumbled. "I love standing in torrential rain."

Sash blinked at her, too surprised to speak.

She slid past him into the shop, shaking out her umbrella. "Has your dad left for Iceland?"

Sash turned to look at her and nodded absently. "Yes, but why are you...?"

"We need to get to the bottom of this. Take that, will you? It's heavy." Verity indicated the suitcase by her feet.

Sash stared at it dumbly. "How did you know I'd be here?"

"I didn't. I thought I'd give it a shot. If you hadn't been, I'd have worked something out. Would have helped if you had a mobile like any reasonable person. I tried to call the landline about an hour ago but nobody answered."

"I wasn't here," he mumbled.

"Well, you're back now so it's all good. As far as my parents are concerned, I'm with Camilla's family in the Cotswolds. They're in Tokyo. It's all covered."

"You can't stay," said Sash slowly.

"I may not have to, but I wanted to give us plenty of time." She nodded at the front door. "The rain's a bit of a bore. You'd better see to that, the poor bear's soaking." With that she trotted towards the flat, leaving Sash standing by the front door.

He watched her disappear into the kitchen. Rain was drumming against his shoulders and rolling icily down the back of his neck. He closed and locked the door, grabbed Verity's case – she was right, it was heavy – and hurried into the kitchen.

Verity was there, standing next to the sink and holding the horse's skull.

"Put that down!" ordered Sash.

"No need to shout, I'm not deaf," she replied, placing the skull on a taxidermy manual. She eyed the scalpels by the sink. "You've got a pretty unusual set-up here," she commented.

"You have to leave," said Sash.

"Yes, yes, all in good time. Where's your dad's study?"

"Oh no you don't!"

"Where is it?" Verity tilted her neck, scanning the short, lit corridor that led to the bedrooms, the living room and the bathroom. She watched Sash. "Not there." She turned to look in the other direction, down the darkened corridor. She glanced back at Sash. His face must have told her what she needed to know. "There," she said.

"No, no way!"

Verity nodded. Suddenly, she seemed contrite. "I'm sorry. I suppose I thought that after what happened in Maths – after I tipped you off about the chair – you might have changed your view of me."

Sash sighed. "Don't do me any favours," he said quietly.

"I'm looking out for your interests, you know! What you have to understand is that they're dumb. Angus and James, thick as a bucket of worms. Especially James – he'll believe anything. Too inbred, that's what I reckon. And James is scared of you, it's obvious. That's why he picks on you. He only does it with Angus and Colin around – get him alone and he's nothing."

Sash didn't reply.

"I just want to help." Verity raised her palms in a gesture of defeat.

"I don't know *what* you want but I can't let you into my dad's study."

"I understand," replied Verity, eyes downcast. "I'll call a cab in a mo', I'll go home." Her fingers idly stroked the horse's skull.

"That would be best," agreed Sash with relief. Perhaps she wasn't as selfish as she seemed. She had warned him about the trick in Miss Freeman's class. It would have been awful if the chair had collapsed beneath him; he would never have lived it down.

"Catch!" cried Verity, lobbing the skull in his direction. It flew towards the wall just above his head and he jumped for it, grasping it through the eye sockets. As he turned to set it down, he saw Verity diving down the corridor and ducking inside his father's study.

"What the hell are you doing?" Sash shouted, racing after her. He stood rigid at the entrance, refusing to enter.

Verity was staring at the "Birds of the World" wall calendar. "According to this, it's 'h-h-e-k-h' now. No, that can't be the right pronunciation. *'H-es-k-h'?* 'B' equals 'b-i-c-o-k-hah'." She mouthed each syllable carefully.

"What?"

"'C' equals 'c-p-e'— No, wait, 'sa-pey'... This is impossible!"

"What are you going on about?" Sash abandoned his position outside the study, pushing past her to look at the calendar.

"Didn't you notice that your dad was kind enough to leave a key, although he left it in that funny Russian writing." Verity pointed to some tiny notes that Max had scribbled at the bottom of the calendar. Sash had missed them on his previous visit. They said:

B = высокий
C = средний
H = низкий

"That's the worst pronunciation I've ever heard," said Sash. "The letters don't have the same sound as English ones. That 'B' sounds like 'V', and the Cyrillic 'H' is pronounced 'N'."

"Well, that makes no sense whatsoever," retorted Verity.

"It makes sense if you're Russian." Sash frowned, forming the words in his mind. "I think 'высокий' means 'high'." He pronounced the word "vis-oki". His anger had dissolved.

He knew that he should back away from the study but he was too intrigued. "I'm not sure about the other words," he mumbled.

"Is it possible that one of them is 'low'? Could 'sa-pey'-whatever mean low?"

"No, that can't mean… Actually, now you mention it, I think 'низкий' could be low." He pronounced the word "niz-kiy". He turned to Verity. "How did you know that?"

"Because rivers have tides. High tides, low tides."

"And medium tides." Sash was suddenly sure he knew what "средний" meant. He blinked at Verity. She was clever; he had to give her that.

"Your dad's been noting down the Fleet's behaviour, trying to work out when it's possible to travel on it. According to his calendar it's – how did you say it? – 'niz-kiy', today."

Now she'd gone too far. "There's no way that he'd think about … about *travelling* on the Fleet. It's underground, how would he get to it? And it's not much more than a sewer, you said so yourself."

Verity shrugged and turned to the desk. "There have to be some clues around here…"

Sash peeked at the shelf, hoping Verity would miss the gosling in the gherkin jar. Could it be that even now he wanted to shield his father from her critical glare? Or was it his own pride Sash was anxious to protect?

Next to the jar he spotted the boating brochure on top of the magazines. Boating. That's right, the brochure had stood out on Sash's first visit and seeing it now made him wonder. Had Verity stumbled on something? He heard a sound and turned to see her moving towards the trunk; the loose floorboards had squealed at the trespass.

Sash shot round, half expecting to see his father standing in the shadowy corridor. He turned back to Verity. Her fingers reached for the trunk.

"You can't look in that, it's private," Sash protested. But as she lifted up the heavy lid he was by her side.

The cavernous trunk had no base – Sash could see the floorboards, on which sat three objects. Two of these he recognized – a torch and a compass. He had seen both resting on top of the trunk during his last visit. The third object was a long enamel box decorated with tiny painted flowers in a distinctively Russian style. As Verity held up the lid of the trunk, Sash found himself reaching inside and lifting it out. He experienced this almost as though watching a film, as if someone else was responsible for the action and he was merely a spectator. With a sense of fear and excitement, he opened the box and both of them peered inside. A lone feather had been placed in a large plastic sandwich bag. The feather was unlike any Sash had ever seen. It was bright red with a golden tip. He glanced at Verity. She was transfixed. Her eyes were slightly moist, her lips parted.

Max had written something on an adhesive label stuck to the sandwich bag: HAMPSTEAD MIXED PONDS: 28.7.1999.

"He found the feather," said Sash. "He found it, probably

105

by chance, and then he started believing that the bird of flames might really exist, and that he could find that too, that he could bring it back to Gully Lane and stuff it… Maybe he wants the fame it would bring, and we could certainly use the money." He spoke the words slowly, eyebrows furrowed like Max himself.

Verity was still holding open the trunk. She started to close the wooden lid, but Sash spotted something on the floor, something that looked like a lever. He hadn't noticed it under the Russian box. Handing the box to Verity, he pushed back the lid until it stood upright without assistance. He scooped out the torch and the compass, setting them down on the floor next to the trunk, and then he lifted the lever. The square of floor beneath the trunk came away almost immediately, snapped down on hinges, and Sash saw only darkness and heard a distant rush of water. Eyes wide, he fumbled for the torch and shone it into the gloom. A metal stepladder appeared beneath him and beyond it a small rowing boat listed on the gentle current.

"Your dad's either insane or he's really on to something," murmured Verity.

"He's insane," Sash muttered.

Verity fronted him angrily. "You don't give your dad enough credit! I think he knows exactly what he's doing. And I don't think he's doing it for money or fame. Have you considered for even a moment that he might actually believe the myth?" She turned back to the trunk, staring down into

106

the darkness. "He thinks the bird will heal wrongs. You heard him talking about taxidermy. The animals he stuffs never grow old or die, they live for ever. And the bird of flames is no ordinary bird. It's special. Magical... So if it lives for ever through taxidermy ... *nothing need ever be wrong again.*"

Sash looked at her doubtfully. Magic, what rubbish, he thought. But, despite himself, he was moved by Verity's words. What if she was right about Max? How well did he really understand his own father?

Verity was already climbing through the trunk and heading down the ladder.

"Have you lost your mind?" said Sash.

"Don't you want to find the bird?" She had reached the boat and eased herself into it. Sash saw it rock beneath her. She coughed a few times. "Prepare yourself, it stinks down here," she warned.

"Find the bird?" echoed Sash. "But there is no bird! It's all a figment of my dad's overactive imagination."

She blinked up at him against the light. "What do you mean? You saw the feather! And you said there was a doorway on the Fleet. When we were in the library. You *said* so!"

Sash shifted uneasily. "I said... What I meant was I could see why my dad thought there was. Which isn't the same thing, because he's barmy." He couldn't believe that Verity accepted all this – that she could believe in enchanted birds and doorways to faraway lands.

"How can you ignore what's going on beneath your nose?"

she scoffed. "Are you blind? You saw the map, and your dad's calendar. You saw the stuff on the internet!"

"I saw the ramblings of a lunatic," replied Sash, wondering again at Max's odd obsession with birds. "That proves nothing. And even assuming just for a moment that he's right – that there is a doorway or whatever somewhere on the Fleet – what makes you think we can find it? My dad's obviously been searching for ages without success."

"We're here now, we might as well try. We may not get another chance in months." Verity's voice echoed in the dank passageway. She was right. Max watched the study like a hawk. "Come down here, will you? We need the torch."

"I really don't think this is a good idea," said Sash, but at the same time he pocketed the compass, climbed through the trunk, passed Verity the torch and eased himself down into the boat. It was hardly big enough for both of them and shook precariously. Two wooden oars rolled beneath Sash's feet.

A putrid smell like sewage and rotting fruit engulfed them. Sash gagged and tried to take shallow breaths. Brickwork arched above their heads. The passage in front of them split into two tunnels. Sash reached out his hand and touched the nearest wall. It was cold and slimy.

"Do you have the map of the Fleet?" asked Verity.

"It's up in the flat. You'd better get it."

"Why me?"

"Because you're lighter. If I try to get up I'll probably tip the boat."

"Well I can't go. You'll leave without me." The torch caught the side of her face, a white half-moon with a crater for an eye.

"I'm not going," said Sash stubbornly. He flicked the torch beyond her, into the darkness. "Anyway we don't need it, do we? It's hardly like the Fleet has hundreds of tributaries. This is the only place it splits as far as I remember." Max had been crafty, finding a flat with easy access to both routes. "It's a simple question of north or south, east or west."

"So what's it to be?"

Sash pulled the compass out of his pocket. First, he thought about the Fleet Valley in the south, which joined the Thames at Blackfriars Bridge. He remembered that it was once as wide as two hundred metres, a busy thorough-fare for boats. It was the mouth of the River Fleet, the artery of London. The valley was downstream so it would be easier work reaching it as the river would carry them. In many ways it was the logical place to start. But if it was easier to reach now, it would be harder rowing back. And it was several miles away, no short distance in a tiny rowing boat. What if the water was rapid down there? What if they couldn't navigate it? A more sensible beginning seemed to be the area they were already closest to, the narrow passages that wound their way to Hampstead in the west, and Highgate in the east. He remembered that it was at Hampstead Ponds that Max had found the bright red feather.

"North, towards Hampstead," said Sash. In the darkness,

he saw Verity nod. He passed her the torch, which she dutifully pointed ahead of her, lighting up the alleyway of the Fleet.

How many times had his father explored this route on his lonely journeys? How would he feel if he learned that his son had snooped through his study with a girl he scarcely knew, reading his notes, opening his trunk ... discovering his secrets?

"Don't tell me you've changed your mind," came Verity's voice. "Sash?"

Sash realized that he had been lost in his thoughts. He looked up at the open trunk and the distant glow from the study light. Would his father ever forgive him if he found out? But how could Sash ignore the discovery of the underground river, now that it had been made? Could he let the water slip beneath him without sparing it a thought, as millions of Londoners did every day? And who cares what Dad thinks? thought Sash with a twinge of resentment. He's the one who keeps secrets. He's the one who dragged me to London. *Useless boy* – that's what he called me. *Can't you do anything right?* He thinks I'm good for nothing. But I can beat him at his own game. Let him know what it's like to be lied to, to be kept in the dark. "I haven't changed my mind," Sash said quietly. He released the rope that tethered them to the wall, reached for the oars and pushed the boat away into the darkness.

They travelled in silence, listening to the eerie music

of the underground river; the swish of ripples against the oars and the occasional splash or scuttle of some dark creature that had made this waterlogged cave its home. Deep within the river's sealed corridors it was impossible to guess whether the downpour continued outside. Sounds bumped against the brickwork, trapped, echoing, so that it was hard to work out distances between a noise and its cause.

Sash realized that he could no longer smell the acrid water, his nose had quickly adapted to it. And yet he knew that the foul odour remained and was hovering around them in the shadows.

There was something oddly soothing about the rhythm of the oars against the water, despite the growing ache in Sash's arms. His mind drifted back to his father. They had lived on Gully Lane for over a year. Sash could hardly believe that during this time, Max had been making journeys along the River Fleet without confiding in him. Secrets. He imagined them shifting in the gloom.

"Do you think there are rats down here?" asked Verity, breaking the silence. Her voice sounded impossibly loud and seemed to hang in the narrow waterway for several seconds.

Sash frowned, paddling upstream against the current. How long had Max devoted to pursuing the bird of flames? Researching on his small laptop ... rowing down this bricked-up sewer... And for what? A handful of daydreams. Sash thought for a moment of East Heath College, of Gully Lane, of the long walk to school past gridlocked traffic.

That was reality. There was no bird of flames; no secret doorway. Life was all you got: there was no point in wasting it hoping for more.

Wasting it as Max has wasted his. "We should go back," said Sash decisively.

"What?" Verity flashed the torch in his face and he winced. She lowered it slightly.

"There's nothing to see here, nothing but a long, dark sewer."

"No!" Verity's voice boomed and Sash almost dropped the oars. She spun her head round. "Wait a minute, there's light up there."

"No, there isn't," said Sash curtly. He narrowed his eyes. Perhaps it *was* brighter further up the tunnel.

"Let's just go on a bit," urged Verity.

"This is pointless," Sash complained, but he started to row again. After a few moments, a distinct but weak haze hung over the water. The small boat drifted towards it until an iron grille came into view on the ceiling of the tunnel. A thin light shone through the bars. Sash clicked his tongue. "It's just a gutter, a manhole to the street. Big deal."

Verity lifted the torch towards the grille. "I need to take a closer look…"

"Be careful!" hissed Sash.

"Chill, I know what I'm doing!" The boat careened as she scrambled to her feet, the light from the torch dappling the walls.

"Are you crazy? Get down!"

"What if the doorway is actually *above* us?" Verity was reaching overhead, trying to grasp the grille. Instead, her fingertips brushed the brickwork of the ceiling. "Yuck, disgusting," she muttered as something like snail slime stuck beneath her nails. As she jerked back her hand, the little boat shuddered.

"Please, Verity, get down," Sash begged, gripping the oars.

"You're not going to force me to go back, not now we're so close!"

"Close? Close to what? It's a manhole, Verity, not some magical doorway. My dad's been down this river a hundred times and never found anything. Just accept it, it doesn't exist!"

"It does exist. It must," replied Verity. "Maybe he wasn't looking in the right place." Her voice was much quieter now. "Let me think a moment."

"Please, just sit—"

"Let me think!" she snapped and the front of the boat smacked the wall of the tunnel.

It began spinning slowly and Sash steadied it with an oar but dared not speak – another outburst from Verity and they could both end up in the water. He didn't like to think about the creatures that lurked in there. Coming out in the boat had been a terrible mistake – he should never have agreed to it.

Verity was clutching the torch and running it over the brickwork and around the iron grille. "We're looking for a door, like the trapdoor to the river, like something with a handle or a knob, something that will appear and say 'open me'. But maybe it doesn't look like a door? Maybe the handle is sort of camouflaged?"

Tensely, Sash watched her shadowy outline as he struggled to steady the boat.

"I need to take a look up there." Without warning, Verity shot up her hand. At first it seemed as though she'd reach the bars – but her fingers skimmed passed them. The boat bucked in agitation. Sash saw Verity only in shades of grey: her hands thrashing in the darkness like a cartoon character suspended above a cliff. The torch hit the bottom of the boat with a thud and everything faded in the dim light from the grille. A moment later Sash felt the boat lurch, heard a rush of air pass him and a tremendous splash as water smacked his face, immediately followed by a gentle swishing.

"Verity?"

Silence.

Sash reached out ahead of him but grabbed only air. "Oh no!" He floundered for the torch that had fallen by his feet, switched it on and shone it across the boat. Verity had disappeared. With a trembling hand he raised the torch over the water. Ripples glided across the surface, but Verity was nowhere to be seen.

"Verity? Verity?" Trying to remain calm, Sash spun the

torch round the boat 360 degrees and watched for movement. He heard something ahead, a scuffling sound. Flicking the torch forward, he saw a rat scrambling across the brickwork. It paused under the glare, whiskers twitching, before diving into the water.

"Verity?" he called. He said it again, louder: "Verity?"

"Verity?" echoed the murky tunnel.

Try the torch again! he told himself, do it slower, you could have missed something! He took a deep breath and repeated the exercise, forcing himself to slow down, to watch closely, running the light over the water.

Nothing.

"Verity?" Sash choked a cry of fear. He set down the torch and started yanking off his trainers, preparing to jump in after her. Perhaps she'd bumped her head and fallen to the bottom of the river. He had to hurry.

"Sash?"

The voice came from behind him. He flashed the torch towards it. Verity's head appeared above the water, hair dripping wet, a wild expression on her face.

"You have to come now! Come *now!*" she commanded.

"The torch…"

"Leave it!"

Bewildered, Sash switched off the torch. He pushed himself off the boat into the icy water. He was surprised to find that he couldn't touch the bottom. The narrow river was deeper than it seemed.

"Where are you?" he called, treading water. His voice floated back to his own ears: excited, unfamiliar.

"Here." Verity grabbed Sash's arm and pulled him down below the surface of the river. He plunged several feet, shutting his eyes and letting her guide him. A moment later she let go. He could feel her pushing ahead of him and diving deeper.

Sash floated upwards and hit his head on something sharp. He raised his hands. There was a spiky ceiling above him – he couldn't get out. He was in a waterlogged cave that must have led off from the river. With a twinge of panic he drove forwards, kicking his legs. For a second his eyes flicked open onto blackness before he clamped them shut. Instinctively he opened his mouth as though to scream and gulped water, strangely salty on his tongue. A tightness developed in his lungs and knotted at his throat. The blackness before his closed eyelids turned to blue. He opened them, realizing that the spiky ceiling had disappeared and light was colouring the water.

A second later he burst free, gasping for breath. Blindly he smacked into a wall of rock. He grappled against it, hooking his arms over it while coughing uncontrollably. His knees scraped the ground beneath him. The water had suddenly grown shallow, no longer icy cold.

For several seconds, all Sash could see was blazing light.

"We've died and gone to heaven!" It was Verity's voice. She was somewhere above him. Sash could hear other sounds too, a rhythmic rising and falling of water, the whoosh and sigh of the sea. Colours began to take shape before him. Verity was perched on top of an oval rock, eyes glowing with excitement. Beyond her Sash saw a tranquil beach lined with palm trees and circled by sparkling water. He looked up, blinking furiously. Above him stretched a brilliant sky shimmering with the light of two suns.

— The Island —

Sash and Verity stood on a clutch of oval rocks that rose from the luminous sea. Clear blue water fanned out around them, dissolving into the horizon. A tropical island hovered in the distance like a mirage. Encircling it, a coral reef painted the water turquoise. Dazzling white sand covered the nearest beach. Palm trees peopled the strand like friendly giants, swaying under a gentle breeze, waving their large green arms in welcome.

South of the palm-lined beach, the coastline swept into lagoons. Just beyond the southern tip of the island, chalky boulders floated above the peaceful water.

Inland, highlands slept under lazy clouds, a mass of indistinct greens. Rainbows floated over the trees. The foliage ended abruptly at northern cliffs, just visible from Sash and Verity's vantage point on the rocks. A series of emerald islands disappeared to the north-west, following the mainland like a kite's fluttering tail. Far in the north-east the sea turned treacherous, charging against a string of tiny islets that pierced the water like teeth.

"It's so beautiful," gasped Verity, hands raised to her face in disbelief. "It's... It's..." She started laughing, then pulled herself together. "I've been to Costa Rica, and Thailand, and even Australia once, and they're... This is the most beautiful place I've ever seen... It's special – magical!"

Sash didn't reply. His head was spinning. The furthest he'd ever been was a school trip to Calais in the north of France. Dazed, he blinked up at the two suns that rose over the island. One looked larger and glowed whitish-yellow, like London's sun when it broke through winter clouds to brighten the streets. The smaller sun was pink and glassy like a lollipop. Two suns. How could that be? Sash rubbed his eyes, as if it was just an illusion that would soon disappear. He felt a sharp stab in his arm.

Verity had pinched him. She smiled mischievously. "It's real... I'm seeing the same thing."

Sash shook his head slowly. He was lost for words.

"It's so bright!" she exclaimed.

"And at home it's late in the evening and pouring with rain," Sash managed.

"Wherever we are is far from home, even if we reached it on a river under London..."

Sash nodded but he didn't really understand. He looked

119

into the watery gap between the rocks on which they were standing. Down it lurked a tunnel to the buried river, only a few metres away but invisible. "My dad's looking for a doorway. Something with hinges, with a door and a handle; something above water level. But it's not a doorway, not in that sense. It's a portal." He licked his lips. "A portal," he repeated.

"Do you think we should explore, now that we're here?" asked Verity.

Sash shrugged. "Now that we're here," he murmured dreamily as they pulled off their sweaters. Verity kicked off her fashionable trainers, tucked her socks inside and left them next to the sweaters in a groove between the rocks. Sash was already barefoot, having left his trainers on the boat in the passage of the Fleet.

The sea surrounding the rocks was so calm that it hardly seemed to move at all. The water was refreshingly cool and inviting. Sash and Verity slid into it easily, pushing away from the rocks and swimming towards the palm-lined beach.

Looking down, Sash saw pastel fish dart beneath him. They hurried for the protection of the reef, which glittered ahead like a vast display of fairy lights. Soon he had reached it too. The cool indigo waters turned to warm turquoise. A violet fish with speckled fins sheltered in the shadow cast by Sash's body. Smiling, he turned to Verity. She had dropped several metres behind and, like Sash, was staring down at the underwater world in wonder.

"Take a look at this fish!" called Sash. Turning from Verity back to the violet fish, his eyes flitted over the dark waters at the edges of the reef. He caught his breath. Something was moving out there, something *enormous*, the length of a van or even a bus. Sash thought he saw a dorsal fin and the judder of a silvery tail. A fist of terror gripped him. But straining his eyes towards the edges of the reef, Sash wasn't so sure. The water sparkled and beneath it the dark contour seemed frozen. He spotted other formations at the borders of the reef. Just rocks – huge motionless boulders. He breathed deeply, awash with relief, and returned his gaze to the coral.

Sash was the first to reach the beach and climb out of the water. He was surprised to find that the sand was only comfortably warm, rather than scorching hot. But it was so fine that it seemed to give way beneath him and he sank into it, struggling to find his balance.

"Look at you!" Verity laughed, swimming towards the shore.

"It's like dust! You try it!"

Verity climbed onto the beach and flopped onto her palms as the sand melted beneath her. "This is difficult," she complained.

"See!" Sash managed a few steps towards the first palm tree before tumbling face-forwards. As he pulled himself into a kneeling position, Verity snorted with laughter.

"You're absolutely *covered* in the stuff!" she cried. It was true, the fine sand had powdered Sash's face and was clinging to his clothes.

"And you're so graceful?" Sash replied. He grabbed part of a coconut husk that lay on the beach and flung it towards Verity. She lunged for it and collapsed on the ground, waving the husk triumphantly and giggling, covered in sand from head to foot. She threw it back at Sash but the angle was bad. He dived for it, missed, and instead rolled along the sand, laughing.

"Missed, Baranovski! See you in detention!" shouted Verity in a nasal, self-important voice, mimicking their Latin teacher, Mr Mills.

Sash reached for the piece of coconut husk and threw it back to Verity, continuing an odd game of catch where the object was to seize the husk while gliding as far as possible along the beach. Verity darted for it but it landed on the soft sand a short distance ahead of her.

"Missed, Tattersall, missed!" chided Sash playfully.

Absorbed in their game, they didn't see the symbol of two triangles etched into the bark of several palm trees. Deeper inland a palm shivered, the shadow of its leaves scurrying over the sand like a monstrous spider. Someone was leaning against it, clutching a dagger – glancing down towards the reef and out to the luminous sea.

"Let's find out what else is here," said Verity.

"But what is 'here'? Where on earth are we?" asked Sash,

dusting himself off and chewing his lip.

Verity shrugged.

They struggled against the sand, weaving between the palm trees.

Verity examined her wrist, scowling. "My watch has gone mad. It's telling the wrong time."

"Isn't it some posh brand that's supposed to work for ever?" asked Sash.

"Yes!" snapped Verity, propelling herself across the sand. "It's still under warranty so I'll get it replaced."

"Are you sure the warranty covers travels through underground rivers?" Sash ran his fingers through his hair. "But how...?" he added. He still couldn't understand where they were or how they'd got there.

Verity scowled at him, grabbing a handful of sand to flick in his direction, but it ran through her fingers like dust.

They went inland under the blazing suns. The murmur of the sea faded and, in time, the fine sand was replaced by rockier ground. The palms gave way to denser, leafier trees that stretched so high it was impossible to see where they ended. Other plants hitched rides on their immense trunks – bursts of golden leaves, bright red fungi and leathery vines. Butterflies fluttered between the branches. The air was moist and sweet, full of twittering calls and the distant howl of animals.

"Can you see anything? Any birds?" asked Verity, peering up into the trees.

"Not really. It's hard to see up there, but I can certainly hear them."

"What if we pass a bird of flames and we don't even know it?"

Sash stopped, remembering why they had come. He listened to the cacophony of trills, warbles and chirrups floating down from the tree canopy. They were lively and pleasant but far from beautiful. "We won't pass it without knowing."

"How can you be so sure?" asked Verity.

Sash shook his head. He couldn't really say. It was like a hunch, impossible to support factually. He glanced at the compass that he'd tucked into his pocket. They were going south-east. If they became lost, they would need to return north-west and make for the oval rocks.

They walked carefully, their bare soles treading over decomposing leaves that littered the jungle floor. A shadow stalked at their heels. Silent as a ghost, someone was skulking behind them, clinging to the shade of the thick tree trunks. Gripping a dagger with tense fingers. Watching the strangers between narrowed eyes.

"This place seems vast. How are we going to find the bird of flames?" asked Verity. "What if we're going in the wrong direction? How can we even be sure that it's here? We need to find fresh water or we'll have to go back. Maybe we should go home through the Fleet and get some provisions. The island's not going anywhere, is it? We've only got half-term before they miss us, we can't just… Sash?"

He had halted suddenly and was looking ahead, ignoring her.

"Sash, what is it?"

Wordlessly, he pointed. Several metres in front of them, glinting between the trees, a stone was just visible. On it, someone had carved an image of a wolf.

"People have been here," Verity gasped.

Sash nodded. Carefully, he edged between the trees until he reached the stone. It was part of a wall built of silvery rock, elevated by half a metre on a platform of earth like a low hill. The wall seemed to have been built in a huge circle. Some of the stones were decorated with images of wolves, fish, feathers and leaves, others with crests that resembled the waves of the sea. Lichen crept across the stones in complex yellow patterns.

"It's some kind of fort, but I don't think it's been in use for a long time," said Sash.

"Why do you say that?"

"It's a ruin. And I think people would have cleared the surrounding trees. They must have. Look up there." Sash pointed at the stones several metres above them. A narrow window was just visible between the tendrils of a vine. At such a steep angle it was impossible to see through it. And yet the jungle was so dense that the window could only be seen up close. "That's for spying. Pointless with trees so near."

"Maybe," replied Verity. "But do you remember that film we saw in Geography on rainforests? It showed how the minute there's any space on the forest floor, because of a fallen tree or whatever, saplings spring up in the light and shoot up as quickly as possible before other plants block them off from the sun. That's their only hope of survival."

"No one's been spying from this building for a long time. If they had some of these trees wouldn't be here at all. They may be younger than others in the rainforest but they're still giants." The trees overshadowing the stone fort must have been ten metres high.

"OK, Einstein, that makes sense, I suppose," said Verity with a wry smile. "There's a lot bubbling away in that brain of yours, isn't there?"

Sash did not respond. He followed the building round to the left. "Look at this design," he said.

"A sort of spiral, like a seashell." Verity traced her finger across the helix carved on one of the stones. She turned back to Sash. "But let's be clear about what you're saying. Are you really suggesting that hundreds of years ago some people found their way through the – what did you call it? – the portal, built a massive thing in the middle of the forest and disap—"

"Shh!" Sash had heard something. Something distant. Something human. "This way," he whispered. Cautiously, he skirted around the fort.

For a moment, Verity hung back, squinting at nearby

shrubs. "Sash, do you think there are wolves out here?" she called after him. "I think that bush just moved…"

"Wolves don't live in rainforests. It's the wrong climate," said Sash, who felt he knew a thing or two about animals on account of his father's job.

"Not in our world maybe," Verity replied. "But here, who knows? If there are images of wolves that means there could be the real thing, right?"

He didn't answer and she hurried after him, glancing back into the undergrowth. As Verity dashed up behind Sash he shot out an arm to block her. Startled, she followed his gaze. Several metres away the fort ended abruptly, continuing again after a space of perhaps four metres. If gates had once blocked the entrance, they had long disappeared. Verity gave a muffled cry of surprise. People dressed in colourful clothes were pouring through the entrance of the fort, some wearing finely woven hoods. They all had short, sandy hair – even the women – and golden skin. Many carried earthenware pots, cloth or stacks of bound palm leaves. Several were clearing the entrance and a short path before it of vines and debris in what must have been a daily battle against the wilful jungle at the fort's doorstep.

Sash moved closer, hidden behind a tree.

"Be careful!" urged Verity, watching the crowds uncertainly.

Sash glanced at her and nodded. He bit his lip and turned back to the fort, his eyes climbing the high walls. Arching over the entrance was a giant statue of a bird in flight. Its body was dark green and speckled with red, like droplets of blood. Its diamond-shaped tail was scarlet. Its mighty wings spanned from wall to wall. The bird appeared to smoulder in the sun like scorching embers. From this distance, it was hard to see what was causing this effect, although it looked as though tiny amber and red jewels had been inlaid at the tips of each carved feather.

Sash shielded his eyes against the glare. "The bird of flames!" he gasped. Before he knew it someone seized his wrist and pulled him back into the jungle.

— The Citadel —

A girl stood in front of Sash, short though roughly his age, staring at him with blue eyes. Her face was framed with sandy brown hair, almost the same colour as her skin, like the other people milling around the entrance to the fort. She wore a wrap-around dress, embroidered with yellow stars and small blue fish, that ended at her knees. She reached up to touch Sash's hair but he drew away.

The girl giggled. "Come," she said. She started back into the jungle.

Sash stared, slack-jawed. Verity was standing a few paces from him. She mouthed "No".

"Come!" repeated the girl, more insistently, and Sash followed dazedly, leaving Verity little choice but to do the same.

"My name is Manah," said the girl.

"I'm Sash and this is Verity," offered Sash.

"Sash and Verity," echoed the girl, forming the names carefully, rolling them around on her tongue. "Sash and Verity. Where do you come from, Sash and Verity?" Although she addressed the question to both of them, she only looked at Sash.

"We're... Not far away."

"What a funny way of talking you have, Sash and Verity, and what strange names," said Manah. "I think that you come from the Trin Isles, do you not? I can tell."

Sash remembered the emerald islands that followed the mainland like a kite's fluttering tail. He said nothing.

"I thought so. Trin Islanders are always so serious!" Manah grinned. "And the clothes..." She frowned at Sash's jeans and T-shirt. "Is this your first time on Aqarti?"

"'Aqarti'?" said Sash. "What do you mean, 'Aqarti'?"

The girl's eyes narrowed. "Why, this is Aqarti," she said, waving her hand towards the fort and the surrounding jungle. "You must know where you are?"

"We're trying to find the bird of flames," said Verity quickly.

Manah's fingers touched her throat, her eyes darting into the surrounding jungle. "Why do you want it?" she asked in a low voice.

"We—" started Sash.

"We've heard it's very beautiful and wanted to see it for

130

ourselves," Verity cut in. She flashed Sash a stern look.

Manah's eyes brightened. "Oh yes! The aruva, the bird of flames. The most beautiful bird of all, the most mysterious. Of course you have heard the story? But there are few aruva now, you know. And they are shy, so very shy. Most people never get to see them, not once in a whole lifetime. Such a shame."

Verity clicked her tongue irritably. "Are they that rare?"

"Oh yes, very rare."

"But the statue…"

"The stone bird at the entrance to the citadel?" Manah lowered her head and shut her eyes. "The Bloodstone Bird," she whispered. Her fingers rose again to her throat.

Verity and Sash exchanged glances.

Manah opened her eyes. "Ancient," she said. "From a time when you could not move without seeing a real one. Not any more. Not unless you know where to search for them."

"Where is that?" asked Sash.

Manah smiled warmly. "Forgive me, Sash, I keep forgetting that you are from the Trin Isles. You cannot be expected to know these things on your first visit. Yes, that is a problem…" she trailed off sadly. "I am so sorry, Sash, but I do not think that you shall get to see an aruva. I hope that this was not the only reason you came to Aqarti?"

Sash felt a rush of disappointment. They had gone so far, only to be denied even a glimpse of the bird of flames. It didn't seem fair.

Verity tugged on the sleeve of his T-shirt. Her eyes were wide and desperate.

"Maybe you could help us, tell us where we'd have a chance of finding one." He added, in an effort at politeness, "If you don't mind?"

Manah clapped her hands together suddenly. "I know what we can do! I know how I can help you! I can show you myself where to find these precious birds! But first we must do something about those curious Trin clothes…"

Making them promise to stay put, Manah disappeared into the jungle.

Immediately Verity turned to Sash. "Let's make a run for it before she gets back!"

Sash hadn't heard her. "She speaks English! Don't you think it's bizarre? We come through this mad portal to this place… Did she call it Aqarti?"

"A sort of English, anyway. Yes, it's all bizarre, but we can talk about that later. Come on!" Verity tugged Sash's arm.

"Are you serious?" He couldn't tell if she was teasing him.

"I don't trust her, there's something weird about her."

"We've only just met her," he returned. "She said she knows where to find the bird of flames. I take it you don't want to go home empty-handed?"

"Did you hear how she called it something else? Aru-something."

"But she knew what we meant. And her offer of help is still the best we've got."

"We don't need her help!" said Verity.

"Don't we?" Sash gestured at the thick foliage surrounding them. Then there was the citadel, with its ancient walls and colourful people. Where would they begin to look for the timid bird? They only had seven days.

"Why does she want to help us anyway?"

It was a good question. Life had taught Sash to be suspicious of kindness, especially from others his own age. Manah seemed so friendly and eager to help them. But hadn't Verity herself seemed friendly moments before she had humiliated him in front of their classmates? Sourness formed on Sash's tongue as he remembered how Verity had ridiculed him. His promise to himself never to trust her flashed through his mind. Suddenly, he wasn't sure who to trust. He stepped away from Verity and peered through the gaps between the branches, where yellow birds like canaries were grooming each other.

Verity scowled. "She knows we're not from Trin or whatever."

"Why do you say that?" asked Sash.

"I can just tell."

Sash shrugged. "So you want to go back to the Fleet?" he asked carefully, avoiding her eyes.

She shook her head quickly, jerking her blonde hair, already stringy from the seawater and humidity. "Fine," she said. "We'll stick with Manah for now. But we ditch her at the first sign of trouble. Agreed?"

"Agreed," whispered Sash.

* * *

Manah returned with a bundle of clothes, a leather water flask and small, rolled pancakes wrapped in cloth.

"No, thank you," said Verity as Manah held out the pancakes.

The local girl stared back, as though in confusion. "But you are my guests now," she said. "You cannot refuse hospitality, that is just... Well, it is just not seemly!"

Sash threw Verity a warning glance. "I'll have one." He reached out and put one of the small pancakes in his mouth. Sweet jelly oozed out of it, tangy and unfamiliar on his tongue. "It's good," he mumbled.

Manah instantly brightened. "Please have as many as you wish. I made them myself with gorpi berries. And I brought you some clothes to wear. It is foolish really but people can be odd around strangers, and if you stay in your own things, everyone will know that you are from Trin. You are so tall, Sash, I hope these fit you." She held up a colourful shirt and a pair of calf-length baggy trousers. "They belong to my brother, Jonto. You remind me of him." She watched Sash, as though fascinated.

Sash's cheeks flashed red as he took off his T-shirt and tried on the shirt. It was covered with finely embroidered leaves and tied across the side with laces. Once on, it strained over his chest and the sleeves were a bit short, but otherwise the fit wasn't bad.

Manah handed him the baggy trousers. "Here, please

take a hood," she said, passing Sash a woven item. "You tie the strings round your neck. It is necessary to protect your head from the sunshine, but maybe you should wear it up all the time to look ... to fit in better."

Sash had never seen a hood that wasn't attached to a jacket or sweatshirt. It felt strange tying it round his neck but he lifted it up over his head anyway, hoping that it would help him blend in. Shyly, he stepped behind a nearby tree to pull on the baggy trousers. He tucked the compass in his pocket.

"And this is for you." Manah passed Verity a knee-length wrap-around dress. It too was colourfully embroidered, with butterflies and other winged insects. There was also a woven hood like the one Sash was wearing. "You know, your hair is very long. We do not wear it that way on Aqarti. Maybe you should cut it? I could help you."

"No. Thanks all the same," snapped Verity, stroking her hair protectively.

"Well, wear the hood," suggested Manah.

Verity held the woven item between her fingertips. "Where is your brother?" she asked.

"He is out hunting." Manah smiled, but a shadow crossed her eyes. "Here, I shall take your clothes and store them away safely in the jungle. As it is your first time on Aqarti, I should think that you want to look round?"

"Not necessarily," muttered Verity rudely.

But if the other girl heard her, she didn't show it.

Manah stalked along the outskirts of the fort and under the stone bird. Sash and Verity followed, hoods raised over their heads.

"You look ridiculous!" Verity laughed, shoving Sash playfully.

"No more than you!" he replied, tugging her hood down over her eyes.

Manah smiled and pulled her hood up too.

From the inside it was clear that the wall surrounding the citadel was circular. The structure had fallen into disrepair. A stone ledge with steps up to the spy windows ran along the inside of the wall but many of the steps had crumbled away. The trees within the citadel had been cut down, leaving a wide clearing where people went about their business. Yet vines sank between the walls and arched out again like writhing snakes. Creepers ran along the stones. Rebellious bushes sprang up in the clearings. Sash saw women pulling them up and collecting them into mounds.

"They travel in flocks here, like birds," whispered Verity.

Sash followed her gaze to a group of dragonflies, which buzzed overhead. Their neon blue wings caught the light like mirrors. He nodded slowly. He hardly realized he was smiling.

People in brightly woven clothes were moving about the citadel. A boy no more than six years old chased several others past giant earthenware pots filled with cotton, spices and seeds.

"Don't you have school here?" Verity was asking.

"School?" Manah blinked at her.

"I mean, don't children have lessons, like Maths and Geography?"

Sash shuddered when he thought about East Heath College. The idea of a world without school seemed too good to be true. Looking around the vibrant citadel he felt heady with delight.

"Oh, we learn all about the island's geography, if that is what you mean?" said Manah. "Here we are in the middle of lowland Aqarti. There is a palm beach on one side of the island, a mangrove beach on the other," she added authoritatively. "Of course, you cannot just go down to the beaches, not without permission from the Keeper." Here she eyed her guests a moment before continuing. "The highlands are wild, they are covered in jungle, although people live up there too."

"Is this where you live?" Sash asked Manah, thinking that to live in this peaceful place, free from the rules and disappointments of his world, would be paradise.

Manah laughed. "No one lives in the citadel, not any more! They only lived here for the years that your people attacked!"

Sash's jaw dropped. So Manah did know that they were different, that they had arrived from far away – and they were not the first. Had Londoners come through the portal on the Fleet and attacked the islanders many years ago?

"It is true," she continued, "the citadel was built during the Middle Period when islanders first arrived from Trin, long before the Great Peace."

Sash sighed with relief. Manah really did think they were from those green islands.

"Only the Keeper *lives* in the citadel, although we do not see him often," she went on. "Everyone else lives in villages. Most are near by in the lowlands, though you would need to know your way through the jungle to find them. The rest are in the highlands."

They were just passing a pot full of prickly red fruit. A short, widely set man stood next to it, talking to a passer-by. As the man's back was turned, Manah scooped up one of the fruits between her thumb and forefinger. She stripped off the skin in a seamless movement to reveal the fleshy white insides, which she offered to Sash. He sniffed the fruit. Manah giggled and popped it in her mouth.

"Where's your village?" asked Sash.

"Look at this," said Manah, ignoring his question and pointing to a number of striped yellow and red fish that a woman was placing on pieces of bark to dry in the sun. The fish were roughly the size of sardines, but their bodies were flat. "Dried fire bass, my favourite. Caught in the atoll reef."

"Are they expensive?" asked Verity.

"What do you mean?" replied Manah.

"Do they cost a lot to buy?"

Manah raised her brows. "Are you asking me how many

other items need to be traded by one village in return for some fish from the village that caught these?"

"Don't you have money?" asked Verity.

Manah's brow crinkled.

Sash stiffened. It was clear that Manah had no concept of money and Verity's questions would make her suspect that they came from further away than Trin. He peered out beyond the striped bass to where a man in fish-embroidered shirt and culottes was fanning embers on which he laid branches. Over the branches, two women draped an enormous eel. It was easily as long as Sash's legs. "Wow!" he said, pointing at the eel in an effort to distract Manah, although he was genuinely impressed by the creature's size. There was something else about the eel that unnerved him and with a wave of disgust he realized that it didn't have eyes.

"Freshwater river eel. Good to eat!" said Manah.

"I wouldn't want to swim with one of those near by," said Verity.

"No, I believe you would not!" Manah agreed, pointing at the sharp little teeth dotting the eel's grinning jaws. "They live in the caves that lead off the streams in the highlands. You are safe as long as you bathe under the suns – eels hate bright light."

"I'll remember that," said Sash, grimacing.

"The streams come together and run down to the citadel. There's a freshwater well beyond the palace, the Well of Tears."

"Why is it called that?" asked Verity.

"Because the animals cried when Bryda the panther and Sivan the razor shark failed to find harmony," replied Manah matter-of-factly.

Sash glanced at Verity but neither of them said anything. After a few moments Verity started to hum a tune. Sash recognized it as *River of Tears*, a pop song that had recently been in the charts. He wanted to warn her to stop – somehow, this song could give them away as outsiders.

But Manah got there first. "What was that?" she demanded, turning on Verity.

"I don't know what you mean," returned Verity, shocked by her tone.

"I thought…" Manah looked around nervously. "I thought you were singing…" She trailed off.

Behind the bartering market rose a building shaped like a stout ice cream cone. Manah saw Sash and Verity looking at it. "That is the Imperial Palace," she said. She drew them closer but stopped at a respectful distance. Covering the palace were more mysterious symbols like the wolves and feathers that Sash and Verity had seen etched onto the citadel's fort. Like the images on the fort, these looked ancient and poorly maintained. It seemed as though several had been removed, or had disintegrated with time; gaps appeared between the carved tiles. Suspended from the top of the cone-shaped building was a flag bearing a symbol of two triangles, with a red triangle next to a black one.

It seemed out of place on the unusual building.

The palace itself was surrounded by a low wall, which looked recently constructed. Stonemasons were decorating the wall with images. These differed from the symbols on the palace and the citadel's fort – they all showed a robed man in various poses. The man's face was hidden behind a mask but his hand gestures and the other images on the stones made it clear what he was doing: in the first he was seated alone on a throne, in the second he was surrounded by animals, in another he seemed to be preaching or singing – Sash noticed that he wore a strange headdress in that one, like a square hat.

"Keeper, bringer of peace," said Manah flatly. "He lives in the palace, or so we are told. He is rarely seen."

"But you can't tell what he looks like," said Verity, pointing at the images.

"No one is allowed to gaze upon his 'timeless face'," said Manah, crossing her arms. "We are forbidden to see his perfect skin."

"What's so perfect about it?" Verity went on.

Manah shrugged. "It is said that he is as beautiful as his own voice. And that he shall never grow old." Manah eyed Sash and Verity for a moment. She narrowed her eyes, glancing over her shoulder. No one was in earshot. She spoke again in a low voice. "But—" she began.

Suddenly a horn sounded.

Manah spun round, tugging at her hood.

"Hail to the Keeper!" somebody cried.

"I spoke too soon. You are in luck," said Manah. "A parade."

Guards handed out ribbons, red and black like the flag that swayed above the palace. Several called out praises to the Keeper. People in the citadel started to clap and cheer. Many hurriedly wound the ribbons round their wrists or waved them in the air.

The crowds parted for a series of colourful marchers. The marchers' clothes were studded with gems and sparkled as they moved. They passed to reveal a palanquin, which was like a carriage but without wheels. Instead, it was carried by guards who wore red shirts and black culottes. Arrows, batons and a collection of ornamental knives hung across the guards' chests and dangled from belts round their waists. The crowd cheered and threw handfuls of petals in the palanquin's path.

As it drew past, Manah bowed her head and looked away. Verity clapped, absorbed in the excitement of the parade. Seated in the palanquin, his hood pulled over his head, the Keeper watched his subjects. His face was covered in a black, plaster mask. Through the narrow eye slits, he noticed the pretty girl clapping her hands with the rest of his people. His glance trailed over her bracelet. His eyebrows furrowed. Such a strange bracelet with a flat, round face... So familiar... Twisting his neck as he moved past her, the Keeper cursed the mask that obscured his view. For a moment, he lost her among the crowds. Suddenly he saw her again. Next to her stood a tall, fair-skinned boy. Although the boy's head was covered by his hood, his dark eyes followed the palanquin. Of course, the boy could not see beyond the Keeper's mask – that would be impossible … and yet those dark eyes seemed to bore through it, to stare directly at the Keeper's face.

It was as though the world had come to a standstill. The Keeper licked his parched lips, watching fearfully. He called urgently to his guards, who scurried towards him.

Manah watched, her fingers rising to her throat. She turned to Sash and Verity, gripping them sharply by their wrists, and tugged them away from the palanquin.

Moments later, a group of guards dispersed through the crowds, spinning their batons. People froze, panic-stricken. A woman whispered to her friend, "They must have found one! It is happening again!"

"What's going on?" asked Sash, noticing a commotion behind them.

Manah steered them quickly through the throng. "Oh nothing," she replied. "Just part of the parade."

— The Iffula —

Manah led Sash and Verity along the side of the Imperial Palace where guards dressed in red and black leant against the wall, twirling their batons gloomily. They passed lavish gardens full of flowers that looked like orchids and smelled of vanilla. Beyond the gardens lay a stone well, which Sash guessed to be the Well of Tears. Not far behind it was the back entrance to the citadel. He and Verity followed Manah past the guards grouped near by. She hunched forward like an old woman, her eyes downcast. But she moved quickly.

"Did you see the parade? Where are you going?" one of the guards asked a man as Sash passed him.

"Yes, sir, I saw it, it was beautiful," replied the man, bowing his head. "Praise be to the Keeper! I am going to my village."

"Are you sure there's nothing going on?" Verity hissed, half-jogging to keep up with Manah.

"All is well," replied Manah, smiling pleasantly.

"Can we slow down then? My feet hurt."

"Soon." Manah kept up the pace as they entered the jungle and started uphill. The high canopy quickly drew over them, allowing only shafts of light to break between the leaves. In the shadows Sash noticed a furry vine dangling from a branch. Curious, he reached out to stroke it but Manah grabbed his hand.

"Do not touch the brown vines," she warned.

She pressed on confidently between the trees. Sash and Verity followed more cautiously, not used to walking barefoot. The floor of the jungle was covered with damp leaves and moss. It made a surprisingly comfortable carpet, provided they dodged the occasional twigs and pebbles.

They trudged towards the highlands without passing a soul, mesmerized by the rhythmic chirping of cicadas. Sash focused on each step. Peering down at his feet he saw that they were dirtier than they had ever been. It gave him an odd satisfaction. He thought of the cleaning ritual that his father insisted on with each new taxidermy specimen. First, any traces of blood were removed with a damp cloth. After that, Max would gently smooth the fur or feathers, his expert fingers searching for damage. He might brush down stray hairs. The final groom came at the end of the taxidermy, once the skin had been treated, stuffed and

mounted. Even then, it didn't do to be over-zealous –
a highly groomed animal betrayed an amateur.

"Nature is imperfect. Rabbits aren't styled by Vidal
Sassoon!" That's what Max always said, proud of the reference to what he thought was a fashionable hairdresser,
although Sash doubted whether Sassoon had cut hair in
decades.

When Sash looked up the world around him had changed.
The light between the trees had dimmed. Sooty moths flit-
tered in gathering shadow. Trills and twitters had given way
to hoots and howls. The lush, colourful jungle that had filled
him with wonder – the jungle of butterflies and rainbows
– had grown eerie in the half-light.

He checked the compass. They were moving northwards.
It was becoming steadily more humid; low clouds of mist
hung in the foliage. Sweat clung to Sash's forehead and he
pushed down his hood to wipe it away. He glanced into the
trees, following the receding light. "That yellow sun sinks to
the south here," he mused.

Verity rolled her eyes. "That's all very interesting, Sash,
but how much longer?" she complained. Stumbling on a low
shrub, she grasped one of the furry vines to steady herself. It
immediately hooked round her hand and started coiling up
her wrist like a boa constrictor. Verity cried out and Manah
leapt round, drawing a dagger from within her dress and
lopping off the vine, which dropped to the jungle floor
and thrashed for a few seconds before falling still.

"I said not to touch the brown vines!" growled Manah.

"What was that? I want to know what's going on!" returned Verity, rubbing her hand in shock.

"We must keep moving, it is almost nightfall. Sash, please pull up your hood."

Verity stood still, arms crossed. "Why do we need to keep moving? Who are you? Where are you taking us?"

Sash stopped and watched. A string of sweat rolled down the back of his neck. He tried to read the compass again but already the face was growing dark and he could scarcely see the dial. Even squinting he could no longer understand where they had gone and, more worryingly, how they would return to the oval rocks. An exit home could be one hundred miles away or just one hundred yards, and he wouldn't be any the wiser.

"Please, we must not tarry," said Manah in a reasonable voice. Her eyes skimmed the darkening jungle. "Let us hurry, it does not feel right."

"What doesn't feel right?" demanded Verity. "We're not going anywhere until you tell us what's going on and where we're going. The citadel ... we left quickly. The guards were looking for something, or someone..."

Manah's head sank until they could no longer see her eyes beneath her hood. "If I tell you, will you hurry?" she asked in a small voice.

"Spit it out!" snapped Verity, and Sash touched her lightly on the arm.

"I am worried that we are being followed. I am taking you somewhere safe in the highlands," whispered Manah.

Sash gazed into the jungle beyond her. Every branch and leaf seemed to twitch with life. Were predators stirring from their slumber? Had something traced their scent on the clammy air? "What do you think is following us?" he asked.

"What, or who?" replied Manah. She lowered her voice. "The Keeper's guards."

"But why? What have we done?" asked Verity, batting away a moth.

Manah sighed. "It is I that they seek."

Sash could just see Verity's raised eyebrow. With a sinking feeling, he looked away. Had they been wrong to come with Manah? Verity hadn't trusted her – it was his fault.

Manah continued. "They think I am a Follower – one who honours Great Aruva – and you cannot do that here any more."

"What do you mean?" asked Verity.

Manah scanned the foliage. "My people revere Great Aruva ... the 'bird of flames', as you call it. We always have, ever since the beginning. My mother's mother, my father's father, and their parents, and their parents' parents before them. She has always watched over and protected us. There are some people who do not believe the story about Great Aruva and the sun, but it is true, it is all true. The aruva is a magical bird and I suppose that is why you want to find it. But you will not find it easily. The Keeper has banned our devotion to the bird. He has even banned the bird itself."

At the mention of Great Aruva and the sun, Sash recalled the excerpts he had read on the internet about the bird of flames. So the Followers really believed that the bird had learned the secret of harmony. He wanted to say something – to share this realization – but Verity was already speaking.

"How can anyone ban a bird?" she was asking coldly.

Manah touched her fingers to her throat again. "How? By training his archers to shoot down the aruva. And every year he kills off more of the birds, and it is forbidden to protect them, and there are very few left. No one is allowed to sing. That is why I was fearful in the citadel when I thought that you were singing." She shook her head. "Only the Keeper sings now, once a year at the joining of the suns. He hates people like me, people who still dare speak of the aruva's power. We are not allowed to follow the aruva – we are only allowed to revere *him*. They say that he is holy."

"But... Isn't the Keeper just an ordinary man who rules your island?" asked Verity.

"He would not say so... No, he claims to be a magician. And it fits a legend about a divine being emerging from the sea in the form of a man. We Followers never really believed that prophecy, but others did. There are lots of old stories passed down through generations. Some have become muddled. It does not matter. Believe what you will, that is what we have always said. But the Keeper does not see it that way."

"So who is the Keeper?" said Verity. "I don't understand."

149

"The Keeper appeared years ago on Rising Beach. Coconut gatherers saw him walking out of the sea, unharmed. And the strangest thing is that just before the Keeper set foot on Aqarti, moments before the farmers saw him, the sky blackened. Do you understand? It went dark, right in the middle of the day! I was not alive then but... Well, everyone talks about it! There are those who thought it would be dark for ever. But then the suns reappeared, and the Keeper arrived. So people praised him as a god or a wizard. He is not one of us – he came from nowhere!"

Sash stiffened but resisted the urge to glance at Verity.

"Couldn't he just have been out swimming or something?" asked Verity.

"That makes no sense. Everyone on Aqarti comes from one of the villages, someone would have known him."

"Maybe he's from Trin," offered Verity.

"Maybe," echoed Manah in a strange voice. "But that still does not explain the swimming. No one enters the water at Rising Beach and survives."

"What do you mean? Why not?" Verity shot Sash a quick look.

"Because of the razor sharks," said Manah. "They are gigantic and they eat everything. They are the most vicious creatures there are! If they smell human flesh they attack instantly. I have not seen it myself but I have heard about what happened to the fishermen who thought they could build a sturdy enough boat... The sharks sliced through the wood and gobbled them up. No one can swim in those waters." Manah's eyes narrowed as she watched Sash and Verity.

"But what about the fish we saw in the citadel? Who caught those?"

"The ones at the market were all netted in the atoll. It is a reef-lined lagoon beyond Rising Beach. The sharks swim around it but mercifully they have not grown legs! So they cannot get in."

Sash remembered the enormous shapes he had seen lurking at the edges of the reef. At the time he had taken them to be boulders but now he wasn't so sure. Feeling hot and anxious, he ran his fingers through his matted hair. Between the gaps in the tree canopy, the light was turning red. A high-pitched cackle echoed through the jungle. He peered into the branches. The jungle seemed to be heaving, pulsing, an immense, complex, living creature. He turned back to Manah. Her eyes glinted beneath her hood. He was suddenly sure that she knew he and Verity were not from Trin: she had watched them swim from the oval rocks.

"You saw us," he said quietly. "You think we're... You think we're like the Keeper."

"Sash!" protested Verity.

"But she saw us," he said.

"I did!" admitted Manah. "I saw you at Rising Beach," she whispered, staring at Sash intensely as if Verity wasn't there. "It is forbidden to go down to the beach, the warning symbols of the Keeper are everywhere but... But I went anyway. And I *saw* you. You *are* like the Keeper! They say that no creature will harm him, that nothing can kill him! They say that he can live for ever! But if you are like him, maybe you can help stop him. You can defeat the Keeper! I called for you, I begged Great Aruva to deliver you, and here you are with your dark eyes, a giant, a silent giant, here you are to defeat the Keeper!" Manah spoke urgently, edging towards Sash with hands outstretched.

"You've got it all wrong. I'm not special! I can't help you," he said. He backed away from Manah, tripping over a stray stone, and fell against a tree trunk. Above him burst a fiendish cackle. Something dived into his hair and he felt a searing pain through the back of his head and another a second later as something sprang on his shoulder and bit his neck. Creatures were swooping down the trunk of the tree. He threw up his hands, swiping at them uselessly, too stunned to speak. For an instant he felt fur. Sharp teeth sank into his finger.

Verity screamed.

"Not like that!" cried Manah. She shoved Sash away from the tree and batted at the creatures with the back of her hand, her fingers flat.

Sash saw one of them fly off his shoulder to land on its back in front of him. The creature squirmed onto its feet, cackling angrily. It was a small, furry animal, no greater than his palm, with short-clawed feet, round ears and a flexing tail. A tiny monkey, Sash realized.

The monkey darted towards his ankle and started climbing up his leg. Manah bent over and kicked it onto the ground again, stabbing it through the back with her dagger. It struggled desperately, its mouth snapping, flashing pointed fangs. Manah wrenched out the dagger and kicked the dying monkey into the undergrowth.

"Why did you take down your hood, you fool?" she scolded, flipping the remaining monkeys off Sash's head and shoulders and spearing them with practiced skill.

Sash blinked at his bleeding finger where one of the creatures had nipped him as Verity pulled his hood over his head. "What were they?" he gasped in shock.

"Iffula – night monkeys. They love fresh meat," muttered Manah. She turned sternly to Verity, wiping the blood off her dagger with a leaf. "You have a loud voice! Guards patrol the jungle and if they were not following us before they will be now. We need to leave at once!"

This time neither Sash nor Verity asked any questions. They hurried after Manah, deeper into the highlands. A warm breeze floated up with them, pressing against their backs, carrying with it the cackles of the iffula.

— The Spiral Net —

Sash trod warily over the dark floor of the jungle.

"Are there any snakes in Aqarti?" asked Verity. Manah had rushed ahead and didn't answer.

Sash turned and waited for Verity to catch up. He marvelled at Manah's boldness in the inky wilderness, without a map to guide her or a torch to light her way.

"We shouldn't be going with her," Verity whispered. "She's using us, Sash. We don't want to get caught up in a battle with their Keeper."

"I don't think we have much choice. If we don't go with her we face a night out here," Sash replied. "But we can leave tomorrow morning, there'll be nothing stopping us then. We can go back to the rocks, back to the Fleet."

"What about the sharks? Why didn't they attack us if they go for everyone else, like she said?"

"Everyone else except the Keeper," added Sash. He had been wondering the same thing. Sharks were wild, primitive creatures. He remembered his father telling him that they had a powerful sense of smell – that some species could pick up the odour of blood a mile away. But humans on Aqarti had different diets. Perhaps Sash and Verity smelled odd to the sharks.

Verity spoke again. "I didn't trust that Manah right from the start. There's something strange about her."

"Well, now we know why," replied Sash. Ahead of them, Manah's dark shape was vanishing among the trees.

"Do we? How can we be sure that she's telling us the whole story?"

"Are we telling her the whole story?" he answered softly.

Verity touched his arm, warning him not to continue. Manah had halted. She turned and placed a finger over her lips, pointing. Three figures came into view between the foliage. They stalked past only metres away, wielding batons: the Keeper's guards.

Sash stood stock-still as the guards passed, holding his breath, his heart thumping. Long after the guards had gone, Manah lifted her finger from her lips and gestured that they should go on in a different direction. They walked in silence, Manah in the lead, Sash in the middle and Verity lagging behind. Every few minutes Sash would pause and wait for Verity, helping her over fallen tree trunks or occasional rocks that blocked their path. They walked uphill all the way, deeper into the highlands, struggling under the poor light, their bare feet sore, their legs trembling with exhaustion.

Without warning, Verity stopped. "Sash, I want to go home," she whimpered.

Sash nodded and glanced at Manah, who was balancing on a boulder a short distance away.

"We are almost there," Manah announced.

Sash turned to Verity. "We'll leave at dawn," he whispered.

The trees of the jungle parted, revealing for the first time a clear view of Aqarti's night sky. Sash had always lived in cities and never seen such a luminous moon. As he gazed up a pattern emerged from the stars, a floating helix that started at the moon and spun outwards across the horizon.

Sash thought immediately of the mysterious symbols that decorated the citadel's fort.

"That is the Spiral Net," said Manah, watching him. "It guards the suns and holds them forever above us, keeping us warm and the world bright. If the suns should fall, our land would be destroyed by fire." Manah pointed into the sky. "Beyond the net is a land that the Keeper cannot touch – a land where music always plays. No one has ever broken through it, no one except Great Aruva."

Peering up at the stars, Sash thought he heard a melody floating down over the jungle. He lowered his face and the music faded. He told himself that it was nothing. It had been a long day and he was tired; his mind was playing tricks.

Ahead of them in a small clearing was a hut raised from the ground on wooden blocks. Its roof was layered with palm leaves. The doors and windows were sealed but light escaped through gaps between the wood, the guttering light of candles.

Manah approached and hooted like an owl. After a pause the door creaked opened a crack.

"Manah?" whispered a man's voice.

"Yes, Tiro, it is I. I have bought visitors who may be able to help."

"Were you followed?" asked the man. He opened the door wider.

Manah looked over her shoulder. "No. But they are out there."

The man nodded and waved them up the low steps into the hut.

In the dim light, Sash saw ten or more people seated cross-legged on woven mats, too many for the small space. At the far corner lay sleeping infants, but most of the occupants seemed to be awake.

The sweet smells of sandalwood and vanilla filled their noses. Candles, surrounded by a ribbon laced with feathers, were placed on the floor among blossom and fruit. Sash in stantly recognized the feathers – they were identical to the one he had seen in his father's trunk — crimson red with a golden tip.

Verity gripped his arm. She must have seen the feathers too. A jolt of energy passed between them.

Manah loosened her hood and walked carefully round the room, kneeling before each of the seated figures and touching the fingertips of her right hand against their foreheads. She started with the eldest. Each of them returned this gesture.

Sash and Verity lowered their hoods and stood awkwardly near the door.

The people in the hut whispered among themselves. Sash heard the word "giant" and shifted uncomfortably. He easily towered over everyone he had seen in Aqarti. He must have seemed strange to their eyes. Embarrassed, he stooped and gazed at the floor.

"They're staring at us," Verity whispered. "I want to get out of here."

Sash wanted to leave too but where would they go? Without Manah to guide them they were lost. They might run into night monkeys — or worse. Sash remembered the haunting yowls that had echoed through the jungle. "At dawn," he reminded her.

Manah gestured towards them. "This is Sash and Verity. They are from Trin but... But I saw them swimming on Rising Beach. They swam over the reef and walked onto the sand unharmed."

People gawped at the visitors, gasping in amazement.

"Let them be seated," said one. Space was made and mats were hastily laid. Sash and Verity sat gratefully, their feet smarting. A young man handed them steaming bowls. "Eat," he said shortly.

Sash raised his bowl to his lips and tasted. It was fish stew, thick and spicy. Immediately he felt better, realizing how hungry he had been.

"We need some brint herb for Sash, he has been bitten by iffula," said Manah.

Her words were met with clucks of concern. A few moments later a girl appeared with half a coconut shell full of paste that Manah daubed on Sash's wounds. It smelled sweet and felt cool against his skin. "Use the rest for your feet, rub it in well," she advised.

Sash offered the coconut to Verity before helping himself. He felt like crying with relief as the sweet paste soothed his battered soles.

The man whom Manah had called "Tiro" sat down on a mat near the front door. Candles lit him from below, highlighting a face deeply etched with lines. Skin strained over the sharp angles of his cheeks, reminding Sash of poorly tanned leather, or examples of taxidermy gone wrong that his father had shown him. Sash could not guess at the man's age but he seemed ancient.

"What were you doing on Rising Beach?" began Tiro with a gravelly voice. He addressed his question to Manah. "You know that it is forbidden. You are reckless, Manah! If the guards had caught you—"

"But they did not catch me," she said. "I knew what I was doing."

"You should not be going anywhere near the citadel. We have spoken of this before. It is far too dangerous."

"I needed to see the Bloodstone Bird!" said Manah. At this, the people sitting round the hut fidgeted nervously.

"Is it safe?" asked Tiro. He held his breath. Others watched fearfully.

"It is safe," Manah answered.

"He would not dare to touch the Bloodstone Bird," said Tiro, visibly relieved. "He would not dare."

"But he grows bolder by the day," said Manah. "Already his guards remove carvings of Great Aruva, Bryda and Sivan from the palace. Sooner or later he may..."

"He shall never dare!" growled the old man, with a force that surprised Sash. "And it is not 'the palace' – it is the Seat of Elders, Manah, and never forget it! I have told you more than once to keep out of the lowlands. They have already captured your brother. Do you want them to catch you too?"

Manah's eyes widened and she blinked quickly, as though holding back tears. "If I had not been at the beach I would have missed Sash and Verity swimming in the sea. Instead, I saw it with my own eyes. Look at Sash! He must be the one we have spoken of, the dark-eyed giant! He will defeat the Keeper – he is the one!"

"But he is only a child," muttered the old man.

"Does that matter?"

"We called for a warrior..." His disappointment was obvious and Sash felt his cheeks flush red.

"That was a mistake," interrupted a middle-aged woman with a long nose. "We should never have called for a warrior! We are not war-like. Not like the Trin islanders," she eyed Sash and Verity critically. "We are a peaceful people; it was not right for us to call up a man or woman of war."

"We have already spoken of this, Zusa," returned the old man. "There is no other way. We need a warrior to fight the Keeper. They say he is a powerful sorcerer, that he can unleash terrible magic. Is he a phantom? He is seldom seen. We all know that no creature can harm him. We must fight like with like."

"No, Tiro! We are forgetting what is important to us. We are different from the Keeper, we seek only harmony and peace, like the aruva." At this, people muttered and clucked in agreement. Sash noticed one or two touching their fingers to their throats. He had seen Manah make the same gesture several times.

"Following the ways of Great Aruva has not helped us," returned the old man bitterly.

"And you think these children can? Do you not recall that in four days the suns will join and the aruva take flight? We know what the Keeper plans to do!" Zusa shook her head sadly.

"He will sing – that terrifying, unearthly voice of his..." said someone else as others joined in. "How can one man sing with the voice of many?"

"And as we fall under his spell he will kill the aruva!"

"It will be like the time before Great Aruva, only worse! The sun's song will be lost for ever! The prophesied war shall begin, a war without end..."

Sash and Verity watched silently, exhausted but anxious, as the debate raged through the night.

"These children cannot help us," said Zusa, appealing to the others with her raised palms. "There is only one thing left for us to do – one last chance to save the birds. We must catch an aruva and protect it from the Keeper. We must compel it to sing. If it sings, the painful wounds that divide the people of this island will be healed and we shall have the strength to unite against the Keeper. To defeat him at last!"

"But that is madness. The only way to catch a bird is to hunt them where they roost. And that would mean—"

"Exactly," said Zusa, and the others fell into a troubled silence.

The heat and sweet incense were making Sash drowsy. He leant against the wall and closed his eyes. Beyond the voices in the hut, he could hear the braying of an animal. It sounded young, like a foal or colt, and its cry filled him with pity.

* * *

Sash awoke to someone shaking him lightly on the shoulder and opened his eyes to see Manah.

"You fell asleep. I know that you must be tired but we need to decide what to do," she said.

Sash glanced across the room. Verity was curled up on a nearby mat. The candles had burned low and the first hint of dawn was peeping through the wooden slats. He heard the twittering of birds in the jungle beyond. "How long was I sleeping?" he asked. He touched his head. The iffula bites still throbbed but only vaguely.

"Not so very long."

"But it's already morning..."

"Almost," whispered Manah. "We are trying to decide whether to send a small group of us to the Impossible Isles – the three islets across the Impossible Sea. Beyond them lies the Endless Ocean. Nothing lives on the Impossible Isles, nothing but the aruva, out on the furthest islet. According to the tales of our ancestors, the birds sleep above a deep pool. They fly over Aqarti once a year at the joining of the suns, to lay their eggs on the white boulders at the tip of the lowlands."

Sash looked at Manah blankly, his mind muddied by sleep.

"Maybe you do not know the story?" she said. She didn't wait for a reply. "Great Aruva was the bird that learned the secret song of harmony from the sun, risking her life by flying into its flames. When she did, she beat her wings and the

163

sun split in two, and Great Aruva flew down to Aqarti. But without harmony the creatures were already at war, and they did not hear her coming. So she flew over the island seven times, singing the secret song of the sun, and the creatures stopped fighting and peace was brought to Aqarti. Now that the Keeper is destroying the birds it will soon be a time of war. At the annual joining of the suns the aruva will fly again from the Impossible Isles to circle over Aqarti. We have spies among the guards. We know that the Keeper has ordered his archers to shoot down the birds before they can sing. And if they cannot sing, they cannot bring harmony, and that will be the end..."

Sash remembered what the woman called Zusa had said: that they must compel a bird to sing, that this would help the islanders defeat the Keeper once and for all. But hadn't the Keeper been on Aqarti for years? The singing aruva had not saved the Followers during this time. It seemed desperate, pathetic even, for them to place their hope on a small flock of surviving birds.

It didn't feel right to express these doubts. Instead, he asked: "Why are they called the Impossible Isles?"

"Because the water around them is so rough that no boats can reach them."

"It is certain death!" called an old woman near by, over-hearing Manah's words. "No one has ever rowed to the Impossible Isles and returned to tell the tale! Our ancestors warned us of such folly – of islets born as the sea burned,

164

born from liquid flames! Have you forgotten the taboo? The sea forbids it!"

Someone protested, and all around the hut Sash heard lowered, bickering voices. Shuddering, he remembered the tiny north-easterly islets that he'd seen from the oval rocks, perpetually lashed by surf. It was clear that these people were desperate to even consider such a journey. "Where's your brother?" he asked Manah. "Someone said he'd been captured."

She nodded. "We were ambushed. Several days ago, in a hut like this one away from the villages deep in the highlands. Guards took everyone ... including my brother, Jonto... You really do remind me of him. Quiet and good-hearted." Manah's voice quavered but she didn't cry.

"Do you know where they are?" Sash asked, looking uncomfortably at his hands.

"Yes, but that will not help me. Followers are taken to the dungeon, beneath the Imperial Palace. The citadel that was once used to keep intruders out is now a useful prison for the Keeper's enemies. He lives in luxury in the palace, rarely seen by his people. While down in the dungeon, Followers are tortured and killed." She wiped her eyes roughly with the back of her hand.

"That's terrible," Sash murmured.

Manah continued as though she hadn't heard him. "It was not always a palace, you know. It was built as the Seat of Elders during the Middle Period."

"When was the Middle Period? How long ago?" asked Sash.

Manah shrugged. "Too long ago to count."

"Is that when the citadel was built?"

"No, not then, not immediately," came a husky voice.

Sash was too sleepy to feel alarmed and turned his head slowly.

The old man called Tiro must have been listening to their conversation, folded into the deep shadows of the hut. "The citadel was built when islanders first arrived from Trin, demanding land. There were battles between these islanders and the people of Aqarti until the Great Peace was agreed. After that, the citadel was no longer used as a fort and the high walls fell into disrepair.

"There are now twenty-one villages. Before them – long before the citadel – there were the seven. Seven is a very important number for us. Seven tail feathers gathered from the southern boulders after the coming of the aruva." The old man indicated the ribbon that wove round the low candles. One by one, the bickering voices in the hut fell silent until only Tiro could be heard. "Seven feathers to remind us of the seven times that Great Aruva circled our island, singing the song of the sun. And so the aruva, to this day, still circle Aqarti seven times to announce their arrival from the Impossible Isles before flying to the southern boulders to lay their eggs.

"In time, the seven villages expanded into the highlands.

Villagers quarrelled over food. Rivalries emerged. With the binding spirit of the aruva in mind, each village selected an elder to represent it before the wider community. A group of seven men and women was chosen to decide the difficult questions of the time, to meet as the suns rose high in the sky, with offerings of fruit and flowers. Everything would be shared; no one would own possessions: not like the Keeper today, with his palace and his gardens, his palanquins and servants. These things were unknown in the Middle Period.

"A magnificent building was erected to house the Seat of Elders, who met in the Great Hall. Our ancestors collected the rocks with their own bare hands, laying them one by one. The shape was intended to represent the aruva's unusual beak."

Sash realized that the old man was referring to the Imperial Palace, the cone-shaped building at the heart of the citadel. He nodded.

"You have seen it?" The old man addressed Sash with so much intensity that they could have been alone in the hut.

"Yes," Sash replied.

"Of course *he* lives in it now," Tiro went on. "But it is not his, and never has been. He banned the Seat of Elders and seized ownership of the beautiful building. Now his guards tear down images of Great Aruva and the other spirit-animals that our ancestors crafted with so much care." Tiro's voice cracked and his eyes filled with tears.

Sash remembered the carvings on the wall of the citadel

and the palace itself: images of feathers, spirals and wolves. But masons had created other scenes – scenes depicting a robed man.

Manah moved over to Tiro and rested her hand on his shoulder. He grasped it, sobbing openly. "The Keeper came... He banned the aruva, our way of life... He... He... He built a dungeon beneath the Seat of... Beneath his palace. That is where he puts us ... Followers who refuse to renounce our beliefs... He does not let us sing... It is the end for us..." He turned to Manah. "I am so tired," he sighed.

Sash looked away, appalled to see an old man in such distress. He had hardly realized till this moment that adults *could* cry. It seemed to him something that only children did. Had his father ever cried, sitting alone in his study? Thinking about Sash's mother, who died so long ago? The thought disturbed Sash.

Verity was still asleep. He had told her they would leave at dawn. And here it was, dazzling between the slats, announcing the arrival of two great suns. This place was dangerous. He knew it was right to leave. Aqarti was enchanting, but poison was woven into the fabric of the leaves, just as the beautiful palace disguised the dungeon below. Yet beyond his concern to return to London, Sash felt a twinge of guilt. How could he go back – to East Heath College with double French, Maths, and Latin, to homework and the taxidermy shop – knowing that innocent people were being rounded up, not because they had done anything wrong but simply for revering the aruva?

Sash suddenly became aware that Tiro was staring at him.

"You are not really from Trin, are you?" asked the old man. He had stopped crying but crystal streaks of dry tears glittered on his cheeks. Peering out of a haggard face, his eyes were surprisingly youthful.

Sash glanced at Manah. She was watching him. Her eyes were wide and she grasped her hands together. He turned back to Tiro. He had agreed with Verity that they would not reveal their true identities. But there was something in this old man's eyes that reminded Sash of his father, that demanded honesty.

Sash licked his lips, preparing to speak as the Followers watched. Without warning the front door flew open and a man burst in. He gripped the frame of the door, panting heavily. Behind him sunlight blazed at last, bleaching the small hut and blinding its occupants.

"Guards, everywhere!" gasped the man.

"The canoe!" cried Zusa. At once she grabbed Manah's arm, dragging her away. "Will we have time to escape?" she called back.

"They are very close! Run!"

"We shall hold them!" cried another man, grabbing a long stick.

"Sash?" Verity had woken, bewildered, to panicked voices.

Manah turned. "Sash, Verity, come with me! Hurry!"

Sash jostled Verity out of the back of the hut behind Manah. Glancing over his shoulder he saw Tiro. The old man sat cross-legged, making no move to leave. His aged fingers touched his throat and fresh tears rolled silently down his cheeks.

Sash froze at the back door. He wanted to beg Tiro to come with him but he couldn't find the words. Outside he heard shouting and a moment later the man in the doorway collapsed, a machete buried in his back. A guard appeared behind him.

"Sash!" shouted Verity. A chorus of howls and whistles shuddered through the trees.

He spun round and flung himself out of the hut, racing after her. Breathlessly they zigzagged between vines and leapt over ferns. Branches smacked their faces and they batted them away. Their feet slipped over fallen leaves. Eventually, the land plunged downhill towards a beach lined with trees – not the friendly palms that dotted Aqarti's western shore, where they had arrived, but a forest of hunching mangroves. As Sash rushed towards them, he saw that these strange trees rose up from the shallows, rather than the land. Their interlacing roots reared over the water, worm-like, distorted reflections of their curving branches.

Concealed in the mangrove swamp, Sash spotted a wooden canoe. Several Followers had already climbed aboard. Manah was passing them leather water pouches, which they hastily tossed on the floor of the vessel.

Verity hopped on and turned to Sash. "What about the razor sharks?" she asked him.

Hearing her, Manah replied. "No sharks, not here. Not *sharks...*"

Instead of relief, Sash felt a twinge of anxiety. No sharks, but other creatures – was that what she meant? The water quivered between the mangroves. Unlike the reef that circled the western side of the island, it was dark; the floor of the shallows was almost invisible. Black shoals of fish no larger than fingernails ducked between the arching roots, the sediment swirling around them.

Sash hesitated. "Someone said that it's madness to attempt this... Something to do with taboo?"

"That... That is nothing," said Manah, but her eyes darted nervously between the mangroves.

"A taboo?" echoed Verity. "That means it's banned. Banned by the Keeper?"

"The Keeper controls all the coasts. But that is not what they meant. My people believe that a curse was placed over the Impossible Isles... That no one but aruva may cross the Impossible Sea. But we do not have a choice..." She beckoned Sash into the canoe.

From the highlands he could hear shouting and floating down from the tree canopy came the bitter smell of smoke. He turned back to gaze into the jungle. They

171

had abandoned the old man and the others. What would become of them?

Manah spoke, as though reading his mind. "They are burning down the hut... There is nothing we can do."

Sash climbed aboard and they pushed away into the swamp.

— The Floating Forest —

They wound through a floating forest of mangroves. Tiny charcoal fish darted away from the canoe as it drifted towards them, hiding among the mangroves' dark roots.

There were six of them on board: aside from Sash, Verity and Manah were Zusa, who had criticized the call for a warrior, and two men, Ren and Laars. The canoe had three pairs of oars resting in grooves towards its prow, allowing only three people to row the vessel.

"We shall take it in turns," said Zusa, who had quickly assumed leadership. She rowed with Ren and Laars while the others sat in silence, shocked by what had happened in the highlands.

Verity leant over to Sash. "Do you ever get the feeling that things are spinning out of control?" she whispered.

"Even time makes no sense any more. My watch thinks that it's four o'clock in the morning."

Sash nodded, feeling disoriented.

Laars was a thickly built man with small eyes and bushy hair. He grunted as he handled his oars.

"Gentle strokes until we pass the lair, we do not want to wake it," warned Ren. He twisted in his seat a moment to study Sash and Verity. He looked older than Laars and was leaner, with hollow cheeks and skinny, muscular arms that worked the oars expertly.

Sash frowned. Had he heard right? Wake *what*?

He tried not to think about the people they'd left behind, nor the danger of their journey to the Impossible Isles. The canoe slunk carefully between the mangroves, sliding past their stilt-like roots. Their leaves were silvery with crystals of salt, patch-working light from the sky above. There was something almost primeval about the floating forest. In the stillness, Sash half expected to see a diplodocus emerge from between the trees, swishing its giant tail. Memories of the dinosaur exhibit at the Natural History Museum in London returned to him. It had been his favourite as a young boy. His father still took him there occasionally, mainly to point out the poor quality of the taxidermy among its collection of stuffed animals. At least, said his father, the Victorians had appreciated this traditional art. Max Baranovski had enormous respect for Victorians. "People with values," he'd always say, "not like nowadays."

Something was drifting on the shady water: the gnarled bark of a dead tree. Growing from the bark was a delicate white orchid. How did it survive on nothing but rotten wood, in this brackish swamp? Sash's hands relaxed against the sides of the canoe, his fingertips stroking the water. It was cool to the touch and with a jolt he wondered what his father was doing at this moment, out in Iceland, braving unimaginable cold.

Light shifted in broken shards on the surface of the water. Glancing up, Sash caught something glinting; it could have been nothing – the feathers of a colourful bird or a bright clutch of fruit. Or was it something metallic? Like the machetes carried by the Keeper's guards…

"I think we're being followed," he said to Manah in a low voice.

She nodded. "It is likely." She leant over to Laars and whispered.

Laars, in turn, bent forward to address Zusa. Sash heard her say "No", and something else that he didn't catch.

"They will stop us before we get out of the swamp. We shall never reach the aruva," said Laars.

"It is not our way!" protested Zusa.

"It is the *only* way."

Zusa fell silent as Laars turned to the others in the canoe and called: "Good, good, keep rowing!"

Sash was shocked by the loudness of his voice – if any guards were near by, they were bound to have heard. He

175

looked to the shore as the canoe floated towards a group of ruddy trees, taller and older than the others rising from the swamp. Sash noticed that the bark of these trees was lacerated, as though it had been scraped by something, and there were grooves on the trunks near the surface of the water. The canoe seemed to falter, trembling between the old trees. Turning back to the shore Sash saw movement, the definite flash of a blade and a glimpse of a guard's red and black uniform. Suddenly they came into view, five of them, wading into the water with weapons raised.

The canoe bobbed gently. No one rowed.

"They've seen us!" hissed Sash. His fingers gripped the sides of the canoe.

Verity too was straining round. "We have to hurry, why aren't you rowing?"

"Do not worry," said Manah, "but keep your arms inside the canoe."

Sash immediately released his grip. After the iffula attack, he wasn't taking any chances. Laars and Ren started jabbing the water with their oars.

The guards were rushing towards them, tripping awkwardly over mangrove roots. The water was shallow, scarcely reaching their knees.

"Halt!" called one, waving his machete.

Another appeared just left of Verity and reached out his hand towards her.

"Now!" cried Laars.

The canoe shot forward as the Followers rowed furiously. It quickly gathered pace, lurching between the trees until the first sight of open water appeared before them.

Sash saw the guards gather between the ruddy mangroves. After a moment, one lunged backwards with a cry and fell into the water. Seconds later another guard stumbled, grasping his legs and howling. Sash watched, stunned. Something was writhing in the water, twisting between the mangrove roots. Two more guards collapsed, leaving the fifth quaking alone in terror. A root-like tentacle reached over the water to snatch the guard's arm, wrenching him down. A short distance away a disembodied human foot floated to the surface.

Verity started to twist round, trying to see what was going on, but Sash caught her eye.

"Don't," he said.

Instantly, she turned her face towards the prow. Perhaps she'd seen enough.

Sash knew he should do the same but he couldn't help himself. He turned back to the ruddy mangroves. The water was still, the guards nowhere to be seen. Even the foot had disappeared. It was as though the guards had never existed. Sash swallowed. He wanted to ask the Followers what had happened – he needed them to explain. But instead he digested what he'd seen in shocked silence.

Zusa was whispering something, a prayer or blessing. Manah and Ren joined in.

177

"Did they all go down?" called Laars.

Sash hesitated. Laars made it sound as though he was referring to things not people. "Yes," he said quietly. Then louder, he repeated: "Yes."

Zusa, Laars and Ren wove the canoe expertly through the remaining mangroves. In minutes they were free of the shadowy forest and out on the sparkling sea.

The Impossible Sea beyond the mangroves stretched endlessly. Rapid waves pulled the canoe away from Aqarti. The tug was playful but persistent, not like the tranquil western coast with its placid ripples. In the distance, the Impossible Isles rose in shrouds of mist. The water encircling them was white, disturbed by powerful currents. Sash wondered how such a fragile canoe would reach them in one piece.

Zusa and Ren began to make clicking sounds with their tongues and Manah joined in. Sash assumed it was one of their spiritual rites – perhaps another blessing for the fallen guards. He was surprised when, after a few moments of the clicking, he spied grey figures darting towards them beneath the surface of the water. They were shaped like fish but were as large as men and women.

Sash cleared his throat. "Dolphins..."

Manah turned and smiled at him. "My people call them 'guardians of the sea'. They are powerful, fearless creatures that share many of our common ancestors and, like us, work together in families, not like those solitary creatures of the deep. The guardians will protect us from... From the worst of these solitary creatures..."

The dolphins started circling the canoe, their heads bobbing over the water, responding to the clicks with their own amiable whistles. There was something thrilling in their playful escort. Sash eased himself deeper into the canoe, his eyes glazing over, as Zusa, Ren and Laars rowed in silence. He didn't know how long he sat like that. Time seemed to pass differently in Aqarti – slower somehow, despite its intensity. He wondered whether the two suns affected the length of the days.

"This is crazy," whispered Verity. "How did we get here?"

Sash lifted his head. Surrounded by the dolphins it was easy to forget the danger that lurked down there, the guards waiting for them on Aqarti or the treachery of the approaching Impossible Isles. He desperately wanted to forget, if only for a few minutes. The islets were still far away. How *had* they got here? It had all happened so quickly. They had just been getting used to their arrival on Aqarti when Manah had appeared. Before they knew it, they were lost in the jungle, then that hut and the guards...

"Our parents will never know what became of us," Verity went on.

"My dad might work it out..." Sash thought of the open trunk in Max's study. The boat would be gone too, lost somewhere on the River Fleet. Max might come looking for them. But if he told the police, no one would believe him. They would assume that Sash and Verity had drowned in the Fleet. Might they dredge the river? He found all this just about imaginable. What he couldn't picture was the sight of Verity's blonde mother with her oven gloves and her husband, a successful City financier, meeting in the same space as Max Baranovski, with his immaculately pressed ties, his thick black eyebrows and fierce brown eyes.

"Do the parentals some good to worry a bit," said Verity.

"What do you mean?" asked Sash.

"Oh..." She looked as though she was about to confide something. "Nothing." The canoe jolted and Verity bumped into Manah. She straightened up and turned to Sash, leaning towards him and whispering, "This is *her* fault. She tricked us."

"I guess she was desperate."

"Don't stand up for her!" snapped Verity, and Manah stiffened, no doubt having heard.

"There's nothing we can do now, we just have to stay calm," said Sash.

"If she'd been honest with us, we'd never have come with her."

"We haven't exactly been honest with her," he pointed out quietly. "The bird..."

"I've been perfectly honest," retorted Verity.

Her voice was so indignant that it set his teeth on edge. Something rigid inside him reacted to that voice. "Oh yes, you've always been straight as a die, haven't you?" he whispered. He flashed his dark eyes at her as the narrow canoe rose sharply on the current.

The nearby dolphins responded with ease to the changing tides, still circling the canoe and whistling.

"What do you mean by that?" demanded Verity.

"Why do you want the bird so much? Why did you want to come here?" asked Sash. If it was hopeless, if they really were about to drown, at least he would know.

"I told you, I'm curious, I—"

"Why did you really want to come?"

"I just need it, OK?"

"Need what?"

"I need the bird – the bird of flames."

"What do you need it for?"

Verity lowered her face. "My life's not perfect."

"Could have fooled me," replied Sash.

"Well, if you're going to be like that..."

"Sorry," he muttered. "Go on."

"It's my parents," said Verity, and to Sash's surprise he saw her cheeks redden. She sighed heavily. "My parents are talking about... About separating." She spat out the words with disgust. "My parents. Can you imagine? I mean, have you met my parents?"

Sash hadn't and said nothing.

"*My parents,*" she repeated more forcefully. "They can't... They mustn't..." Her eyes were wide and dewy. "I've tried reasoning with them but it hasn't worked. They say that sometimes people just stop loving each other. I need something magical, something that will make them care, like they used to. I need the bird of flames."

Sash gaped in surprise. "You can't really believe... Are you saying that you think the bird has some special power? You've lost it, Verity! How can you be so stupid?"

Verity's eyes narrowed. "I am *not* stupid! Why do you have to doubt everything? The bird *is* magical. It will sing and … and my mum and dad will be happy again."

With a start Sash remembered the day when he'd been forced to play rugby, the day the crest had been ripped from his blazer. Hadn't he seen Verity whispering urgently into her mobile, talking to her mother? He had hardly registered it then, stalking to the changing rooms straight after practice. But now it made sense. "If they get divorced you'll have two rooms, won't you? Two of everything, isn't that how it works? And they'll both feel guilty so they'll buy you tons of extra stuff. And take you on more expensive trips, like Costa Rica and Australia." Sash was trying to be funny but it wasn't working.

"I don't *want* them to get a divorce. I'm their only child. We were so happy, the three of us. People talk about parents staying together for the sake of the children. It happens all the time!"

"Maybe, but divorce happens all the time too. It's not the end of the world."

"How would you know? I'll be forced to choose between my parents. You don't even have a mother!" cried Verity, and Manah wheeled round in her seat. Perhaps she had been listening for a while – Sash couldn't be sure and he no longer cared. Verity's last remark had reminded him that they weren't friends and never would be, that she had used him as a way of reaching the aruva, which she wanted for her own ends. In a flash he was standing outside the long driveway to her Hampstead home. He suddenly knew that he would always be on the outside.

"I'm sorry," Verity stammered. "I didn't mean it."

Sash set his jaw. Don't listen to her, he told himself. Who cares what she thinks? He turned away from Verity to gaze at the turbulent sea.

A little later, Verity spoke again. "I tried to apologize but of course you won't listen." She sighed, immediately exasperated.

Sash ignored her, refusing to meet her eye.

"That's right, just shut it all out," she continued. "Shut out anything that doesn't suit you. At least I'm trying to improve my parents' situation. All you do is hide away. You never say what you're thinking – you're distant, Sash. It's as if you've given up, you just don't bother. But it doesn't have to be like this. You can change things! You know what your problem is?" Her voice rose over the rolling waves: "You're surrounded by all those horrible dead things, all those ... corpses. You're so quiet and frozen you might as well be one of them!

But you're not dead, Sash – you've just forgotten what it is to be alive!"

Staring down at his hands, Sash smarted with rage.

But Verity hadn't finished. "I suppose you think you're better than me. Better than everyone! You don't need friends; you don't need anyone. You don't even want the bird! Oh no, you're too good for that. So why are you here, Sash? What are you searching for anyway?"

Silently, he fumed. How dare Verity speak to him like that? How *dare* she judge him? What did this Hampstead princess know about him, about his life?

"Is everything all right?" asked Manah worriedly.

"Does it look all right to you?" Verity snorted. "We're out in the middle of the sea in a tiny canoe, chased by guards and destined for certain death! What do you think?"

Zusa, Ren and Laars glanced back a moment before rowing on.

"I am sorry," said Manah. "Really, I am. In a way, I suppose this is my fault."

"In a way?" echoed Verity. "In what way isn't it your fault?"

"For once in your life, just shut up, Verity!" Sash exploded. "You're not helping! You're just a selfish, spoilt little brat!" He fell silent, shocked at his own outburst. He didn't look at Verity. Instead, he focused on his fingers, the tips of which he tried to join together with difficulty against the movement of the juddering canoe.

"What did old Tiro say? 'We called for a warrior'?" scoffed Laars. "Warriors indeed!"

"That is enough," said Zusa. "There shall be no fighting among ourselves. We need to remember the bravery of Great Aruva. To stay strong, we must work together!" She clicked her tongue and the dolphins whistled back, as if in agreement.

Sash continued to stare at his hands. He didn't know whether Verity was angry or upset, he had no idea how his words had affected her. He had the sensation that Manah was craning round Verity and studying his face.

"Guards!" cried Manah, pointing in the distance.

Sash turned to see three painted longboats slicing through the water from Aqarti. Two of the longboats were already alarmingly near, while the third lagged at a distance. Closing behind the third longboat was a narrower one painted pink. A moment later it disappeared from view, leaving Sash wondering if he had just imagined it. He blinked at the sparkling water. Suddenly, the pink boat reappeared, and Sash realized immediately that it wasn't a boat at all, it was a creature: it was *alive*. It had a pointed, serpentine face. Its long, pink body was covered in glittering scales and a series of small fins. Its bulging red eyes were lid-less and as it opened its mouth – easily the size of a car door – it revealed several neat rows of triangular teeth.

Sash gripped the canoe, faint with fear.

"It will not touch us," Manah assured him. "The dolphins

protect us." She was leaning round Verity, who was trans-fixed with horror.

The guards in the third longboat were struggling to keep up with the others, oblivious to the danger behind them. Sash wanted to warn them somehow but they were too far away – too far to hear him, no matter how loudly he shouted – far from the protection of the playful dolphins. He shut his eyes as the snake-headed creature sank its teeth into the longboat. He heard the wooden frame shatter between its fierce jaws.

The shrieks of the guards were carried away by the wind.

"A sea serpent took the third boat, but the other two are still gaining!" cried Manah to the Followers.

"We can do no more!" Laars shouted back. "We cannot row harder!"

"Can I help?" Sash called across the waves.

"Yes! Slide up in front of Manah and grab my oars," shouted Zusa. "Stay down or you will fall out!"

Sash edged past Verity without meeting her eye, stoop-ing low. He eased past Manah and took a seat behind Laars. Zusa passed Sash the oars.

"It is a circular movement: both oars down in front of you at the same time, paddle straight down, understand? Then flip them round and repeat the motion," instructed Laars. "Copy me."

Sash grasped the oars and soon got the hang of paddling.

"They are gaining on us!" yelled Manah.

Zusa, released of her rowing duties, was surveying the sea. "Take heed everyone, rough currents are upon us!" she called.

The sturdy Laars set the pace, smashing his oars against the water, and Sash struggled to keep up. Already his arms were throbbing, unfamiliar with the rhythmic, downwards paddling. Progress was difficult and Sash knew they weren't moving fast enough, that the guards with their superior longboats would soon catch them. The jagged Impossible Isles were still in the distance, dangerous and elusive.

The canoe jumped and zigzagged for a few metres before straightening up.

"That's a rip!" It was Verity's voice, rising over the crashing water. "Find the rip tide, we need to get onto it, it'll carry us!"

"What do you mean?" called back Zusa.

"Just now, when the boat jumped, it was a rip tide – a strong current that rides out to sea. It's dangerous but it's fast!"

"You mean a wolf current," said Zusa slowly. "I see... Laars, we must find it."

"Everyone knows it is lunacy to cross a wolf current! We shall all perish!" barked Laars. "Are you going to listen to this outsider? She is just a child!"

"They are almost on us!" cried Manah.

Sash stole a quick look over his shoulder and gasped. The two remaining longboats had closed in quickly and were only ten or fifteen metres away.

"Find the tide, Laars. Do it!" shouted Zusa. Her voice thundered with authority.

Laars jammed his right oar against the canoe and fanned out the left as Ren and Sash kept paddling.

The nearer longboat shunted them from behind. "Stop! Stop in the name of the Keeper!" commanded a guard. Something sailed past Sash's ear: an arrow.

"Down, everyone!" cried Manah and added, for Sash and Verity's benefit, "The tips are poisonous!"

Despite their efforts, the small canoe was actually slowing down, meeting the resistance of bucking currents. Laars grunted, raised his right oar and again jammed it against the canoe. He fanned out his left oar. Reluctantly, the canoe veered to the right and suddenly leapt off the rapid tide they had briefly bumped against earlier.

"That's it, grab it!" shrieked Verity.

Laars levelled out his oars and the canoe lurched onto the rip and sprang forward, as though propelled by an invisible motor. Water spurted in Sash's eyes but he paddled on blindly. In a moment, the canoe was flying ahead of the longboats and the dolphins had fallen away.

"Now straighten up!" cried Verity. "That's it!"

Sash paddled frantically, abandoning efforts to keep time with Ren and Laars. They were moving so quickly that it was almost impossible to catch the water beneath his oars. Pain seared through his arms and shoulders.

"Good, good!" called Zusa. The longboats had dropped far

behind. Beyond them Aqarti was no more than a green haze.

The canoe gathered speed, racing with the current. Laars and Ren lifted their oars and Sash did the same – they were no longer able to help it on its way.

"We are losing them!" exclaimed Manah.

"Do not speak too soon!" yelled Laars.

One of the longboats had found the rip tide and was making chase. With its superior size and weight, it was already gaining on the small canoe.

"Where is the other longboat?" shouted Manah. "There was a second boat..."

Verity searched the sea behind her. "I can't see it."

"The sea serpent must have taken it too. But the other one is catching up with us!"

"Oh no!" Zusa spun round. There was a new problem. The first of the Impossible Isles was looming out of the water. "We shall run aground on the islet! What do we do?" The howling wind drowned out her voice.

"What's that?" cried Verity. "I can't hear you!"

The canoe leapt onward, building speed all the time. Sash could see the waters swirling recklessly around the islet, exploding in white bursts of foam. They would be dashed against the fortress of stone.

"Ahead of us!" yelled Sash.

Rocks as sharp as broken glass glanced the base of the canoe, slicing long gashes in the wood. Fountains of water gushed through.

Verity gasped as she saw the islet but quickly found her voice. "Break off the rip tide by steering to the left. You have to do it fast. The rip is narrow, if you break off it, we'll slow down straight away!"

"Laars, Ren, Sash, I need you to steer left when I tell you to," shouted Zusa. "Do you understand?"

The guards' longboat was speeding behind them, the islet just ahead, as water burst through holes beneath their feet. Sash nodded as the others cried, "Yes!"

"Oars left of the canoe. Ready?" Zusa glanced towards the nearest islet. They were so close that her voice was lost beneath the roar of the water breaking against the rocks. "Now!" she screamed. Sash grasped the command from her contorted face.

Ren and Laars thrust their left oars against the canoe. Sash copied them as they outstretched their right oars, steadying the vessel as it jack-knifed the rip tide. The prow broke out against a slower current, shying violently. The canoe careened in the wrong direction, back towards Aqarti. A wall of water slapped their faces and thrust them sideways.

Sash heard the thunder of surf as the longboat flew past them and smashed into the rocks, shattering into splinters. He saw the guards sink beneath the tossing waves, their bodies limp and broken. The Followers passed only metres away, soaked by spume. Zusa directed Ren, Laars and Sash as they wove between the islets, steering skilfully, their arms trembling against the pressure of the turbulent water.

They sat in a basin of seawater that was filling the canoe – already it was tipping onto its side. Verity and Manah scrambled to scoop out the water with cupped hands.

"We're sinking!" cried Verity.

"We are here," sighed Zusa as the last of the islets rose into view.

Clinging to columns of black rock, iguanas braced themselves against the surf, their small yellow eyes twitching curiously. The horned lizards watched the arrival of the vessel. The visitors stumbled out before tugging the canoe onto higher ground, their bare feet slipping on the islet's pebbles. Sodden and exhausted, they staggered inland.

Weaving overhead, sea birds battled against northern gales. They made for the shelter of the islet's jagged hill. The iguanas looked on as another vessel landed further down the pebble beach. A longboat. Its red and black flag jittered in the wind.

— The Impossible Isles —

An endless wind blew across the islet, chilling the air in spite of the two suns that glowed above. Furious surf battered the rocks, dissolving into clouds of mist. Drenched by salt water and kneaded by wind, few plants clung to the shallow soil. A single hill rose beyond banks of cloud, overlooking sea that rolled on north for ever.

"The Impossible Isles!" gasped Manah. Like the others, she was soaking. Her short sandy hair hung flat against her face and droplets of sea spray clung to her lashes. But her eyes were wide with excitement. "Can it be true? Are we really here?"

"We did it!" sighed Zusa, smiling broadly.

"This one did it," muttered Laars, ruffling Verity's mottled blonde hair, not unkindly. To Sash's surprise, Verity allowed this. "How did you know all that, young warrior?"

"Surfing in Costa—" Verity caught herself. "I picked it up somewhere."

Sash was surprised by how cheerful they sounded. Turning away from the others, he peered at the sea. Waves crashed against the islet's black rocks. Gorse, peppered with thorns, crept over the pebbles at his feet. Overhead the hazy sky was a shifting canvas of greys, blackened by the silhouettes of screeching terns. How could the bird of flames live here?

"What is this place?" he said to himself.

A cold hand touched his shoulder and he turned to see Ren.

Ren's grey eyes matched the sky, misty and unreadable. "Our ancestors called it the shadow land."

Sash shivered and turned away.

They found a cave in a cleft of rock, protected from the shrilling wind. Zusa and Sash went in search of gorse to fuel a fire. They tugged the branches from the soil, snagging their hands on thorns. It took hours to gather enough gorse, by which time their fingers were scratched and sore.

Near the entrance to the cave, Ren used his flint dagger to light a meagre fire of salty gorse as Zusa and Sash looked on, too tired to help or even speak. Laars and Verity went in search of food while Manah collected handfuls of moss to cushion their sleep.

As Ren struggled to maintain the fire, the group cooked thick slabs of mortus roots that Laars had managed to unearth. The roots were full of a sweet juice that helped to quench their thirst. The skin had a meaty texture and although it was almost tasteless they ate greedily.

The pink sun sank north below the horizon, trailing a violet haze. The camp fire burned low. Shielded from the wind, the rocky ground was warm. Verity and the Followers lay down on clumps of moss and soon fell asleep.

Despite his fatigue, Sash felt restless. In this dismal place on the fringes of an unknown world, he thought of how close they had come to death, and of those who hadn't made it. He wandered out of the cave, through a pall of mist, to gaze at the sea. Against the darkening sky, he could hardly follow its outline as the water hammered the rocks. The second sun was sinking south beyond Aqarti, no longer visible in the distance. Already, the moon was glowing overhead, surrounded by spiralling stars.

Shutting his eyes and listening to the crashing waves, Sash thought of his argument with Verity. For a moment he allowed himself to wonder whether she was right. Did he really hide from life? Was it possible that in an effort to avoid trouble, he was missing out on so much more?

No! Sash thought with a flare of anger. He opened his eyes to the complex spiral of stars. He felt a sense of longing, a pang of regret. He looked away. He was tired. He was letting Verity's words get to him. She had said them to upset him, to gain the upper hand. They didn't mean anything. Only stupid words.

Sash yawned, his head dizzy, his arms throbbing. Wearily, he made his way back to the shallow cave and lay on a mattress of spongy moss. In seconds he was tumbling into sleep.

When Sash awoke the two suns were high in the sky.

Laars was sitting cross-legged, weaving gorse twigs together next to a pile of moss.

"I must have slept for hours," said Sash.

"None of us have been long awake. The journey was tiring. Ren is fixing the canoe. The others are gathering what they can for a meal." Laars kept weaving.

Sash stretched. His arms ached from paddling and his whole body felt stiff after a night on the floor of the cave.

Manah and Verity appeared cradling amber mortus roots, as bulbous and shiny as aubergines. Sash didn't look up. He hadn't spoken to Verity since their argument in the canoe – since she'd revealed her real reason for seeking the aruva.

The others arrived and the group sat in silence, eating the fleshy roots. Near by the crash and hiss of the sea drowned out other sounds. If the aruva were singing, Sash couldn't hear them.

Laars had woven his twigs into a large, bell-shaped carrier. He reached for a handful of moss, which he used to line the bottom. "It is ready," he said. He raised his eyes, which met Zusa's, and something passed between them.

"It is the only way," she whispered.

After they ate, the Followers formed a circle and held hands, murmuring blessings led by Zusa.

Verity and Sash watched in silence. Soon the blessings were over and the Followers parted. Laars scooped up the gorse carrier. It had a loop at the top through which he slid his hand. They had packed it full of mortus roots and leather water flasks.

They stepped out of the cave into a light made hazy by moist wind. Sash looked around. The ground was a mixture of rocks, pebbles and sand, with clawing gorse and the occasional tuft of yellow grass. Behind them in the distance lurched the islet's only hill, which Sash thought for a moment to be snow-capped before realizing that it had been stained by thousands of droppings from sea birds. It reached into the clouds, narrowing at the top like a cone. Its shape reminded Sash of the Seat of Elders, the building in the citadel now used by the Keeper as a palace.

Zusa turned to the others. "It is time to find Great Aruva's Pool," she said.

"It will be somewhere on the beach, it has to be," said Laars. "That is where water collects. There are few plants further inland, and little rain. Of course the mist is every-where, but not enough water for a puddle or a pool." He blinked through the damp air, gripping the woven gorse carrier. "It must be along the coast," he added to no one in particular.

Zusa nodded, leading the way down towards the shore. The sea grew noisier, battering the rocks below them. They crunched over the pebbles, taking small steps. Sea spray drenched their clothes.

"Look well, everyone," Zusa shouted over the wind. "Walk slowly and steadily, in case we miss something."

"How can we miss a deep pool with a group of aruva above it?" replied Laars. He and Ren started wandering along the ragged coastline, treading carefully over clumps of gorse.

Sash drew level with Manah. "What's that about a pool?" he asked.

Verity sidled up and listened too, although she made a show of ignoring him.

"It is as I told you in the hut," said Manah. "The aruva live above a deep pool of water. Not the sea – a place where they drink and bathe. That is what our ancestors told us. And it must be along the coast, as it is full of little lagoons."

Sash licked his lips. They were chapped and salty. He could see various pools of trapped seawater dotted about the rugged beach. Zusa, Laars and Ren were busy approaching these, looking in and glancing overhead.

"So we must check them all," said Manah.

"There could be thousands," Verity pointed out.

"Yes, that is true, but the islet is small. If we walk around the coast we shall have to see *the* pool eventually."

"But what are we checking them for?" asked Sash.

For a moment Manah seemed unsure. "To see whether

they are deep. If they are only very shallow that means they cannot be Great Aruva's Pool."

"And the birds live above this ... this pool?" pressed Verity. "But where exactly? There are no trees here. Not even a hedgerow. Just miles and miles of gorse. Where do the birds perch? Where do they nest?"

Manah shrugged. "Our ancestors were never wrong."

Verity clicked her tongue impatiently. "This all sounds completely ridiculous. Can't I stay behind in the cave? There's no point in all of us going. I'm tired as it is."

Sash rolled his eyes. Brat, he thought.

"We must search for the birds together – we do not know what is out on the islet, it is better that we do not separate," said Manah. "We shall find it, we have to." She looked away. "Our ancestors were never wrong," she repeated like a chant. She hurried to catch up with the others.

Verity followed at a distance, leaving Sash standing alone. He glanced out at the sea, feeling again the dismal clutch of the islet. The Followers and Verity trod between the pools and puddles, skirting past inhospitable tangles of thorny gorse. Slowly Sash followed, peering into each small lagoon with a sense of pointlessness. Once or twice he turned round, blinking through the salt air. He thought he'd heard a shuffling sound, or maybe a voice. But it was nothing, just the tide dragging the pebbles, and the ceaseless howl of the sea.

* * *

198

For hours the group walked, chilled by the wind as they combed the coastline for Great Aruva's Pool. Ren was in the lead and had disappeared from sight. Zusa and Laars followed, with Manah just behind. Verity strayed further inland.

At least she's ignoring me, thought Sash. I don't have to talk to her, to pretend to be friends. He tried not to think about the things she had said on the journey to the islet. He could feel her words rising up inside him and, frowning, he struggled to push them away. They weren't friends and never would be. That's all he had to remember. *He would always be on the outside.*

Wind pummelled his face and tangled his hair. Sash rubbed salt from his eyes. He noticed something a little further towards the coast, something that looked like a pond. He approached it, stumbling on pebbles and stopping to steady himself. Crouching, Sash saw that it was little more than a puddle in which strings of seaweed twisted. The water was only as deep as his elbow. A crab scuttled out of it and hurried towards the sea.

Sash tried to remember what he was looking for. What had Manah said? "The aruva live just above a deep pool of water. Not the sea – a place where they drink and bathe." Thinking about this properly for the first time, the instructions made no sense to him. All the pools and lagoons dotting the coast were full of seawater. Did Manah mean to say that the birds drank and bathed in this salty water? Was that likely?

Of course not! said a voice in Sash's head: his father's voice. You saw the Bloodstone Bird at the entrance to the citadel. Elaborate tail features; bright colours; a beak built for seeds or fruit. Did it look like a sea bird to you? Sash imagined Max standing above him, furrowing his brows in despair at Sash's foolishness. *Useless boy... Can't you do anything right?*

Sash stood up. He needed to tell the others that they'd got it wrong – that they wouldn't find aruva on the beach. He stepped round a sprawling mass of gorse that blocked his way. Zusa, Laars and Manah were far ahead. At first, he couldn't see Verity at all. Then he spotted her leaning over what must have been a pool of water and tapping it with her bare foot. She seemed to wobble as she did this, falling into the pool. Serves her right, thought Sash irritably. He was tired, his muscles still ached from the rowing and his eyes burned from the salty air. He sighed, glancing back at the gorse. Looking more carefully, he thought he could see something within it, a large, low object. A breaker leapt over the islet's fortress of rocks, collapsing with a roar and dousing Sash. He ran his fingers through his wet hair, distracted from the gorse. This was pointless. No song bird could live happily in these conditions. What sort of strange creatures would?

The roar subsided and for a moment Sash thought he heard something, like the screeching of terns. He looked up towards the towering hill, where sea birds circled overhead. There it was again, that sound.

"*Sash!*"

He dropped his gaze with a start. It wasn't sea birds he had heard – it was Verity. He scanned the rugged coastline but she was nowhere to be seen. He began to run along the pebbles but slipped onto his hands and knees.

"*Sash!*" shouted Verity.

He scrambled to his feet and hurried towards her, more cautiously this time. The Followers were nearer to Verity but the wind carried her voice in his direction. Another great wave broke over the rocks, its spray crashing over Sash's head. A bank of thick white fog sank over the beach. Sash blinked through it, lurching across the pebbles, his hands outstretched as though in a game of blind man's bluff.

"Where are you?" he called.

"Over here!" Verity cried back. "I fell into something. I can't get out! I'm sinking!"

"OK, don't panic, just keep talking so I can find you!" said Sash.

"Don't panic? Why would I panic! And you ask me to talk! What am I supposed to talk about?"

Sash followed the voice, knees bent, keeping low to the ground so he wouldn't trip over the pebbles. "Anything," he replied.

"Fine, I could tell you about skiing. This stupid fog reminds me of Chamonix one year. I was with my parents, back when they could still bear the sight of each other.

Of course they wouldn't dream of going away together now."

Sash staggered forward, groping the air. "I thought you said they were together in Tokyo at the moment?"

"That wasn't strictly true. My dad's in Tokyo. My mum went to stay with her sister in New Zealand. They thought it would give them some... Oh, help, I'm sinking deeper!"

"Try not to move, I'm almost there!" Sash crept towards Verity's voice.

"It's a sort of sandpit, and the sand is sinking! Don't fall in or you'll be no good to either of us!"

"I won't." He knelt down and started feeling towards the edge of the pit. It was further away than he had imagined and he couldn't quite reach it. Sand and pebbles stuck to his fingers. He ignored them, reaching out and shuffling forward.

"Yeah," Verity went on, all of a rush, "I made you think that both my parents were in Tokyo, didn't I? Even Camilla doesn't know the truth. I don't want people meddling in my business. You understand, don't you? You're a private person. People don't need to know everything. And there's no need, not if my parents work it out and drop this idiotic divorce stuff."

"Is that really likely?" asked Sash, edging closer. "From what I can work out, adults do what they want." His out-stretched fingers grazed the moist sand of the pit and he drew them away. "They may tell you it's what you want,

202

or what you'd want if you knew what was good for you. But really it's what they want. If your parents are fixed on divorce—"

"Not if I have the bird of flames!"

A gust of wind raced across the beach, disturbing the fog. Sash could just make out Verity's outline. The thick sand had closed over her waist and was climbing round her chest. Her arms were raised above it.

"I'm here!" called Sash. He gripped the rocky side of the pit with one hand and reached out with the other.

Seeing Sash, Verity flailed towards him but lost her balance, floundering backwards up to her shoulders. "Help!" she shrieked as one arm flew back to sink beneath the sand.

"Try not to move!" said Sash. "Just stay still."

"Easy for you to say!" mumbled Verity, but she obeyed him.

Sash shuffled his knees up beneath him, took a deep breath and again extended his hand, this time further. Verity reached out to him. Their fingers brushed each other as the heavy fog resettled.

"I can't see you!" cried Verity. "Sash, I'm sinking!" All trace of humour had left her voice, replaced by brittle fear.

"I'm just here," he said. "Keep your hand where it was." He reached out as far as he dared – further – hanging over the pit. He couldn't feel her fingers. He tried again and this time he touched them. He seized Verity's wrist. She closed her fingers round his wrist. Sash tried to ease her towards him.

She wouldn't budge. The fog lifted enough that he could see her again, but it was no use. Verity was too deep and at this angle he didn't have the foothold to reach forward and drag her out. If only he could somehow hook his legs onto the land.

"I'm sinking, Sash!" Her fingers loosened round his wrist.

Sash's eyebrows furrowed in concentration and he pulled again. She was slipping out of his grasp. His heart hammered in his chest and he set his jaw, straining with effort. He held her tightly, tugging harder. If I could only use both hands, thought Sash, even for a few seconds... The hand that clutched the side of the pit let go, meeting his other hand round Verity's wrist. Gradually, he was able to heave her through the thick sand.

"I'll have you free in a sec," Sash panted. He gave Verity one last lug that took her to the edge of the pit. But he was leaning too far forward. Both hands gripped Verity's wrist – neither was free to hold him back.

Sash plunged face-first into the pit.

— Great Aruva's Pool —

$\int$ash sank into clinging darkness. Every jerk of his shoulders sent him deeper. In minutes there would be nothing left of him – he would disappear entirely, never to be seen again.

He kicked his legs, still hanging above the sand, and suddenly he felt hands wrapping round them, grasping his waist, heaving him out. A moment later he was free, coughing up sand as Laars and Zusa lifted Verity onto the beach beside him.

The fog had drifted and the pink sun floated irresistibly above the distant hill. Manah placed a hand on Sash's shoulder and offered him a water pouch. He gurgled several mouthfuls and spat them out, retching, unable to drink. Damp sand clung to his lips, face and hair, inside his nose and ears. When he blinked, he could feel it weighing on his eyelids.

"Give yourself a moment to rest," said Manah.

"Well, that almost ended in disaster," said Verity, accepting some water from Zusa. The cheery sarcasm had returned but there was still an edge to her voice. Seated on a flat stone near Sash, she watched him anxiously. She too was covered in sand but unlike Sash it ended abruptly at her neck, forming a neat ring round her throat. Above this, Verity's skin seemed dazzlingly pale.

"We did not know that there was quicksand on the islet," said Zusa.

"A sand mire," said Laars. "I have heard tell of such things."

Zusa nodded. "We should not have let ourselves become divided. If we had not heard you..."

Verity shivered. "Have you found Great Aruva's Pool?" she asked.

"No," said Zusa quietly.

"We have been searching for hours." Laars thwacked some pebbles with his heel. "Verity and Sash were almost lost to a sand mire, we are all hungry and tired, and there is no sign of the bird. So much effort, and for nothing."

"It makes no sense," said Zusa. "They dwell above a deep pool. We learned that from our ancestors."

"Whatever you say, Zusa," said Laars mockingly. "All those tales about the pool. Islets born from the boiling sea. None of them is true."

Ren appeared behind them. "I have been all the way round

the coast, searching. I did it quickly. I did not check inside caves... I might have missed something..."

"You did not find the pool?" asked Zusa despondently.

Ren stepped over a clump of gorse and sat on the ground next to them, indifferent to the wet pebbles. Even through the lingering mist he looked exhausted. "Not even a feather." He sighed. "And there is something else."

Zusa frowned. "What is it, Ren?"

"I felt a growing unease as I circled the islet. I sense that there are others here. That we are not alone."

Sash looked up. Hadn't he heard something too – a dragging sound or a voice? He wondered if he should say something. But what if they thought he was imagining things? He took a sip from the water pouch.

Laars shook his head. "There are no others here. The long-boats were destroyed. Two were taken by the sea serpent, another crashed against the first islet. No people live on the Impossible Isles. It must have been in your mind. There are odd sounds on this islet from the wind and the sea."

That settled it – Sash wouldn't say anything. What would be the point? He rubbed the sand from his face. He didn't look at Verity. He felt confused by what had happened – he no longer knew where he stood with her. He knew what it meant to dislike her, to be enemies. Enemies made sense. But the thought that she might have suffocated in the sand mire filled him with terror. He cupped his hands round his mouth and breathed deeply, staring at the cone-shaped hill where terns and gannets darkened the sky. He wanted to be far away. He thought for a moment of London, of Stuff the World, of East Heath College. No, not there. Not anywhere.

Manah sighed. "We could have got the wrong islet. What if the birds do not live here at all? If they did, we should have found them by now."

"We are in the right place," Zusa protested. "Our ancestors were clear – the furthest islet, the one with the hill. Great Aruva's Pool *must* be near by."

"Where, then? Perhaps our ancestors were wrong," said Laars. "The story makes no sense – the sea cannot boil. Islets are forged of earth, not liquid flames."

There was something peculiar about the hilltop. Something about its shape. Beyond it rolled the Endless Ocean. Had its waters really boiled? Millions of years ago, before fish and seaweed? Before gorse and terns? Hadn't Sash learned that his own world had erupted in flames long ago, forging craters and mountains? His dark eyebrows knitted over his eyes. He imagined the earth deep at the bottom of the ocean, tearing like a gash, releasing blood-like, liquid fire. "Some islands are forged of flames, in a way," he said. "Out in the middle of nowhere, in the sea."

"What did you say?" asked Manah.

"Liquid flames… That sounds like magma… Like the fluid that bubbles miles below the surface of the earth."

The Followers watched him blankly.

"His head was in the sand mire too long. It has addled his mind," said Laars dismissively.

"You mean a volcano!" exclaimed Verity, clapping her hands, ignoring Laars. "You think there's a volcano on this islet?" She stared intently at Sash.

He didn't look at her. "A lot of islands start life as volcanoes, don't they? Dr Clifton taught us that," he said, almost to himself. "And sometimes, when a volcano burns out, water fills the space where the magma used to be. It's a sort of natural well, the purest water you can find."

Overhearing part of this, Zusa reached out and gently squeezed his arm.

Sash turned his head, startled. He wasn't used to being touched.

Zusa's eyes were wide and hopeful. "You think there is a pool somewhere else on the islet?"

Sash nodded, looking beyond her into the distance. She followed his gaze to the curious hill that disappeared into the clouds.

At daybreak the next morning, Sash, Verity and the Followers left the cave and started towards the hill. It rose eerily in the distance, its peak lost beyond impenetrable clouds. Iguanas clung to the lower rocks. Blue-winged gannets and small black terns huddled above them.

They reached the foot of the hill. The rocks rose sharply,

hostile and impassable. But between the rocks were caverns, deep corridors, just wide enough for a person to climb through. Several forked ahead of them and vanished into the hill.

"We could split up," said Laars, clutching the gorse carrier.

Zusa shook her head, throwing an anxious look towards Sash and Verity. "After what happened yesterday I think we should stay together." She took the lead through one of the corridors and the others followed, with Sash bringing up the rear. Mist billowed around their bare feet and sea birds swooped overhead. Sash slipped on the rocky ground. He turned for a moment to look behind him. The entrance to the corridor was lost in a blanket of fog.

Mounting the hill, Sash felt a wave of excitement. Were they actually going to see the aruva – the bird of flames? He reminded himself that this was the reason he had broken his father's rules, had entered the River Fleet and had come to Aqarti. What would the bird look like? He had only seen the feathers – the one in Max's trunk and those used for rituals by the Followers. Then there was the statue suspended in the citadel. Could the aruva be that large? Could its beak really be cone-shaped?

Of course, he could have been wrong about the pool inside the extinct volcano. If so, they were all struggling on this difficult journey for nothing. He tried not to think about that now. He studied the ground. For several seconds his feet disappeared beneath him in the fog, only to reappear as the chafing wind blew it away.

Ren's voice floated down to him. "It is slippery up here. Slow down and tread carefully."

As Sash turned the corner round the boulder, he shivered. The flank of rock that had blocked the worst of the wind fell away. Cool air rushed over him. Goose pimples rose on his arms and legs. He paused and turned towards the foothills, concealed behind the boulder. He thought that he'd heard something. A voice, perhaps. Like Verity's voice yesterday that he had mistaken for the screeching terns. No, not like hers. Verity was further up the hill with the others, not below him in the foothills. What he had heard sounded like a deeper voice; a man's voice.

His heart started banging. "Is anybody there?" he called.

Ren stood a few paces above him. "Who are you talking to?" he asked.

"No one," said Sash.

Ren's grey eyes narrowed. "It is this place," he said quietly. "Murmurs and echoes. It is the curse of the shadow land."

They walked on in silence. Sash focused on keeping his balance. His long legs weren't used to climbing. The steep corridor twisted further round the hill, in the face of the wind. It whipped his cheeks. Only for the seconds that the wind dropped was Sash reminded of the warming suns above. Thousands, perhaps millions, of years of these conditions had smoothed the rocks on the northern side of the hill into panelled stepping-stones, into a causeway built for monumental footsteps. They rose steeply but with surprising symmetry for a stairway sculpted by nature.

The giant steps were easier to climb than the sharp angles of the southern corridors. Slowly the group mounted the causeway.

Sitting uncomfortably on the rocky steps, they stopped to rest. Gorse clung to the hillside, clutching at their ankles. Seed pods hid beneath the spindly leaves.

"Aruva like gorse seeds," said Ren, gathering the pods carefully. "Help me to collect some." He glanced at Sash and returned to the pods. He cracked them between his fingers and small seeds tumbled out, flat and brown like chocolate discs. "No good for us. Poisonous. One or two seeds cause sickness at once – vomiting and fever. Larger amounts kill."

Sash nodded. He plucked some seed pods and fumbled to crack them open, tucking the small seeds in his shirt.

"Not again," mumbled Verity as Manah passed her a mortus root from the gorse carrier, but she said it feebly, in a resigned way.

Sash chewed on a piece of leathery root. He closed his eyes and tried to imagine the flavour of spaghetti bolognese with grated cheese, one of his favourite meals. Max was good at cooking spaghetti – he took it off the boil before it got soggy, not like the slop they served at school. Sash did his best to remember the taste of the spicy tomato sauce. He wiped a trickle of mortus juice from his chin with the back of his hand. "It's strange to think of aruva as actual birds," he ventured. "All I've seen is the statue in the citadel." That and Dad's red feather, he added, in his head.

"The Bloodstone Bird," said Ren, and the other Followers touched their throats. "Not just a statue, young friend. The Bloodstone Bird stands for all that we believe in. It is the symbol of Great Aruva's power on our land."

Manah nodded. "The Bloodstone Bird has an energy of its own – the life energy that flows through all things."

Sash frowned. None of this made much sense to him.

"Can I ask you something else?" said Verity. "Sometimes – like just now, when Ren mentioned the Bloodstone Bird – I've seen you put your fingers like this." She demonstrated, touching her fingers to her throat. "Why do you do it?"

Sash, who had seen the Followers doing this too, was interested in their response.

"Before the Keeper arrived, our people wore aruva tail feathers on string round our necks," said Manah. "Like the feathers used in our rituals, we collected them from the southern boulders after the birds took flight for the Impossible Isles. We would touch them for luck, before a difficult task or if we feared something bad might happen, to feel Great Aruva's courage and strength. It is a habit that the Followers have maintained, even though we dare not wear the feathers."

"A dangerous habit," added Laars, chewing the end of a mortus root. "We do it without thinking, but it sets us apart as Followers. It is a way that the Keeper's guards might recognize us."

"That is true," Zusa agreed. She paused, staring out to sea thoughtfully. "There is something else you should understand about the Bloodstone Bird. The statue means even more to us today than it did in the past. It has come to represent our struggle against the Keeper. There it stands, at the entrance to the citadel that he now claims as his own. But as Tiro said, he dares not touch it."

"Why not?" asked Sash. If the Keeper lived in the palace facing the statue, it would be the easiest thing in the world to have his guards take it down.

"He would not harm the Bloodstone Bird. The people of Aqarti are peace loving but that would be too much — there would be an uprising. Many are sympathetic to the Followers. They feel for us, but fear to speak. Such an act of barbarism would unite all in horror. It would lead to the Keeper's overthrow. As long as the Bloodstone Bird watches over our land, there is still hope." Zusa smiled at Sash kindly and he felt a pang of sadness. Perhaps she saw this, for she spoke very gently. "Eat, Sash," she said. "You shall need all your strength for the climb."

After their meal they set off again up the giant causeway. Progress was slow and all Sash could see in front of him was the sombre Ren. Each smooth rock drew them into the northern wind while the land below disappeared into mist.

What a lonely place, thought Sash. An odd, *timeless* place. Timeless. Sash suddenly remembered one of the first things that Manah had said about the Keeper: "No one is allowed to gaze upon his 'timeless face'." Did anyone actually know what the Keeper looked like? How about the coconut gatherers who had seen him emerge from Rising Beach? How long ago was that? What else had Manah said? That the sky had blackened just as the Keeper arrived on Aqarti, but that was before she was born.

Puzzled, Sash focused on the Keeper for the first time. It wasn't just that the man's face was covered. Even with the mask, with the hood and robe, he was rarely seen by his people. Hadn't the Followers told them that? But where did he go? Where *could* he go in a place as small as Aqarti? Where did he come from anyway? Sash struggled up another steep step. His thoughts returned to the oval rocks and the gateway to the Fleet. The sea surrounding the rocks was inhabited by ferocious sharks – sharks that had left Sash and Verity alone. But they attacked everyone else. Everyone else except the Keeper…

Ren had come to a halt. Peering past him, Sash saw that they had reached the end of the steep steps. Ahead was a plateau, a flat hilltop. A sharp tooth of rock sprang in front of them, around which clung a bank of cloud. Beneath the cloud was a faint glint of cobalt-blue water. Great Aruva's Pool, thought Sash in amazement. It really must have been a volcano once, perhaps in Aqarti's earliest history. For a

215

moment he imagined the trembling ocean exploding into ash and flames.

Zusa and Ren skirted around the water, which was roughly the size of a small, circular swimming pool and seemed unfathomably deep. Laars followed them. They approached the rock tentatively and knelt down before it. Sash stood still. He didn't understand why they were kneeling. It was just a pinnacle of stone, grey and pock-marked, craggy and formidable. It blocked both suns and the northern wind, a shady shelter from the elements.

Manah stood next to Verity by the side of the pool. Sash was about to ask them what they were doing. The wind rattled over the hilltop. An arrow of sunlight pierced the clouds. Sash's jaw fell open. Settled into the grooves of the rock were mounds of bright green feathers – balls the size of cats or small dogs. The feathers were speckled with drops of red and tipped with shimmering blue and amber; the tops of the folded wings were green too but scarlet feathers were tucked beneath them. The long, diamond-shaped tails were fiery red, edged with gold. Caught in the light, the feathers glistened as though ablaze.

Sash gaped, cheeks flushed with heat. At last. *The bird of flames.* Here, real, before his eyes. It was almost as though the rock hummed with their beauty, with their power.

There were ten of them nestled between the crags. One drew an emerald head from beneath its wing and watched the humans. It raised its cone-shaped beak a moment, nodding, as though in acknowledgement, before resting it again inside its wing. Despite the scarlet wings and tail feathers, the aruva was more green than red.

"They're beautiful," sighed Verity.

"There used to be dozens," said Manah. "Can you picture it? The whole rock would have sparkled. And just wait till you see them in flight!"

"They are such gentle creatures," murmured Zusa. "It is dangerous to be so comfortable with humans near by. They trust too much."

Sash agreed with this comment. Hadn't people always taken advantage of the wildlife around them? Used it for their own ends, without a second thought? Wasn't the Atlantic starved of prawns, the North Sea drained of cod? The aruva was just another dodo – friendly and fearless, an easy target. In his own world they'd have been extinct years ago. The rush of excitement he had felt on first sighting the birds was waning. Huddled against the rock, they seemed small and vulnerable, far from the majestic statue at the entrance to the citadel. Was this what he and the others had fought so hard to find? Sash thought of the move to London, of his father's study, of the long hours that he'd spent alone as Max disappeared on secret journeys on the Fleet. Was this really the bird of legend, the bird that split the sun in two? Was this what his father had sacrificed everything for?

Laars had set down the gorse carrier and emptied out the remaining mortus roots and water pouches.

"Great Aruva shall forgive us," whispered Zusa.

Laars stood slowly. The birds raised their heads in unison and watched with sea-blue eyes. As he crept forward they warbled excitedly. One began hopping on its crag, flapping its wings as though preparing for flight.

Laars stiffened. Zusa rose and edged to the left, indicating that Ren and Verity should move to the right. Manah pulled back along the side of the pool a few paces. Soon Zusa, Laars, Verity and Ren had formed a semicircle round the rock.

Zusa turned to Sash, who was still standing alone on the far side of the pool. "Come and help us." She beckoned.

Laars lifted the carrier and Sash suddenly realized what it was really for. How could he have failed to see it sooner? *A cage to catch a bird of flames.*

"Come!" urged Zusa. "Quickly, before they fly away."

They had chosen their bird. The smallest one. It was watching them, warbling. Zusa and Laars took a cautious step towards it as Verity and Ren held their ground. Zusa glanced back at Sash.

He shook his head. This wasn't going to work. Did they really believe they could capture a bird and keep it alive, taking it to Aqarti in secret and protecting it while the others flew home to be killed by guards? Did they think that a wild creature would survive in a small cage, would cope with the perilous journey by sea – would sing to command?

Sash swallowed, an acid taste in his mouth. "You're

making a mistake," he said. Silently, he willed the small aruva to fly away. If it really had magical powers, now was the time to use them. He urged the bird to sing. Instead it started shuffling nervously, making no move to escape.

Sash cleared his throat. "You mustn't—"

"Shush!" hissed Verity. For a moment, their eyes locked. Hers were wide, the whites gleaming. He saw there a desperate hunger, a desire for the bird beyond reason. She turned back to it, outstretching her hands.

Sash watched a moment longer as Zusa and the others closed round the confused aruva. Walking away, he heard a rising chorus of warbles followed by an ear-piercing screech. The throb of beating wings as the aruva was captured. No songs. No earthquakes. No flashes of thunder. The bird of flames scarcely put up a fight.

With another screech came a drift of fog that masked the land in a white veil. Heading back towards the causeway, Sash felt weak, as though he might be sick. He stumbled and fell onto his knee. Wincing, he touched the grazed skin. Drops of blood clung to his fingertips. Briefly he heard a voice. He looked up in time to see a hand clutching a stone as it swung into view, emerging from the mist like a ghost. It smashed into his skull and he slumped backwards. As his eyelids closed he could hear the screeching bird and the lash of the furious sea.

— Spring Tide —

The bird was squawking and scrambling in the cage, trying to flap its wings.

"Hush now, hush, aruva," Zusa crooned to no effect. She turned to the others. Laars held down the cage while Ren sewed it up with a string of plaited gorse. "The mist is clearing. We should fill our water pouches from the pool and return to the cave to rest. We travel back to Aqarti tomorrow morning."

"How do you expect us to depart this dismal place?" asked Laars. "The currents all pull towards the islet! And even if we fight against them, we shall never travel beyond the rocks. The canoe is damaged, it cannot last long. We are trapped. Just as trapped as this aruva. They are called the Impossible Isles for a reason."

"We will prevail," said Zusa, staring at the captured bird

through the gaps in the cage. Occasionally, its cone beak poked out, pecking at the gorse. The remaining aruva flapped and warbled in distress.

"They think that we are going to harm it," said Manah.

"If only we could explain to them," said Verity.

Ren and Laars started filling the water pouches from Great Aruva's Pool.

Verity turned to watch them. Suddenly, she remembered: "Where's Sash?"

Manah lowered her face. "He did not agree with what we were doing. I suppose that he must have returned to the cave."

"He shouldn't be wandering off alone, it isn't safe. He's annoyed about the bird. But it's the only way. What else could we do?" Verity stepped cautiously over the slippery ground around the pool, making for the giant causeway that led down towards the sea. Mist rose in ripples, dappling the waves below. In and out of the mist wove gannets and terns. The shore heaved with movement. "We had no choice," she called back to Manah. "He'll just have to…" The words evaporated from her lips. She bent down.

"Have to what?" Manah was at her side. Her eyes traced the rocky ground just right of the steps. A swirl of cloud distorted a dark puddle of water. As the cloud lifted, Manah realized it was blood.

Verity dropped down the first steep step, skidding for a second before straightening up and taking the next step.

"Be careful!" urged Manah.

"There's been an accident! He's hurt!" was Verity's reply. Billows of mist rose up to meet her, as though she was treading on clouds rather than the hard, flat stones beneath her soles.

Manah spun round to the other Followers, who were walking slowly around the pool towards the steps, Laars holding the gorse cage. The aruva on the rock pinnacle still clucked nervously, but the bird in the cage was silent.

"Something has happened to Sash!" cried Manah.

Zusa and Laars hurried towards her and she gestured at the puddle of blood.

Ren followed slowly, deep crinkles etched onto his brow. He crouched and gazed at the blood thoughtfully. His eyes trailed over the ground. "The boy fell," he said. "Here. Where it is uneven." Ren pointed at a patch of rugged rock speckled with lichen. "A hard fall. Painful. Not serious."

"Then where is he?" Manah wrung her hands anxiously.

Laars looked over the causeway, down to the thundering sea. "Maybe..."

"No!" Manah protested.

Ren shook his head. His finger floated over the ground beyond the puddle. Tiny droplets of water clung to the rocks, but immediately after the puddle these differed in size, as though they had been disturbed and recently regrouped. Several of the droplets had merged together in sequence.

"Dragged," said Ren.

"What do you mean?" asked Laars, still clutching the gorse cage with one hand – reaching for his dagger with the other.

Before Ren could answer they heard Verity shouting from the causeway below. "Hurry!" She had made it down halfway to where the group had stopped to eat. A compass lay at her feet – the compass that Sash had taken from his father's study. Her fingers trembled as she lifted it. The plastic face was broken but the dial juddered, pointing towards the Endless Ocean.

Reaching her, Manah stared at the compass. "What is it?"

Verity snatched her hand away. "It belongs to Sash."

"Perhaps he dropped it on the way up," Manah reasoned.

Verity shook her head fiercely, starting again down the steep steps.

The others followed more warily. Creeping fog made it hard to see anything beyond a metre away. After a while, the causeway twisted south into the shade, and the steps narrowed and became the dank corridor.

Verity sat at the bottom, panting with exhaustion. "Where *is* he?"

Ren joined her on the rock, his grey eyes peering through the mist. A knot of thorny gorse snatched at his ankle. He turned to look at it. A scrap of black fabric clung to the gorse, fluttering in the wind like a flag. "Guards have been here," he said quietly.

"Guards?" gasped Manah, standing just above them.

"They have taken him," added Ren.

"Guards? Here?" Manah's eyes flitted towards the beach, invisible through the fog. "The middle longboat. We thought that the sea monster... But we did not see it go down..."

Verity stared at Ren in disbelief. "You walked all round the islet! You would have seen a longboat, wouldn't you?"

Ren shook his head. "Perhaps it was concealed somehow. Hidden in a cave, partially buried..."

"So where are they?" asked Manah.

Zusa appeared behind her. "They must be taking him back to Aqarti," she said.

Verity buried her face in her hands. Nobody said anything as this grim possibility dawned on them.

Finally, Laars spoke the words they were all thinking. "They will never get across the Impossible Sea."

Zusa reached forward and rested a hand on Verity's shoulder. "He is gone," she whispered. "May the ocean welcome his soul."

They sat on moss under the shelter of the cave, eating mortus roots and barbecued crab to the sounds of the driving surf. Verity knew that she would never think of the sea in the same way as she used to, as a holiday resort, a place for sport and fun. There was a reckless danger to the swirling waters. The aruva sat huddled in the cage, refusing pieces of vine that Manah offered through gaps between the gorse.

"Do you still think we should leave in the morning?" asked Laars.

"What choice do we have?" replied Zusa.

"We cannot reach Aqarti," he said flatly. "The currents around this islet ... I have told you... They flow inland. We cannot escape them. The canoe is not strong enough, and neither are we."

"We will prevail," repeated Zusa.

"How will we prevail? Would that we could fly over the rocks! There are whirlpools between them that will take us down. It is hopeless!"

"But we have to try," Zusa insisted. "And if we die, we do so for a cause. A great cause."

"What is the use of having a cause?" said Laars bitterly, hurling an empty crab shell out of the cave. He licked his fingers.

"It is the last thing we have to hold onto."

"So out we go to the Impossible Sea, out to certain death, we and the poor bird..."

"There is no shame in death," said Zusa simply.

Verity shivered and pushed away her hunk of root.

"The moon falls before the yellow sun tonight, falls atop our land," Zusa went on. "I shall give our rites to it before tomorrow comes."

Verity looked up. "Will it be a full moon tonight?" For some reason, this reminded her of something.

"Do you care if it is? Do not tell me that you believe

in paying rites to the moon," said Laars.

"You do not?" asked Zusa. Her eyes widened and for the first time Verity saw signs of doubt.

"I stopped believing in anything the day the Keeper came. The day he destroyed everything."

Verity ignored the exchange. "The sun sinks towards the white boulders in the lowlands, doesn't it?" she asked. She was sitting up, her lips parted.

Zusa and Laars weren't listening. But Manah addressed Verity. "The great yellow sun sinks towards the white boulders – the pink sun towards Trin. Once a year they join and the aruva fly. That is in two days…"

"Zusa said that the moon falls before the yellow sun tonight," said Verity.

"What is it?" asked Ren.

His deep voice was so unexpected that Verity hesitated. She had almost forgotten about him.

"You have thought of something?" he pressed. Suddenly Zusa and Laars were listening too.

"It's just something I was taught recently. I don't know if it's the same here, but … but when a strong sun … a sun like your yellow sun … when that shines behind the moon, and the moon is near to us, and it sinks in the sun's direction, there's a gravitational pull."

The Followers looked at her blankly.

Verity sighed. "There's something called a spring tide – a very high tide that happens only once a month as a full moon rises. The moon sort of drags the water along with it, back in its direction, creating a powerful current. It's a bit like that rip tide that we rode on the way here, but instead of a narrow strip of current it's as though the whole sea is dragging along behind the moon. It's that powerful."

"What are you saying?" asked Zusa. "Are you telling us that this special tide is on its way?"

"Yes. Maybe... I'm not saying it will be easy. It'll be a fast current, probably quite rough, but... Well, it's better than nothing, isn't it?"

"This tide sounds hard to believe," said Laars. "A tide so magical that we need only push the canoe out onto the water and it will carry us south towards Aqarti, rising right up over the rocks to leave us totally unharmed?"

"Just forget it!" Verity sprang to her feet and backed away into the dark shadows of the cave. Tears were running down her cheeks.

Manah approached slowly.

"I wish I could go back in time," cried Verity. "I made Sash come here. He didn't want to... It's all my fault." Her voice echoed through the cave's hollow passages.

"No ... no, that is not true, Verity. You came because we needed you," said Manah. "You did not have a choice. You may think you did but... But we needed you – both of you. Everything happens for a reason."

"Do you really believe that?" said Verity, rubbing her eyes.

Manah nodded.

"Sash thinks I'm selfish, and I am, aren't I? If only I hadn't pushed him into all this. But I wanted the bird, I wanted it *so much*. I thought he could help me, that I could just take it. I've been so stupid."

"Perhaps Great Aruva called you," said Manah. "She must have realized that you have a part to play in our struggles."

Verity was no longer listening. "He said I was a brat, and he's right. I was a brat, always thinking of myself, taking what I wanted just like that, because I could. But that Verity is finished. As of this moment she doesn't exist." She turned to face Manah. "Cut my hair!"

Manah blinked back at her. "Now?" she asked.

"Please. Right now. With that knife you carry." As Verity spoke, fresh tears rolled down her cheeks.

Manah hesitated. "But I thought you did not want to have your hair cut?"

"I changed my mind."

Manah nodded and drew her dagger from within her dress. She took a handful of Verity's hair and started cutting it away. Clumps of tangled blonde locks floated onto the floor of the cave. Verity stared at them. "I changed my mind," she repeated to herself.

Zusa, Laars and Ren were sitting round the fire in silence. The flames flickered against the walls of the cave, casting an amber halo around them. The mortus roots gave off a sweet, pungent aroma as they crackled in the heat.

Ren prodded the fire with a stump of gorse. "She was right about the wolf current," he said.

Laars nodded but said nothing.

Zusa stood and walked to the entrance of the cave. She spoke decisively but with her back to the others. "The first sun falls. We do not have much time..."

The pink sun had already sunk beyond Trin. Verity and the Followers stood next to the beached canoe. Ren had done his best to patch up the holes. The water's edge seemed far away – much further than when they had rowed onto the shore.

"It is true," said Zusa. "See how far the water has escaped. It aches to reach Aqarti."

"So do we," said Laars.

The wind rose over the hill and cleared the fog from the sea. The dark mass of Aqarti was just visible in the south-west. Beyond it, concealed between oval rocks, lay a secret passage to the River Fleet. To the Fleet, to Max Baranovski's study, to a taxidermy shop on a forgettable London street.

The moon appeared above Aqarti. The yellow sun sank, blazing a tail of violet and red.

Manah and Verity climbed into the canoe and held the gorse cage with the aruva carefully between them. Zusa, Ren and Laars guided the prow onto the water and slid inside. For a moment the canoe held back, as though unwilling to embark on another perilous journey. They eased it onto a wave and it leapt into the air, riding the powerful current. It flew over the jagged rocks without a graze.

Back on the islet, sea birds roosted and iguanas sought shelter from the wind. Hidden by darkness, two guards watched the disappearing canoe.

"How could they have known that this strange tide would happen? Did they summon it? Can they...?" One of the guards turned back to the looming, cone-shaped hill, shuddering. "This is dangerous magic. This is—"

"No, that cannot be possible, only the Keeper has power," said another guard. "They have nothing. They cannot control the elements."

"Then why are we letting them escape? They have a bird... And the Keeper wants the girl with the strange bracelet, that is what we were told."

"It is clear that the Followers have mastered a rich understanding of the ocean... Without them we might never leave this place alive. It is better that we follow at a distance – we can catch up with them on Aqarti. We have the boy. The girl is less important. She was too far away on the hill, we would have had to fight the others to reach her. The boy was alone, an easy target." The guard watched as the small canoe disappeared into darkness. "I was sure that the Followers would find our longboat hidden in the gorse bush when they made that odd journey around the coast. They are not as cunning as everyone thinks they are."

"But what of the tides? They bend them to their will! People say they can. And did you see how they summoned the wolf current? And sea creatures too! The beast of the mangrove swamp; the serpent of the ocean!"

The other guard's eyes flashed. He glanced over his shoulder. "Be careful what passes your tongue. This is reckless talk. All I know is that we can finally leave this treacherous place. Tell the others: we leave now, before the tide changes."

Four guards pushed the longboat onto the water as the other two onboard paddled. Sash lay unconscious on the floor of the boat, his arms bound behind his back, his mouth gagged.

"Is he alive?" asked one of the guards, prodding the captive with the tip of an oar. The boy made a muffled sound but his eyes remained shut. "It is not our custom to gag the Followers," he commented. "It is not usual. Who will hear him out here?"

"We are under orders," said another, throwing him a meaningful look. "From the palace."

Vaulting over the islet's fortress of rock, the longboat rose onto the sea. Waves leapt towards the moon, towards Aqarti in the south-west. The yellow sun had disappeared and with it the colourful sunset. In moments the sea was a shifting black mass, the sky a spiral web of infinite stars.

— Captive —

The sensation of heat bearing down on Sash's eyelids was powerful and immediate. This was followed by a shot of pain through his forehead. He tried to lift his hands to his temples but they wouldn't move. His eyes flicked open into glaring sunlight.

"Get up," ordered a voice above him.

Sash tried to rise but slumped back without the use of his hands. He felt groggy and for a moment he wondered, disoriented, if he had been in an accident. He remembered the Royal Free Hospital in north London where Gertrude Trench had been admitted. He pictured beige corridors and fluorescent lights. He thought he could smell antiseptic.

Arms seized him and lifted him out of the longboat, setting him onto his feet. His right leg immediately gave way but hands held him upright until he found his balance.

His knee throbbed from his fall on the rock plateau and his head thundered.

Sash saw mangroves to his right and before him loomed dense jungle. A flock of violet parrots colonized a nearby tree, preening and chattering with noisy clucks. Two cobalt butterflies quivered above Sash's face and deep from the jungle rose chirps from cicadas. Instead of antiseptic, the fragrant smell of the damp rainforest filled his nose. With a wave of happiness, Sash realized he was back on Aqarti.

The happiness was short-lived. He tried to speak but couldn't. A gag was tied tightly round his mouth. He shook his head, which sent waves of pain through his skull but did nothing to loosen the gag. His arms refused to move because they were bound at the wrists. Tingling with fear for the first time since gaining consciousness, Sash took in the situation. Seven guards in red and black uniforms stood around him, batons raised.

"Forward!" commanded a guard as he nudged Sash with his baton.

Sash tried to protest through his gag.

"I said move!" barked the guard as another reached for a machete at his belt, waving it threateningly.

Sash took a small step, tripping and almost falling on a snaking mangrove root.

"Hurry up!" hissed the guard. "The Keeper is waiting!"

Only one of the guards was bright-eyed and neatly dressed, and he seemed to be the leader. The other six were dishevelled and Sash guessed that they, too, had recently disembarked the longboat. They must have captured him on the Impossible Isles and taken him back to Aqarti. Sash's heart beat rapidly, his initial grogginess forgotten. Treading carefully he felt anxious, alert. With a start, he thought of Verity, Manah and the others – were they OK? Surely the guards would not have left them unharmed?

The group walked through the jungle in silence. Sash struggled to recall how the guards had caught him. Had they been watching him on the extinct volcano, lurking beyond the mist? The thought brought back Great Aruva's Pool, the screeching bird, the determined look on Verity's face... Concentrating on not stumbling, Sash counted the days they had been in Aqarti: one night in the Followers' hut, two nights on the Impossible Isles... Or was that three nights on the Impossible Isles? How long had he been un-conscious? He thought suddenly, urgently, about Max. His father would be worried sick. No, wait, he reminded himself. Max would still be in Iceland. On a taxidermy jaunt – wasn't that how Verity had put it? There was nothing out of the ordinary about Max's trip. He was always coming and going. Even when he seemed to be home, you couldn't be sure that he really was, hiding away in that study of his... There one minute, gone the next...

After walking for hours, the wilderness of the jungle ended and Sash found himself standing at the rear entrance to the citadel. Something was going on around the main entrance, he could see that immediately. Beyond the bartering market, guards were scaling the furthest wall, clutching vines and climbing makeshift ladders. Dozens of locals stood by, whispering behind raised hands. Above them glittered the Bloodstone Bird.

"Keep moving," grunted a guard, shoving Sash forward. People turned to watch them, saw the guards and looked away, as though Sash was invisible. He understood more about these islanders than he had on his last trip to the citadel. He guessed that they acted in fear of punishment, not because they weren't curious or didn't care.

"Praise be to the Keeper," murmured one or two people as the guards passed.

"What is happening?" a small girl asked, gazing at Sash.

"Hush!" cautioned her mother, clutching her wrist and leading her away. "It seems as though another Follower has been caught."

Peering back at Sash, the girl caught his eye. "What will happen to him?"

Sash looked away.

The girl's mother placed a protective hand on her shoulder. "It is better not to ask, my child."

The guards led Sash through the orchid gardens that he had noticed on his tour of the citadel. Colourful birds darted between the blooms and butterflies rested on petals, lazily fanning their wings. This close, the beautiful flowers and smell of vanilla were intoxicating. It was hard to imagine anything bad unfolding amid these peaceful gardens.

Sash assumed that he was being taken to the dungeon beneath the Imperial Palace. Instead, he was led through a corridor to the centre of the cone-shaped building. The guards smoothed down their shirts and culottes and he noticed one polish the metal of his machete. A nervous energy passed between them. Sash watched this change curiously. Was he about to meet the Keeper?

The Great Hall at the centre of the palace was large and round, with a ceiling that funnelled upwards, ending in a wide hole, a circular skylight. Sash's captors slipped away but he was not alone – further guards were posted at seven doorless entrances spaced evenly around the circular hall. There were no windows but light flooded in from the hole where the roof opened to the sky. Sash remembered Tiro's explanation of the Middle Period of Aqarti's history when the building was known as the Seat of Elders. He imagined seven old women and men sitting in a circle, with the light casting a perfect sun on the floor between them. They would have burned candles, with dusty incense twisting slowly through the still air. Sash pictured ribbons laced with feathers and offerings of fruit and wild flowers. The Great Hall would have been more colourful and inviting than it was today. Now it was barren, without decoration. No, that wasn't quite right: on a shelf near one of the entrances, Sash spotted something that looked like a box, the only item in the hall. A length of colourful fabric covered it entirely. Sash started to take a closer look but at that moment a man appeared from the opposite exit.

"Follower, get away from there!" spat the man as he glided across the hall in a red robe like a cassock. The guards standing sentry by the exits closest to the box darted in front of it and crossed their arms protectively, although Sash was nowhere near.

The man wasn't the Keeper – Sash guessed that immediately. He was small, like other locals – he might come up to Sash's shoulders at most – and the podgy face was unmasked, unlike the Keeper who, according to Manah, never showed his "timeless face". And he was old – Sash couldn't guess how old. The robe looked too long for him and dragged heavily across the stone floor. A ridiculous outfit considering the hot climate.

Sash tugged at his wrists but couldn't free them. Perhaps even without the use of his arms, he could overpower this squat man, kick him down and run. But the guards at the entrances watched silently. It was hopeless, he was surrounded.

The man stopped a short distance from Sash, panting and red-faced. "Follower," he managed breathily, jabbing a stumpy finger at Sash's face. His pale blue eyes bulged. "The Keeper has..." The man took a deep breath, drew some cloth from his sleeve and dragged it over his forehead.

237

"I am the Keeper's Senator. The Keeper has commanded your arrest. He has ordered it personally." He paused again to draw breath. "*Personally*," he repeated for emphasis. "Soon you will be taken to the dungeon to fester with the rest of your kind." The man crinkled his nose disapprovingly. "But first I wanted to lay eyes on the one that the Keeper so despises – the leader of the Followers' underground! The worst of Aqarti's rebels!"

The leader of the Followers' underground? thought Sash. How had they reached that conclusion? He struggled against his gag. This was pointless – he couldn't even reply.

"Oh no, Follower, oh no!" snapped the man. "The Keeper has warned his loyal servants that you would try to trick us, to implore us to untie you, or worse, to release the gag so that your mealy words are free to do their damage. I shall not release the gag!" The man mopped his brow again, his cheeks ruddy. He turned to one of the guards. "Get rid of this giant! Take him to the dungeon. That will soon cut him down to size!"

Several of the guards approached Sash, their batons raised. He bowed his head, ready to follow them. He was exhausted and outnumbered. They would take him down to the dungeon and he'd probably rot there. In several days his father would return from Iceland to find the trunk open and Sash gone. He would never find the portal, the under-water cave from the River Fleet that opened on the shores of Aqarti. Sash could hardly bear to think about it.

"Good boy, good Follower," jeered the man.

Keep your head down, thought Sash. It doesn't matter what he says. If you respond, it will only get worse. Just ignore him. But even as Sash thought this, his bound wrists stiffened and his hands formed fists behind his back. For a moment he remembered Verity's words: "All you do is hide away. You never say what you're thinking." But he couldn't say anything, not now with the gag, and what would be the point?

"Be gone with you," puffed the man, growing in confidence at the sight of his captive's obedience. "Not so big now, are you, Follower?"

The words echoed in Sash's head. Anger crackled through him. It was almost as though he *was* a rebel, as if he really revered the bird of flames, as the Senator thought he did. *Sash Baranovski, leader of the Followers' underground.* It was ludicrous. These people had no idea about Followers. They thought they were dangerous. They imprisoned them, torched their homes, banned their beliefs. But why? Sash thought of Tiro, the old man who had stayed to burn to death in the jungle.

The Senator smoothed down his robe. "Fool of a Follower," he muttered.

It wasn't much of an insult but it was enough. Sash snapped, lunging at the Senator and butting him with his shoulder. The man tumbled onto his bottom, the voluminous robe flapping around him, his sweaty face lost behind folds of fabric. Immediately guards leapt at Sash, forcing

239

him to his knees. He felt a baton in his ribs and spluttered through his gag.

The fallen man jostled with his robe until his sweaty red face emerged, glowering with rage. "You will pay for this, Follower!" he cried in fury. To the guards he shouted: "Get him to the dungeon! Cut out his tongue – he shall never speak again!"

Panic-stricken at hearing these orders, Sash thrashed and kicked wildly. Guards gripped his arms and dragged him towards the exit near the shelf with the box draped in fabric. One of the guards tried to seize his ankle but Sash kicked him away, thrusting the guard against the shelf. The fabric shuddered off one side of the box, revealing a large, silvery corner. Sash glimpsed a round panel and something that looked like switches. He saw the words "Waterproof" in squat, rounded letters. A tape cassette clattered to the floor. Someone had written NESSUN DORMA (FWC 1990) on it in capitals. *Nessun Dorma*. The words seemed strange but oddly familiar. He strained to take a closer look but the guard returned and clouted him across the jaw. Hands closed round his arms and legs and dragged him down to the dungeon.

Deep in the humid highlands, Manah knelt before a cage woven from palm and twigs. They had transferred the captured aruva as soon as they returned to Aqarti, concerned that the gorse carrier with its rough, uncomfortable edges was the reason that the bird refused to eat. But it crouched within the new cage, ignoring all offers of berries and seeds. Manah reached her fingers between the bars and touched its feathers gently, hoping it would move. The aruva was silent and motionless. Only its staring blue eyes betrayed life.

"What now?" Laars was pacing impatiently beneath a giant fig tree. "Soon enough they must find us. Nowhere is safe."

"Ren is watching for guards. He will know if we were followed," replied Zusa. "It is safe enough. Safe as anywhere can be. Nobody knows about this place."

"Ren is not perfect. He failed to discover the longboat on the islet. And some do know about this place." Laars shook his head. "Some who were taken to the dungeon. They may speak. They may betray us."

"They will not betray us," murmured Zusa.

Verity sat cross-legged in a pool of sunlight, inspecting the compass. "We have to find Sash," she said. "We have to help him."

"He cannot have crossed the sea. He is beyond our help," said Laars. His voice was gruff but his fingers instinctively touched his throat.

"We don't know that!" Verity protested, rising to her feet. "They might have made it back – we did! We owe it to him—"

"We have a duty to ourselves, and to the aruva, to stay alive," said Zusa sadly. At the mention of the bird, they all turned to Manah and the woven cage.

Manah glanced back at them. "It will not eat; it will not drink. It does not even move any more." She lowered her eyes. "I think it is dying."

Verity's fingers tightened over the compass. She watched the aruva thoughtfully for a moment. The bird wouldn't survive here, it needed somewhere safe to recover, somewhere *really* safe. Her eyes trailed from the cage to the surrounding jungle. None of the Followers thought it possible that Sash had survived. Verity tugged absently at her short hair. She felt sure that he was near by, somewhere on Aqarti. If she could only find him they could escape back through the portal. They could get out of this place. She looked again at the aruva. They could *all* get out of this place.

"Aruva like gorpi berries, is that not the case? Have you tried those?" asked Zusa.

Manah shook her head, standing up. "I shall gather some. Verity, do you want to help me?"

"I'll watch the aruva," said Verity quietly. She didn't meet Manah's eye as she sat down next to the cage. She waited, examining the compass and glancing again between the trees, until Manah had left in search of berries. She rose slowly. Zusa was talking to Laars. They weren't looking in her direction. She scooped up the cage with the silent bird. Backing behind a clutch of ferns, Verity started quickly towards the lowlands.

After a while, Manah returned with a handful of gorpi

berries. She stopped in her tracks. "Where is Verity?" she asked.

Zusa and Laars turned around. Zusa shrugged. "She was just..."

Manah's eyes bulged. *"Where is the aruva?"* she cried. Scarlet berries tumbled to her feet.

Verity had vanished – and so had the bird of flames.

The guards hauled Sash down the stone steps into the dungeon. Once no more than the foundations of the palace, the earth had been dug out to form small, grey-walled cells with slits for windows, leading off a narrow corridor. It was dingy and airless, lit by tiny peepholes cut just below the ceiling. The holes faced the Keeper's gardens. Occasionally butterflies fluttered through the peepholes to find themselves lost inside the dungeon. They never lived long down there.

Sash hardly noticed his surroundings. He tugged at his wrists but the bindings held tight. Guards clutched his arms and legs. They half-carried, half-dragged him through the dreary corridor. He heard a muddle of voices, crying and shouting.

"Help, please help!" someone begged. Hands reached out of the high windows along the corridor, groping the stone with blackened fingers.

The guards threw Sash into a tiny cell. Three held him down as another drew a machete from his belt. Sash saw the shimmering blade and struggled frantically. His pulse hammered at his temples. His jaw felt paralysed and he was unable to swallow. Saliva gathered in his mouth, soaking the gag.

I'll choke to death! he thought desperately, jerking his face away.

The guard pressed the machete against Sash's throat and he immediately fell still. The icy metal stunned him. His heart thumped violently. It felt like it was tearing, as if it might suddenly stop.

Another guard wrenched off the gag and Sash choked back saliva. Someone grasped a handful of his hair, holding his head still. The machete rose above his face. Flashing across the blade Sash saw huge, terrified eyes. His own eyes.

Sash screamed.

— A Promise —

Verity stalked through the undergrowth, clutching Max's compass in one hand and the cage with the aruva in the other.

"You're heavy!" she complained, frowning at the bird through the bars of the cage. She had only been walking for a couple of hours and already her arm ached from the strain of carrying the aruva in the humid jungle. She leant against a tree trunk. "They don't believe me. Your lot, the Followers. They think Sash drowned in the Impossible Sea. But they're wrong. I know they're wrong." Verity stuck her finger through the bars and was surprised when the aruva jabbed at it with its beak. "Peckish, are you?" said Verity. "Great. We try to feed you non-stop from the minute we catch you and now you're hungry. I suppose I'll have to find something. I, who know nothing of birds. Can't you hang on till we find Sash? He knows about animals. Wait a moment, aren't those the gorpi things that Manah was going to get you?" She had spotted the scarlet berries on a bush.

"We'll find Sash, and I'll say sorry for what I said about him not having a mother. For other stuff too... I'll rescue him and he'll have to forgive me. And the three of us will disappear through the portal into London. You're going to love London! I can't say that you'll fit right in there but maybe it's good to be different." She broke a branch off the gorpi bush. "Sash is different, isn't he?"

She plucked some berries from the branch and fed them to the eager bird.

The guards shot to their feet. Sash's head rolled back against the stone floor. A large red spider was creeping across the ceiling. For several seconds he gazed at it, unthinking. He heard the clamour of prisoners from nearby cells. When he blinked he imagined a flurry of hands reaching out through window slats. Floating in front of these were the words "Waterproof" in squat letters and a tape cassette with NESSUN DORMA (FWC 1990) printed in capitals.

He turned his head to peer out of the open door of the cell. He could see the guards bowing and fawning and a figure looming in the dark passage just beyond them. In a floor-length black robe with a mask covering his face, it could have been some sort of monster, or even Death itself, like the Grim Reaper of films and comic books. Sash blinked. The figure had vanished. Had he just imagined it?

He ran his tongue along the inside of his teeth and turned to stare at the spider, which had stopped and seemed to be watching him. Memories of the poised machete, only seconds old, were melting away. Even now he could scarcely take in what had happened. But he would never see a spider again without an inward shudder of horror.

Verity stood behind a hefty tree trunk on the outskirts of the citadel. She smoothed back her short hair. It felt curious against her fingertips, almost as though she had fallen asleep as Verity Tattersall and woken up as someone else – someone from Aqarti. She hadn't seen her reflection and could hardly imagine what she looked like. Back in London, she would have checked her appearance in a mirror half a dozen times a day.

The aruva in its cage pecked at the ground between the bars, cheeping. Verity leant forward, tugging up her hood. Over the chirping cicadas she could hear a stir from the citadel.

"Something's going on down there," she said out loud. "Sounds like trouble." She glanced at the aruva. It tilted its crimson head and watched her with a cool blue eye. Verity smiled at it grudgingly. "You know, you could put a stop to all this. All you have to do is sing. Not so hard, is it?"

A twig snapped. Verity spun round. She froze and, as

though following her lead, the aruva froze too. It didn't protest as she carefully picked up the cage and started down towards the citadel.

Fern leaves rustled. Manah stepped out in front of Verity. "Where are you going?"

Verity gasped in surprise. She glanced over her shoulder, intending to run in the opposite direction. Ren appeared behind her.

"I... I'm going to help Sash," Verity stuttered.

"With the aruva?" asked Manah, eyeing the cage.

"I was going to leave it up here while I go to get him."

"'Go to get him'? Do you think he will be sitting in the sun, waiting for you? He drowned in the Impossible Sea, Verity," said Manah, quite firmly. "I am sad about it too, but there is no point—"

"You've known him for five minutes!" Verity protested. "And he didn't drown. I'm sure he didn't!"

"Perhaps not." Manah shot a nervous look towards the citadel. "But that means that the Keeper has him down in the dungeon. You will not be able to free him. If it was that easy we would have freed them all by now, my brother, Jonto..."

"Well, let's try then!" Verity made a move towards the citadel but Manah blocked her path. "I cannot let you do that, Verity."

"You can't stop me!" Verity clutched the cage and tried to push past Manah.

The cage didn't budge. Ren also held it between his narrow, muscular hands.

"We are doing this for your own safety!" said Manah. "You do not know the jungle as we do. The guards prowl it unseen by all and they will catch you. They know you escaped to the Impossible Isles with us. They will throw you in the dungeon where you shall be no help to anyone!"

"Let go of the bird!" ordered Verity, but Ren did not loosen his grip. He stared at her steadily. "Fine!" she snorted. "I don't need the bird. Just take it, will you?" She let go of the cage. But hesitating, she looked back at the aruva.

"Do not go to the citadel," pleaded Manah. "You need to be near the bird. Come back with us to the highlands and help protect it."

"But Sash..." began Verity. Her voice faltered. She was no longer sure.

"It is too late, we cannot help him. We have to think of the aruva."

"Take it then! Just take it," spat Verity. "You've obviously given up on Sash but I'm not going to!" She pushed past Manah towards the citadel.

Manah watched her anxiously. "Shall I go after her?" she asked Ren.

He shook his head. "No. She will be caught."

As though to illustrate his words, two guards appeared from the bushes outside the fort. They closed round Verity.

"You have no right!" they heard her cry.

"I tried..." said Manah. "She would not listen."

"We must get the aruva to safety," said Ren.

Manah nodded and followed in silence as he carried the cage into the jungle.

Sash rolled onto his side and coughed for several minutes, his eyes shut, his chest heaving. The gag was gone but his wrists were still bound. He opened his eyes to red fabric. Someone was standing over him. Immediately Sash thought of the robed man he had seen in the dark passage beyond the cell. The Keeper, it had to be.

Sash shuffled against the wall until he was seated upright. The guards had disappeared, the door behind the tiny cell was shut, and standing in front of him was not the Keeper but his puffy-faced Senator.

The man was breathless, even more agitated than he'd seemed up in the palace. His flushed cheeks almost matched his scarlet robe. "The Keeper has told ... has a-a-asked me that is, to order you to..." The Senator took a deep breath. Sash noticed that his pudgy hands were shaking and he stammered when he spoke. "First I should say that ... that he does not want you harmed... He is angry that I ordered your tongue out, he needs you with your tongue intact." His words poured out all in a hurry. He glanced at the door to the cell.

"I cannot enquire as to who you are," mumbled the Senator. His eyes bulged. "Although you are obviously not just anyone, not just another Follower... Not even the leader of the Followers' underground." He eyed Sash a moment before continuing.

Sash opened his mouth. At first, no sound emerged. He tried again. "I don't understand," he managed in a cracked voice.

"Never mind that!" returned the Senator. "It is not for us to understand His Excellency's whims. He is not seen for days, then wanders silently around his grounds. He is not a man of words. He does not need to ... to explain himself to us. We are just servants. It is ours to obey – to obey without question..." He glanced at his hand and Sash noticed that the man was clutching something in his pink fist.

Sash blinked at the Senator, dizzy and bewildered. The Keeper had appeared, had spared Sash's tongue. Why? It didn't make sense. Was the Keeper trying to protect him, is that why the guards brought him back to Aqarti? Who was this mysterious man, who scarcely spoke, who was not seen for days on end and sang once a year with many voices? Why wasn't Sash allowed to meet him – what was the Keeper trying to hide? What sort of man hid his face behind a mask? With a start, Sash thought of the flat at Gully Lane. Of the ceremonial mask that hung on the living room wall. He licked his lips. "What do you want?"

The Senator started pacing back and forth in the tiny cell, mopping his sweaty brow with his sleeve. "I need you to... That is, the Keeper has ordered me to tell you to—"

Sash coughed again. He tried to breathe slowly, shutting his eyes. He opened them to see the Senator staring at him worriedly.

"You are not dying, are you?" the man demanded. He looked again at the door. He seemed terrified.

"Can I have some water?" asked Sash.

"You are not dying?" repeated the Senator. He knelt forward and gripped the collar of Sash's shirt. His small blue eyes searched Sash's face.

Sash flinched. "No! I'm just thirsty."

"Water soon," replied the Senator. "Do you see this?" He held a hand up and opened it to reveal a metallic cylinder. He cupped it carefully, as though displaying a precious gem.

The object was so close that it blurred before Sash's eyes. For a moment he didn't recognize it – it seemed unreal in the setting of the gloomy dungeon. But then he realized what he was looking at.

"What is this?" asked Sash.

"I thought you could... The Keeper said you would know," replied the Senator.

"I do. I mean, it's a battery."

The Senator nodded, although he clearly didn't understand.

"Where did you get it from?" asked Sash.

"The Keeper... He created it from some great spell... But he needs you to get more. As many as you can – no less than three. His are old. He said you would… He said you would know what to do. The guards will lead you to Rising Beach. They will leave you there. And you will go and get more of these, ones that work because …" – the Senator threw his hands in the air – "… because they are needed… And the Keeper does not have time to get them, he is busy preparing for the joining of the suns. He needs you to do this thing, and if you do, he will spare your friend with the unusual bracelet."

"What bracelet?" Sash shook his head.

"The Keeper called it a 'watch'."

"Verity," breathed Sash, suddenly remembering that she had been wearing a watch – that it had stopped working properly on their arrival in Aqarti. His head was spinning. It was all too much to take in. The Senator knew about Verity. Which meant that they had caught her – or that they were tracking her, and would have her soon enough. Despite this, Sash allowed himself to hope that she was far away in the highlands with the Followers or, better still, back in London in her beautiful Hampstead house with the glittering Mercedes. Thinking of London made him feel miserable and abandoned. It seemed so far away. He fixed his eyes on a crack in the stone floor. How would Verity readjust to life back there? Would her parents really get divorced? Would she ever think about Aqarti? Would she remember him?

He thought again of the robed figure in the passageway. The Keeper wanted him to get some batteries. But why? What could someone in a land without electricity want with batteries? A local could not possibly know about this technology, any more than they could know about watches. Again Sash remembered the hulking razor sharks that lurked at the edges of the reef. Manah had said that they ate everything in sight. Everything but him and Verity. *Everything but the Keeper.* What else had she told them about the Keeper? "They say that no creature will harm him, that nothing can kill him! They say that he can live for ever!"

Sash frowned. Why couldn't the Keeper ask Sash for the batteries himself, rather than sending a servant who did not understand – a servant who, Sash guessed, was not meant to understand?

The Senator continued. "You will go back to where you came from. You will go and get these ... these 'batteries'. Remember, no less than three! You will return by first light tomorrow, before the suns join in the sky. Return with the 'batteries' to the palace. You are ordered to keep them dry. It is vital that you return with these things. You *must* be quick. You must be here tomorrow at first light."

"Why does the Keeper want batteries?" asked Sash.

"His Excellency did not explain his reasons to me and it is none of your concern," replied the Senator. "He simply said, 'None shall sleep – none shall sleep until I have more of these.'" The Senator waved the battery.

Sash cleared his throat. "Why should I?" He knew that people bowed down to the Keeper, that it was impossible to resist his will. Because they think he's magical, like a wizard, thought Sash. But how could anyone really believe that? The Keeper didn't have special powers – people had made that up, like Santa Claus, the tooth fairy and the Easter bunny. The Keeper was just a man. Verity was wrong: magic didn't exist. With a sense of sorrow, Sash recalled the aruva on the rock pinnacle. He remembered how easily one had been trapped. *No songs. No earthquakes. No flashes of thunder.*

"Your friend with the 'watch' might have escaped us on the Impossible Isles, but not any longer. She has just been caught and … and if you do not go, if you refuse, or if you fail to return" – the Senator's eyes bulged – "your friend will perish in the dungeon with the rest of your kind. Believe me, they do not last long down here. I give her one moon. Less…"

Sash gulped.

"You see," the Senator went on, "you have no choice. Not if you want to meet your friend again. If you go, and return with the…" His brow crinkled. He shoved the battery towards Sash. "With some of these things by tomorrow at first light, the Keeper is prepared to let you and your friend go home. Go back to your own land. Whatever he means by that. He is a merciful man, a great and merciful man."

"How can I believe you? What if I come back with the batteries and the Keeper changes his mind?" asked Sash.

"His word is his honour. And anyway," said the Senator, "you are in no position to argue. Here!" He tucked the battery inside Sash's shirt. His hand was shaking and the metal was hot from his grasp.

255

Sash watched him. "You're scared," he said. He bit his lip. He hadn't meant to say it aloud.

The Senator met his gaze. His voice was shaky. "Do what the Keeper says," he muttered. "Do whatever he says..."

"Why did he gag me? Does he normally gag Followers?" asked Sash.

The Senator shook his head.

"It's because of what I know about him. What I can guess..."

"Because you can find more 'batteries'?" asked the Senator, confused.

"Sort of... Because it means that I know where he came from. And it isn't the middle of the ocean."

"That is enough!" cried the Senator, eyes wild. "He said that I was not to learn anything from you!" He struggled to his feet. "And you must not say a word to the guards – not a word! If you do, your friend's life is forfeit! Do you understand?"

"It doesn't have to be like this!" said Sash. "You can rise up against him. He's only one man!"

"Do not say another word!" The Senator backed towards the door.

"I haven't told you a thing," assured Sash. "It's OK." Despite everything, he pitied the small man.

The Senator nodded, mollified. "I know nothing," he agreed.

* * *

Guards marched Sash down the gloomy corridor. He passed cells where heavy wooden bars had been lowered against the doors, locking their captives inside.

"Hurry up!" snarled the nearest guard, prodding Sash in the small of his back. "His Excellency told you to be quick!"

"I'm going as fast as I can. If you'd just untie my wrists..."

"Do not be insolent with me!" warned the guard.

"Sash! Sash, is that you?" someone cried.

Sash looked up to see a small hand reach out of one of the slits. There was a watch on the wrist.

"Verity?"

"Sash! You're alive! I knew it!" She whooped from within her cell. "Where are they taking you?"

"I have to go somewhere now, but I'll be back," he shouted. "We'll get out of this!"

A guard gripped the back of his neck and wielded his machete. "One more word out of you and you will not be going anywhere!"

Four guards walked Sash out of the dungeon and into the blinding light of the citadel. They led him through the bartering market. A crowd of people still gathered round the main entrance.

"Watch out!" someone yelled.

Ropes had been tied round the Bloodstone Bird. Guards were standing beneath these, tugging.

Sash remembered what the Followers had told him about the statue. It was the symbol of Great Aruva on Aqarti, of power, resistance and faith. They had assured Sash that the Keeper would never touch it, that the Bloodstone Bird was safe.

With a terrible cracking sound, the statue stirred. Billows of dust rained from its damaged body. For a few seconds, the bird swayed dangerously. The spectators stepped back, hands covering mouths. Everyone held their breath.

Sash remembered Zusa's words: "As long as the Bloodstone Bird watches over our land, there is still hope."

A giant, jewel-encrusted wing shattered. The statue collapsed with a mighty thud that echoed through the jungle.

— A Perfect Sky —

The guard cleared his throat. "The Keeper awaits you in the Great Hall," he said solemnly.

The Senator nodded. He hurried through the stuffy corridors of the dungeon and climbed the steps to the palace. The air lifted as he clambered above ground but the Senator didn't notice. He leant against the wall, breathing heavily.

As he approached the Great Hall, he wrung his hands. They were moist with sweat. Silently, he cursed the robe that dragged behind him. He stepped through one of the seven doorways and blinked against the bright light pouring through the hole in the ceiling. Unusually, there were no guards posted at the exits. At first he thought he was alone – that there had been a mistake. A shadow flitted beyond the light against the far wall. The Senator jumped. Through the haze stood a tall figure in a floor-length robe. He could hardly see him. The light seemed to distort his shape, to blur his outline.

The Senator pressed a hand against his heart. It pounded so hard, he was sure that the Keeper would hear it. Didn't he hear everything, after all? The Senator swallowed. "The boy has been dispatched to get the batter— ... the objects you desire."

The figure took a step closer, towards the light. "What did you call them?" he asked.

"The objects... The..." The Senator's voice was trembling so much he could hardly speak. He took a deep breath. Beyond the high walls he could just hear the twitter of birds. Nothing could happen to him here, now, in this ancient, sacred chamber – safe beneath the light of two suns. "It is all in hand, Your Excellency."

The figure stepped under the perfect circle of light that dazzled the stone floor. His robe rustled like the feathers of a hawk. He raised one arm. Something glinted within his wide sleeve. With his other arm, the Keeper made a beckoning gesture.

Unwillingly, the Senator approached. His eyes locked on the sliver of metal. "I do not know anything!" he spluttered. "I m-m-mean, I do not know what the batteries are, what they are for! Please, Your Excellency, *I do not know anything!*" His bottom lip quivered and he bit it, drawing blood.

The Keeper towered over him and rested a hand on his shoulder. "Of course not," he murmured.

The Senator gazed up at the masked face, his eyes wide with hope.

The bird's stone head tumbled a few metres and came to rest against the base of the citadel's wall. Guards began smashing the ruins with rocks. Glittering gems leapt from them like sparks. The crowd looked on in silence. Sash turned away, disgusted at seeing the ancient monument destroyed, knowing what it meant to the Followers.

The guards led him through the lowlands jungle. Eventually the mossy ground beneath his feet grew sandy and light blazed beyond the high trees. At the first swaying palm the guards untied him.

"The Keeper has ordered us to leave you here," said one of them. "He told us that you would know what to do."

Sash nodded.

The guards lingered, watching him curiously. They could not understand why they had been ordered to let the prisoner go, here at the start of Rising Beach, forbidden to all since the Keeper's arrival.

Sash hesitated, rubbing his wrists where the rope had dug red circles. He wasn't going to start towards the sea with guards watching – he didn't want to give the game away. Verity's survival depended on his safe return. Not that he really cared about Verity – he didn't even like her... But if he failed she'd be left in the dungeon, and he didn't want that on his conscience.

After a few moments the guards moved away, disappearing into the jungle.

Sash sighed. He made his way towards the soft white sand, remembering how he and Verity had fooled around on their arrival. His feet sank into the warm waters of the sea. But he didn't head in straight away. He watched the borders of the reef. The dark shapes of razor sharks were unmistakable. What if they came after him this time? What if his days on Aqarti had made him smell more familiar, more inviting to a shark's delicate nostrils?

Although both suns were still high in the sky, the moon was already visible. In a matter of hours it would be dark. He only had until sunrise. Nervously, Sash waded into the water and swam towards the oval rocks. The razor sharks bobbed like giant buoys. Their powerful nostrils sniffed the water. They nudged each other out of the way, craning to take in the moving shape, to work it out. But none of them approached Sash and, silently, he swam past.

He eased himself onto the oval rocks and peered down the watery gap between them that led to the underground river. In a groove just above it, Verity's jumper was neatly folded on top of his own, next to her pink and white trainers.

He plunged into the waterlogged cave. A few moments later he rose in the Fleet. The tide was higher than it had been before, the ceiling only a metre or two away. Someone on a boat would struggle with so little space above them – but Max's boat was nowhere to be seen. The underground river was icy – colder, even, than Sash had remembered. The tunnel was lit by the weak light from the grille overhead. Treading water, he scanned both directions. The boat was lost to the darkness, no doubt far downstream, beyond Kentish Town, beyond Gully Lane. Next to Sash along the curved walls were iron steps heading up towards the grille. He hadn't spotted them before. Excitedly he realized that it could be another way out.

He dragged himself up the steps until he reached the grille. Even close to the bars he could only see dull light drifting through and not where it led. He felt no wind and heard no noise above. His father's voice floated into his head: *Foolish boy! You do not remember that it was raining the last time you were here? Did you see rain fall through the bars?*

Sash pushed away the image of Max. But it was true – the grille could not be a manhole to a street, as he had initially concluded. It led to a room, an indoor space. Sash couldn't guess where the grille would take him, but it had to be better than the freezing river. He rammed the iron railings with all his strength but they refused to budge.

Exhausted, he eased himself back into the River Fleet. He would have to swim with the current and hope to spot the light from his father's study. Otherwise, he would be lost in these tunnels for ever, or until he ran out of strength... But what if the light bulb had blown? He couldn't think about that now. He wasn't sure how long he could hang on in the freezing water. He swam with the current as quickly as he could, taking gasps of air and doing his best to keep his head above water. The high tide made him feel more trapped than ever. How far was the flat and Stuff the World? He tried to guess the distance that he and Verity had travelled several days ago by boat. How long had it taken them to reach the portal? He wasn't sure.

He swam in total darkness, trying to control his shaking muscles, struggling to fend off a growing dread that he would never find his father's study. When eventually the water took on a silvery glow, Sash cried out with relief. He swam with renewed vigour until he saw light streaming through the open trunk.

He climbed the ladder with trembling arms and hauled himself into his father's study. He had never been so happy to be home. Even the gosling in the gherkin jar seemed pleasantly familiar.

Sash lowered the lid of the trunk and sat on it heavily, panting and shivering. He needed to be back in Aqarti tomorrow at dawn. He had the evening and all of the night. School was out and Max was in Iceland – Sash had plenty of time to get the batteries, go to Aqarti and return to London again before his father came home.

At last, he began to relax. No one knew he was here so he wouldn't be disturbed.

"Is anybody home?" The wheezy voice carried down the corridor.

Sash caught his breath. It was Gertrude Trench.

* * *

The Keeper retired to his private rooms, past rows of guards in red and black. The Great Hall was deserted. The twitter of birds rose beyond the high walls. Aqarti's two suns shone brightly, casting a circle of light at the centre of the hall. Within this circle, the Senator lay motionless. His hands rested at his sides, the palms still damp with sweat. A trickle of blood escaped beneath the folds of his robe to roll lazily over the stone floor. His eyes gazed, unseeing, through the ceiling of the palace – into the perfect sky.

— After Sunset —

Gertrude Trench ambled through the kitchen. "Aleksandr?" she called. She leant against the table and glanced along the two corridors. She had been down the short one a couple of times to have tea with Max in the living room. Usually she joined him in the shop. She had never been down the other corridor – the one leading to Max's study. She started towards it, pressing heavily on her walking stick. Was that a patch of water on the carpet or just a stain? She strained to see. It looked like a damp footprint or two.

"Mrs Trench?" Sash appeared along the shorter corridor by the door to his room. He was dripping wet and a towel was wrapped round his waist.

The old woman blushed. "My dear boy, I am sorry. But... A shower? In the afternoon?"

Sash flushed. "I... Sport. Good to see you out of hospital!"

He forced himself to smile, although the muscles in his jaw were tense. *In the afternoon.* What time in the afternoon? He hadn't even thought about the time. No one seemed to care about it in Aqarti. Was it midday? 3 p.m.? When did the shops shut?

"Thank you, Aleksandr. I've been in Ipswich with Philip. That's my boy. Not really a boy any more, but he'll always be a boy to me!" She broke into a raspy laugh which quickly turned into a cough.

"Are you OK?" asked Sash. He watched her awkwardly as he dripped onto the carpet.

"Yes, my dear." The old woman tapped her hip. "The doctors say I'm not dead yet! So Philip suggested that we pop back to my flat to pick up some bits and pieces. I didn't have a chance to take that nice Verity's phone number, so I thought I would check up on Stuff the World, just in case. Max gave me a key for emergencies. Well, what do you know? Here you are!" She tottered towards Sash and patted him on the back. "You're shivering!" she wheezed in surprise.

"I forgot to turn on the hot water," mumbled Sash. He thought quickly. "I was playing rugby against Middleton Secondary – that's a school up the road in Camden. I thought it would be easier to pop back here to get changed after, as it's so close… I'm off back to Verity's now." Lying wasn't all that hard, once you got the hang of it.

Gertrude Trench eyed him critically. "You seem a bit battered." She pointed at the bruise on Sash's forehead

267

from his blow on the Impossible Isles and a scrape on his shoulder.

Sash stepped back. "Mmm. Rugby. It's a rough sport."

"And you enjoy this rugby?" asked the old woman. Her eyes trailed down to Sash's feet and along to the entrance of his room. Poking out of the open door was a piece of colourful fabric embroidered with leaves.

Following her gaze, Sash kicked the fabric behind the door. "I'll..." He cleared his throat. "I'll just get dressed." Sash backed into his room, taking a deep breath. That was close. He seized the digital clock by the bed. 17.36. Could that be right? His heart was thumping. Wouldn't hardware shops shut at 5.30 p.m.? He gripped the clock tighter. It occurred to him that he didn't even know what day of the week it was. He closed his eyes and concentrated. He'd been knocked out on the Impossible Isles and had awoken on the shores of the floating forest. The guards must have been under orders to take him straight to the Keeper. He couldn't have been unconscious for more than a night. Which meant that he'd been away less than five days. He and Verity had discovered the Fleet late on Saturday evening, perhaps at 9.30 p.m. or 10 p.m. *And yet it had been sunny in Aqarti.* So it must be Wednesday afternoon. He had left Aqarti in broad daylight but the moon had already hung in the sky. So by now it might be starting to grow dark. He threw open the curtains. He didn't have much of a view from his window – just a small yard where the rubbish was kept. Darkness had settled over the bins.

Verity stood on tiptoes, trying to look out of the slit in the cell door. She scanned the tiny cell, searching for something to stand on, but it was empty.

"What a bore," she mumbled, as though she had just missed a bus, or had been told to learn French verbs for a test. But her voice trembled.

"Is someone there?" called a voice from the next cell.

Verity leapt back to the door. She called quietly. "I'm Verity. Who are you?"

"My name is Jonto." It was a boy's voice.

"Jonto..." Verity had heard that name before. "Do you have a sister called Manah?"

"Yes! You know Manah? How is she?"

He had such a warm tone that Verity instantly liked him. She thought of the last time she'd seen Manah, standing at the edge of the jungle with Ren and the caged aruva. Manah had warned her not to go down to the citadel, but she hadn't listened. "She's well, really well," Verity replied. "She misses you. She talks about you a lot."

"Really?" said Jonto. "Wait, I think there may be a guard coming."

They both fell silent for a few moments as they heard the tap of a baton against the wall of the narrow corridor.

"Hello?" called Jonto. Then, in a quieter voice: "I think that he has gone."

"What will happen to us?" Verity asked.

"Once they take you down in the dungeon..." Jonto didn't finish.

"My friend Sash got out. We'll get out too," said Verity with forced cheeriness.

"Yes," said Jonto, though it was clear from his voice that he didn't believe her. "It is the annual joining of the suns tomorrow. The aruva fly from the Impossible Isles..."

"I know," said Verity, thinking of the colourful birds on the dismal islet. "The Keeper plans to ... to finish them off."

"Does he? I can guess..." said the boy.

Verity realized of course that, like his sister, Jonto was a Follower. She understood what it would mean to him to learn of the birds' fate.

"And the Keeper will sing," he added.

"Yes, so I'm told. What's so special about his voice anyway?"

"Have you never heard it?" He sounded surprised.

"No ... I..." She wasn't sure what to say. She could hardly tell Jonto that she wasn't from Aqarti.

"It is amazing. *Other-worldly*. No one else sings like that. Well, no one is allowed to sing now... But even if they were, they could never sound like that. His voice is the key to his power. Even though we cannot understand the words. It is a spell. Only aruva sing more beautifully. And from what you just told me, they will not be singing any more..."

* * *

Sash threw his towel on the bed and looked around the room. His favourite trainers were in Max's boat, lost on the River Fleet, and his jeans were somewhere in Aqarti. He found a sweater and an old pair of jeans that were short at the ankle and some trainers that were splitting at the back. He grabbed the sodden clothes from Aqarti. Small brown discs scattered across the bedroom floor. Seeds gathered from gorse on the Impossible Isles. He had forgotten about them. What had Ren told him? Devoured by aruva; poisonous to humans.

Sash chucked the clothes from Aqarti into a plastic bag. He pocketed a few pounds in change that were strewn on a set of drawers, together with the gorse seeds. He stepped out of his bedroom fully dressed.

Entering the kitchen, he noticed Verity's suitcase next to the dining table. "I better put this away," he mumbled, carrying it into his bedroom. A moment later he was back in the kitchen, grabbing his parka.

"Do you have to go somewhere?" asked Gertrude Trench doubtfully, seated at the dining table.

"I … I promised Verity. I need to get back to her." It was true, but not the way it seemed.

"She's a lucky girl." There was a hint of regret in the old woman's voice. "So you're off to Hampstead?"

"That's right. My things are still there."

"Philip will be here soon! We're returning to Ipswich."

"Verity's expecting me. It's fine." He began towards the shop. He glanced back. Gertrude Trench looked bewildered. "But, thanks," he added more gently. His eyes fell on a stack of tapes. Classical music. His father liked to play it in the shop. Sometimes he brought his old tape player back to the kitchen, when he was working on an animal. Sash frowned. One of the tapes had PAVAROTTI handwritten on it in capitals. He grabbed it and shoved it in his pocket. He started again towards the shop.

"Aleksandr, stop right there!" the old woman puffed. She stood up on her second attempt and followed him through the flat. "If you wait, Philip will drop you at Verity's. I would like to speak with her parents."

"Sorry, I'm late," Sash said vaguely. "Would you mind locking up?" He was through the shop and heading towards the front door.

Gertrude Trench stood at the entrance to the shop, clutching the doorframe. She sighed in exasperation. "For heaven's sake, Aleksandr, can't you stay still for five minutes? Just watching you is exhausting! And you should really dry your hair before going outside!"

Sash was hastily unlocking the front door. He fumbled with the keys, dropping them and missing the keyhole a couple of times.

"At least give me Verity's address!" said Gertrude Trench.

Sash disappeared down Gully Lane.

She called after him. "I could pop by with Philip before

going to Ipswich. Aleksandr? *Aleksandr?*" The old woman's voice cracked and she started to cough. Rummaging through her handbag, she drew out a packet of cigarillos. "Boys," she mumbled. "They never change."

As soon as he had turned the corner onto Kentish Town Road, Sash began to jog. First there was the mini-market. They were bound to sell batteries, but the range was always dubious. There were two or three hardware shops on the high street, but it was much later in the day than he had thought and they might not be open. Sash ducked into the mini-market. The batteries dangled on pegs behind the counter, next to cough sweets and headache tablets.

The girl at the till filed her nails and stifled a yawn. She could only have been a few years older than Sash. Despite the liberal use of blusher, her face was wan, her eyes tired.

This is London, thought Sash suddenly. Everyone looked exhausted and sun-starved. Not like Aqarti. Of course people here were free, without a controlling Keeper. Free in some ways but not in others.

"Yeah?" said the girl.

"Could I have some single A batteries, please?" he asked.

She shrugged. "What ones are they? We've only got them." She peeled a couple of packets off the pegs.

Sash read the labels: AA and AAA. "You don't have any others?"

"Did you say A? Them big ones?"

273

"Yes, that's right." Sash nodded enthusiastically.

"Yeah, I know them."

Sash was filled with hope. "Do you have any?"

The man in the queue behind him started tapping his foot impatiently.

"Sorry, we ain't got none," replied the girl. "Try one of the hardware shops."

Sash thanked her and left. Back on the high street he broke into a run. When he reached the first hardware shop, he almost punched the air with relief – the front door was open. Sash stepped through the entrance.

"We're closed!" a man snapped gruffly. He was filling the shelves with tins of varnish from open boxes on the floor.

"Could I... Please may I get some batteries?" asked Sash.

"You deaf lad? I'm only here for a minute. Till's closed. You'll have to come back tomorrow." The man kept stocking the shelves.

Sash stood at the entrance, biting his lip. Tomorrow would be too late.

"You still here?" asked the man. He put down one of the tins with a grunt and placed his hands on his hips.

"Please... It's an emergency! I've got money. I really need some batteries."

"Emergency? Can't you manage without your iPod for one night?" muttered the man.

Sash fought the urge to rise to the insult. He didn't have an iPod. And he wanted to point out that iPods used their own rechargeable batteries but that wouldn't be helpful right now. He took a deep breath. "Please, I don't want to put you to any trouble. But it's..." It's a matter of life and death, thought Sash, but no one would believe that. "It's really important."

"I said no, kid!" The man stared at Sash in disbelief. "Go on, get on with you or I'll call the old bill."

Reluctantly, Sash backed away. The last thing he needed was police officers sniffing around, delaying him with questions. He jogged towards another hardware shop, almost passing it in his haste. Closed. Sash thumped the door in frustration. Now what? The other shops would be shut too. Surely somewhere in London would sell single A batteries and be open, but right now Sash couldn't begin to imagine where.

He withdrew to a nearby bus stop, where he could stand without looking suspicious. So that's it, he thought. I tried. There's no more I can do. I don't owe her anything. He imagined Verity back in Aqarti. She was crafty – she'd be OK. Girls like Verity landed on their feet. He glanced down the high street, towards the turning to Gully Lane. It was time to go home, to abandon this foolishness. But his feet didn't move.

Verity's voice floated into his head: "It's as if you've given up, you just don't bother." I tried, Sash silently reasoned. I didn't just give up ... I tried. "But it doesn't have to be like this. You *can* change things!" her voice retorted from his memory.

Sash leant against the bus stop. "Damn," he murmured. His thoughts were racing.

"Getting in?" someone shouted.

Sash looked up with a start. He hadn't noticed the bus pull up. Number 46 to Hampstead. He began to shake his head. From the corner of his eye, he saw a car stop under a nearby streetlamp. A middle-aged man climbed out. He opened the passenger door to a tumble of copper hair. Gertrude Trench. She pointed down the street in Sash's direction.

The doors of the bus started closing. Sash shot up his hand and tapped on them. Rolling his eyes, the bus driver opened the doors. "Make your flipping mind up," he grumbled. Sash hopped on and the bus sped away.

It was rush hour and the bus was packed. Sash climbed onto the top deck and found a seat near the back. He would go to the school. They were bound to have batteries there.

He drew the tape cassette from his pocket and turned it over in his hand. PAVAROTTI. He thought about the Keeper. It was a huge risk to let Sash go to London. He could refuse to return, or come back with others. The Keeper must really need those batteries, thought Sash. He must *really* need them... He remembered the words "Waterproof" and a tape cassette with NESSUN DORMA (FWC 1990) handwritten on it in capitals.

The Keeper was not alone in his love of classical music. Max liked it too. Sash thought about his father, a secretive

276

man who was preoccupied with birds. He often came and went... Even when he seemed to be home, you couldn't be sure that he really was... Sash's dark eyebrows knitted over his eyes. He thought again of the tape player he had seen in the Keeper's palace – a waterproof, portable tape player. And that tape: NESSUN DORMA (FWC 1990).

The gates of East Heath College were open when Sash arrived and he noticed a number of cars in the nearby car park. He paused for a moment on the driveway. It was still half-term, wasn't it? Yes, of course it was.

The atrium was lit. As Sash approached he could see the caretaker, Mr Priestly, standing near the double doors. It seemed odd that he would be there this late on a Wednesday. Sash didn't wear a watch but he guessed that it was seven o'clock by now. Mr Priestly was a solemn man with little patience for students. If he set eyes on Sash, he was bound to be suspicious. Glancing over his shoulder, Sash skirted around the building, searching for another way in. He ran his hands along the windows. None of them budged. He considered breaking one – after all, this was an emergency. But they might be wired to an alarm. Would security or police be alerted?

Sash crept round the back of the school that overlooked the playing fields. He stopped in his tracks. The Head of Games, Mr Healy, was dressed in a suit, grasping a cigarette and a glass of wine. He was speaking with Mr Greene, the rugby coach. Mr Greene was also smartly dressed. He puffed on a pungent cigar. They stood several metres in front of the door to the gym. It was wide open.

Sash wondered what the teachers were doing there. Either way, he couldn't let them see him. They would want to know why he was there.

"I know, Paul," Mr Healy was saying. "But the new pavilion won't be ready for cricket season."

"That's a real shame, Matt," said Mr Greene.

Sash found it strange to hear them refer to each other by their first names. It was easy to forget that teachers even had them. And it was odd to see them smoking – they were sports teachers, after all, and the students were forever being warned about the hazards of tobacco.

Sash was about to duck through the open door into the gym when he heard rapid footsteps coming from inside. He shrank back.

Angus Slaughter appeared. He was wearing the rugby team blazer. There must be an event on. Which meant that James Goodwin-Black would be near by, Sash realized grimly.

Angus cleared his throat and the teachers turned to look at him.

"Mr Crawford sent me to let you know that the speeches are about to start," said Angus. He took a couple of steps towards the teachers. There was a swagger in his walk.

Guiltily, Mr Healy flicked his cigarette onto the playing fields.

"Ah yes, Slaughter, having a good evening?" asked Mr Greene. He patted his favourite student on the back and continued to puff on his cigar undeterred.

"Oh yes, sir," fawned Angus.

Sash crinkled his nose with distaste.

Mr Greene pointed across the playing fields. "We were just talking about the new pavilion," he said as the others followed his gaze.

Seizing his opportunity, Sash dived through the door and sprang behind a heap of mats. A moment later Angus and the teachers turned and went inside. They bolted the door behind them and wandered past Sash on their way out of the gym. Before leaving, they flicked off the lights.

Sash crouched in darkness for several minutes. It must be some sort of rugby dinner. This complicated matters. He was no friend of the rugby team. He would have to avoid them at all costs. He got up and made his way to the exit. The corridor was lit but the classrooms that branched off it were dark. He hurried towards the audio lab.

Sash clicked the door of the lab shut behind him. He threw open the cupboards and began to rifle through them. Kettle leads, cables and plugs were crammed inside. He saw a small, waterproof all-weather torch, which he gratefully bundled into one of the large pockets of his parka. He found several packets of AAA and AA batteries, and a single square D battery loose on a shelf.

There was another audio lab a few doors down. Sash

crept into it and started searching through drawers. Size A batteries were large and old-fashioned. Perhaps no one used them any more. Perhaps you could only get them from specialist suppliers. He struggled to push away these thoughts, to keep the fear at bay. But he could feel it gnawing at him. Perhaps... Perhaps... He stepped away from the drawers. This was hopeless. Panic seized him suddenly, shot through his chest. Breathlessly, he spotted something metallic near the back of one of the open drawers, behind boxes of tiny Dictaphone tapes. Holding his breath, he reached inside and pulled out a heavy packet. He read the label: 4 A BATTERIES. He read it again. He took out the battery that the Senator had given him. It was the same size.

Pressing the batteries against his chest, Sash backed away from the drawers. He was standing next to a hi-tech recording suite, complete with a large tape player, CD drives and MP3 player. A digital display flashed 19:42:06. Sash hardly noticed the modern technology, but the tape player made him think. He reached into his pocket and pulled out the cassette with PAVAROTTI written on the side. On a whim, he slid it into the machine and pressed play. Immediately, the audio lab was filled by the sound of string instruments, the trilling of flutes, the rumble of drums. A choir sang softly in a foreign tongue. Then another voice, a rich, deep, beautiful voice. It soared and for a moment Sash closed his eyes, allowing it to carry him away. He couldn't understand the words but it didn't matter. A powerful piece of music:

how would it sound to people without modern instruments or technology? If one man claimed to be responsible for this music, how would people who knew nothing of Sash's world be able to challenge it?

As he listened, Sash realized that he knew this song though he wasn't sure why. Perhaps because Max played it sometimes. No, it was more than that. For some reason, Sash identified the music with football. That was it! "FWC 1990" must refer to the 1990 Football World Cup. Now that Sash thought of it, he was sure that the Italian opera singer, Pavarotti, had sung some sort of anthem for the games before Sash was born. Pavarotti had died quite recently – a few years ago – and they had played *Nessun Dorma* on the news. Suddenly realizing how loud it was, Sash jumped to switch off the track. He noticed a small microphone attached to the side of the tape player. It extended from the machine on a lead. Sash didn't need to be back in Aqarti till dawn tomorrow. It wasn't even 8 p.m. He had time.

His fingers closed round the microphone. Then, bringing it to his lips, he pressed RECORD.

Sash hurried down the corridor. He would return to Gully Lane, to his father's study and the River Fleet. He checked himself over. The coins he had grabbed from his bedroom were stuffed in his jeans pocket, together with seeds from the Impossible Isles. Deep in the pockets of his parka were two plastic bags – one held a tape cassette, a set of

281

four A batteries and a small, waterproof torch; in the other bag were the shirt and culottes from Aqarti, covered with embroidered leaves and soaking wet.

As he approached the dining hall, he heard raised voices. The rugby team was singing. Sash winced. The roar — half-shout, half-bleat — was about as far from Pavarotti's sublime voice as it was possible to be. He edged up to the door of the dining hall and took a quick look inside. There was the team, celebrating a recent victory over rival St Paul's. The remainders of a meal littered the table.

Sash backed away. He felt a hand on his shoulder. Turning, he saw James Goodwin-Black.

James folded his arms. "Well, well, well, Baron Oiksky. What a wonderful surprise."

— None Shall Sleep —

Roars of "'Swing low, sweet chariot'" rose from the dining hall. James mouthed the words silently. He was flanked by Angus Slaughter, who had undone the top two buttons of his shirt, had lost his tie and was looking even more smug than usual.

"I don't have time for this," said Sash. He took a step forward.

Angus blocked his way. "Oh, I think you do."

The silent giant, Colin Williams, appeared behind Sash. They had him surrounded.

"So, what brings you here?" asked James.

"Nothing," said Sash.

"'Coming forth to carry me home!'" boomed voices from the dining hall.

"Nothing, eh? Well, it's all the same to us," said James.

"Sporting of you to drop by. I feel we may have got off on the wrong foot, what with your Maths homework, and that mix-up with the chairs."

"Yes, you seemed quite fond of my chair," said Angus, narrowing his eyes.

Sash sighed impatiently. "I *really* don't have time for this."

"Now!" spat James.

They pounced on him. Sash felt a fist sink into his stomach and doubled over.

"Priestly!" hissed Angus. The caretaker had turned down the corridor and was heading towards them. They shoved Sash through a door marked NO ENTRANCE which led onto a stairwell. He struggled but Colin grabbed his arm and wrenched it behind his back. They marched him awkwardly down the stairs.

James rifled through Sash's pockets. "Got any money on you?" He grabbed a few coins and a couple of the gorse seeds.

Sash couldn't let him find the tape. "Let me go!" he said, twisting out of Colin's grip. He tripped down the bottom steps. Colin, James and Angus stood above him, blocking the exit. Although the stairwell was lit, the space beyond it was gloomy. It smelled damp down there. Sash squinted for a moment, searching for escape routes. The basement seemed to stretch endlessly into the darkness. He couldn't be sure that there were other ways out. Even if there were, they might be locked. What time was it? He had to make his way back to Gully Lane, to Stuff the World.

"Trapped like a rat," said Angus. "Too bad."

"What's this then?" James inspected one of the seeds. "Chocolate Buttons? God, you're a baby!"

Sash cleared his throat. "Don't touch them," he said. He remembered what Ren had told him: one or two seeds made you sick. Larger amounts could kill.

"Really, Baron Oiksky, I had no idea you had a sweet tooth." Greedily, James popped the seed in his mouth. He screwed up his face. "Yuck!"

"This isn't funny," said Sash.

James took a step down the stairwell, wiping his mouth against the back of his hand. "You should know that there are two things I never joke about: rugby and *revenge*." He turned to the others, proud of himself.

"We did warn him about the drains, didn't we, Goodwin-Black?" said Angus. His hair glowed orange under the strip lights. He swaggered down the stairwell, joining James at the bottom. Colin loomed above them, gormless, thuggish.

"We did," James agreed.

"This is stupid," said Sash. "I don't have time."

"Is that right? Your busy social schedule won't allow it, is that it?" James snorted. "I can just imagine all your friends waiting for you."

"It must be hard to be that popular," Angus jeered.

Sash spun round and bolted. They jumped off the steps and raced after him. He smacked blindly into a stack of

285

chairs that crashed to the ground, but he kept his footing. Surrounded by a blanket of darkness, he stepped lightly in his old trainers, listening for the clatter of shoes close behind. He skidded round a metal filing cabinet and hugged the wall as the others rushed past. What terrible luck, thought Sash. He had survived the beasts of Aqarti, the merciless guards of the Keeper, only to return to a handful of rugby bullies.

They had stopped near by. He could hear them talking in loud whispers.

"He won't know what's hit him!" James was saying. "Just as well it's Friday tomorrow, he'll need the weekend to recover. *If* he recovers..." A muffled laugh. A scrabbling sound.

"It's definitely here somewhere," whispered Angus.

"That caretaker really did drown down there, it's a well-known fact," said James.

"God, you're gullible," sighed Angus.

"It's true!" James protested.

"Shhh! He'll hear us!"

"Here it is," mumbled Colin.

Sash heard dragging sounds as metal scraped metal. When the dragging stopped he heard something else – the gurgle of running water. A shiver of fear awakened in him. He pressed harder against the metal cabinet. The drains. James and Angus had taunted him about them. That myth about a careless caretaker. And what had James said just now? That it was Friday tomorrow. That wasn't right. Sash had been in Aqarti just under five days. He had left around 10 p.m. on Saturday evening. So it had to be Wednesday, not Thursday...

"Baranovski?" called James. For once, he used Sash's real surname.

Sash held his breath. He could hear them approaching clumsily, whispering among themselves and laughing. He sidestepped round the metal cabinet. *Today is Thursday.* How could that be right? There were a couple of possibilities: James had got it wrong or Sash had been unconscious for more than one night.

"We've got something to show you," called Angus.

The gush of water from the uncovered drain mimicked the pulsing blood through Sash's veins. There was another possibility: that time on Aqarti moved at a different pace; that a day in Aqarti was longer than a day in London. *That while only five days had elapsed on Aqarti since Sash and Verity's first arrival there, six had elapsed back home.* Sash stepped beyond the cabinet, edging along the wall. Days seemed endless on Aqarti, the land of two suns. He remembered waking up on his first morning in the highlands and wondering how it was that night had passed so quickly. The candles had burned low and the first glimmer of dawn had glittered between the gaps in the wooden hut.

But what had Verity told him as they sat on the canoe in the floating forest? "Even time makes no sense any more. My watch thinks that it's four o'clock in the morning."

Perhaps it really *had* been four o'clock – *four o'clock in London.*

Sash bit his lip. What did all this mean? He thought about his departure from Aqarti, of the Bloodstone Bird broken and brought to the ground, of the moon already visible in the sky, despite the two suns. In a matter of hours it would be dark. He had arrived into dusk in London, into a grim winter evening. How many hours of darkness would there be here tonight? Sash counted from 5.30 p.m. until 8.30 a.m. Fifteen hours. Perhaps even more.

He had banked on having the whole night to get batteries and return to Aqarti. He only had until sunrise. But if a night on Aqarti was only four hours long, and if nightfall had followed his departure by an hour or two, that meant he only had five or six hours in London before he had to be back. He had arrived at the flat on Gully Lane at about five-thirty in the afternoon, London time. By ten-thirty in the evening the suns would start rising on Aqarti. *What was the time now?*

Sash stood still, pressed back against the wall, looking out towards the stairwell. Colin and Angus were moving away from him, their arms outstretched in the darkness. James had split off from them and was shuffling towards Sash.

"Bar-a-nov-ski?" James called in a singsong voice. If Sash reached out his hand he could grab him. He could easily overpower James, who was a coward without his sidekicks. But what would be the use in that? Sash thought fast.

James had stopped. He was licking his lips. He made a belching noise.

Sash stepped lightly away from the wall. Pressing his face close to James's ear, he murmured: "Make a sound. I dare you."

James flinched. "We were only—" He belched again.

"Quiet!" whispered Sash. They were almost touching. He could smell James's sweat.

James froze, as though caught in a snare. "I don't feel so good..."

Sash glanced up. The others were shuffling about in the darkness, silhouettes against the light of the stairwell. "That's because I've put a Russian curse on you. That's what I do to people I don't like. How does it feel?" The words sounded ludicrous to Sash's ears.

But James nodded furiously. "I'm sorry," he gasped. "I didn't mean anything. I feel terrible..." He was trembling, clutching his stomach. Bile rose in his throat and he swallowed hard.

"That's nothing. It'll get a lot worse."

"Make it stop! I'll leave you alone from now on, I promise," James whimpered. "None of us will go near you... Please make it stop! I've got pains. I feel dizzy."

"Good," hissed Sash. "You need to be taught a lesson. I have things to do. Stuff that has nothing to do with you, or rugby – stuff you wouldn't understand. I don't care about your stupid games. But if you waste any more of my time you'll regret it. Understand?"

"Yes," breathed James.

Sash's voice was scarcely a whisper. "Understand this too. I'm sick of seeing you bully year sevens. I'm on to you. If I see it again, I swear to God, you're dead."

"I won't go near them… I promise. I promise!" His whole body was shaking.

Sash took a step back. "Get lost."

James melted, as though released from a spell. He staggered forward.

"Wait!" breathed Sash. "What's the time?"

James turned for a moment to stare at him. The whites of his eyes were yellow in the dim light. He blinked.

"The time?" Sash repeated.

James looked at his watch. He pressed a tiny button and the face shone green. He cleared his throat. "It's nine-twenty. But why…?" He retreated a few paces, gawping at Sash in confusion. Suddenly he doubled over and threw up noisily. Then he turned and fled, hunching like a chimp. He stumbled towards the others, jostling them up the stairs.

Sash stood alone in the basement. He felt the blood drain from his face. *Nine-twenty*. Almost sunrise in Aqarti. How would he make it back to Stuff the World and through the portal in time? He started towards the stairwell but stopped in his tracks. There it was, the gushing of water. Sash groped in his pocket for the bag with the torch. He flicked the light round the room. There was an opening the size of a large manhole where James, Angus and Colin must have pulled off the grille covering. Under it ran water, with iron rungs disappearing beyond the surface. Hidden below water level, Sash realized, only metres away, was the portal to Aqarti: directly beneath the school. It had been there all along.

Sash threw off his parka, his trainers and jeans. He struggled into the cold, wet shirt and culottes. He turned the empty plastic bag inside out and dropped the other one inside it. He knotted the top of both tightly and tied them to the lace of his shirt.

Clutching the torch, Sash took a deep breath and plunged into the icy water.

— The Keeper's Voice —

Sash clambered up the oval rocks. He blinked into the sky. A halo of white light was rising over Aqarti's northern horizon. Far in the north-east, he could just make out the flinty Impossible Isles. He thought of the aruva above the pool, preparing to travel to Aqarti's southern tip. Perhaps they had already taken flight.

He gripped the plastic bag with the batteries and tape. Bobbing near the border of the reef, he could see the contours of enormous sharks. Beyond them, the tropical beach rose deliciously from the sea. Sash felt a rush of the awe he had experienced the first time he'd seen Aqarti's western coastline.

He sank into the limpid waters and swam towards Rising Beach.

* * *

The cell door creaked open and Verity stepped back.

A grim-faced guard stood by the door. He pushed half a coconut towards her, full of grey goo. "Breakfast," he muttered.

Verity sniffed the coconut suspiciously. There were figures gathered in the corridor, other guards handing out food to people in nearby cells. She could hear a woman sobbing. "My child is sick, please..."

"Are all the prisoners Followers?" she asked the guard.

He nodded.

"What's going to happen to us?" She studied his face.

The guard licked his lips. His right hand strayed to his throat, which he brushed with his fingertips. "I cannot answer your questions," he said quietly.

His gesture was familiar. Verity had seen it before on Aqarti – the touching of the throat. It was a habit shared by those who revered the bird of flames, recalling the lucky feathers they once wore round their necks. "You're a Follower," Verity whispered.

The guard gaped. He glanced fearfully over his shoulder.

Seeing that she was right, Verity spoke quickly. "The Keeper's going to let us die down here, even the old ones. Even the babies!"

"Enough!" pleaded the guard. "If the others hear you—"

"Then what? It couldn't get any worse for me, could it? You're a Follower, you understand."

"I understand nothing!" whispered the guard, withdrawing from the cell.

"But these are your people." Verity's fingers clasped the coconut shell. Her bottom lip was quavering.

The guard was out in the corridor. He met her eye briefly before tugging the door behind him. Still a crack of light escaped between the door and its frame.

Verity stood for a long time, cradling the coconut shell. She pushed it away and stood behind the door, listening. Silence. She nudged the door. Nothing happened. She pushed a little harder. With a reluctant groan it began to move.

The citadel had been transformed. There was no trace of the Bloodstone Bird that had once hovered over the entrance. Red and black ribbons were everywhere, draped over the high walls and fluttering from vines. The centre of the citadel had been cleared, the bartering market gone. Women were busily pulling shrubs from the earth and piling them in mounds. People were pouring through the entrance, bearing baskets of fruit, petals and sweets. Several had painted red and black triangles onto their arms with berry juice. Dotted around the walls of the palace, guards with bows gazed into the sky – archers awaiting the arrival of the birds.

Clutching the plastic bag tightly, Sash passed between the crowds towards the Imperial Palace. Hunching at the palace walls, masons were hurriedly finishing their carvings of a robed man.

A group of guards polished their machetes near by. Sash approached them. His shirt and culottes clung damply to his skin. He hoped they wouldn't notice. "I have an urgent delivery for the Senator," he said.

The guards surrounded him, eyeing him suspiciously. "What sort of delivery?" asked one. "Show us."

Sash shook his head, clutching the plastic bag protectively. "It's private."

"Private?" scoffed the guard. "Nothing is private... Who are you?"

This wasn't going well. The two suns were already creeping over the highlands. There was an odd hue to the sky, an amber tinge. Silently, Sash kicked himself. He might have guessed that this would happen. He should have devised a proper plan, rather than simply agreeing to return with the batteries. "I can't tell you anything, the Keeper doesn't want me to," he said.

The guards laughed. "The *Keeper* does not want you to?" replied one of them, a stout man with a shiny face. "I see you are on good terms with the Keeper!"

"You speak strangely," said another guard. "Which village are you from? You do not look familiar."

Sash shifted impatiently. "Could you get the Senator? He'll explain."

The red-faced guard took a step towards Sash. "The Senator is dead."

"Dead?" The hairs rose on Sash's neck. His mouth was dry. He remembered the puffy-faced man who had visited him in the dungeon. The Senator had been terrified. "But

I saw him only yesterday…" It was yesterday, wasn't it? His sense of time was growing muddled again. He cleared his throat. "In that case I need to see the Keeper." He had never spoken to the Keeper, Aqarti's ruler. What made him think that the guards would let him meet him now, before the joining of the suns? Verity was in the dungeon. She was counting on him.

"He needs to see the Keeper!" The red-faced guard laughed. Suddenly his face grew hard. "I think we should talk about who you are and what you want with the Keeper. A few nights in the dungeon may help."

The pink sun was climbing just above the yellow one, as though being chased. Someone stepped forward, blocking the light. The guards turned. Towering at the entrance to the palace was a masked man in a floor-length robe. He waved away the guards and pointed at Sash. Then he spun round and disappeared into the palace.

The guards watched, speechless, as Sash hurried after him.

Verity crept out of the cell. The dingy corridor was empty. She could still hear the faint sound of a woman crying.

Pushing the cell door shut behind her and lowering the bar so that nothing would seem out of place, she sidled up to the neighbouring cell.

"Jonto?" she whispered urgently.

"Verity?" he replied in disbelief.

With hasty glances along the corridor, she lifted the bar that had been placed across the cell door. She tried to pull it open but it was too heavy.

"Push the door!" she told him. "Hurry!"

Verity stepped back and a moment later the door swung open.

A boy who couldn't have been much older than her stared at Verity in disbelief. Then he smiled, an awkward, toothy grin.

Verity smiled too.

"How did you...?" Jonto began.

"One of the guards! He's a Follower, he—" She hesitated. She had heard something, a distant footfall. "Quick, let's go."

Jonto followed her, after pushing shut the door to his cell and lowering the bar so that it was locked, as though he was still trapped inside. Verity was already halfway down the corridor when he called to her.

"Wait!" he whispered.

Verity froze. "The guards..."

Jonto waved at the other cells. "We cannot leave them."

The woman's sobs had lulled into a low moan. Verity was about to protest. She stopped herself. Quietly, she said: "*That* Verity is gone. She no longer exists." She raised her hand to her short hair. It was feathery against her fingertips. She nodded. "All right, but we have to be quick."

Verity kept watch as Jonto lifted the bars on the cells One by one, the prisoners flooded out.

297

* * *

The black robe fluttered down the corridor as the Keeper disappeared into the Great Hall. Guards were posted at each of the seven entrances. Sash stopped alongside one and took in the scene. Dusty light shone from the hole in the ceiling and beneath it several men were decorating a platform with red and black streamers. Against the far wall stood the Keeper: tall, motionless. A hood covered his head and a black, plaster mask concealed his face. Around him, the hall was abuzz with activity. A ritual was already taking place, with children throwing handfuls of petals over the stone floor.

Sash untied the plastic bag. He took out the batteries and tucked the bag awkwardly beneath his shirt. He could feel it sticking to his chest and the torch poked between his ribs, making a small bulge. He tugged at his shirt. He might need that torch to get home – he didn't want some guard helping himself.

He crossed the hall, almost colliding with a girl who was busily scattering flowers. He approached the Keeper, holding out the batteries. Sash felt his heart thumping in his chest. The man stood over him, peering at him from behind his mask. His eyes were dark and seemed familiar. Sash held up the batteries in cupped hands, so that only the Keeper could see them.

The Keeper nodded slowly.

Sash swallowed. "Where's Verity?"

The Keeper pointed across the hall. Sash followed his gaze to the box covered by fabric that he had seen on his last visit. It still rested on a shelf beside one of the exits.

"It's a tape player, isn't it?" said Sash. "You want me to put in the batteries?"

For a few moments the Keeper didn't move and Sash wondered if he'd heard. Then he nodded again.

Sash started towards the tape player but hesitated. "What about Verity? You promised..."

A guard was eyeing him curiously. "Your Excellency, is this boy bothering you?" he asked.

Again the Keeper pointed at the box. Sash moved across the hall towards it. He lifted the fabric away to reveal an old-fashioned portable tape player. He found the panel at the back and replaced the batteries with shaking hands. He looked over his shoulder. The Keeper was watching him from across the hall.

"Your Excellency." A woman in a ceremonial red dress was approaching her leader. "A guard told me that you are ready. Shall we begin?" Another woman, similarly dressed, stood nervously behind her.

The mask must have affected the Keeper's peripheral vision – he had to turn to look at them. Sash saw his chance. He slid his hand beneath his shirt and pulled the tape cassette from the sticky plastic bag. He focused on the tape player. Heart drumming, his eyes darted across the buttons. It was hard to read the writing on them – the light

299

flowing down from the hole in the ceiling was flushing red, streaked with amber. Sash stabbed the buttons frantically, searching for EJECT. He stole a glance at the Keeper, who was addressing the women in the red dresses.

The guard was still studying Sash from across the hall. He began to approach. Struggling to keep the panic from his face, Sash struck the button marked STOP and the door to the tape player creaked open, revealing a tape cassette with the words *NESSUN DORMA* (FWC 1990) written in capitals. It was the same tape Sash had seen on his previous visit to the Great Hall, before being led to the dungeon. He lifted it out of the player with trembling fingers. Hastily, he slotted in the other tape.

"You! What are you doing?" barked the guard. He was only a couple of metres away.

The guards at the nearest exits gripped their batons, suddenly on the alert, the women in the red dresses froze, and the Keeper wheeled round.

Sash sprang back, pulling the fabric cover over the tape player.

The Keeper pointed directly at him.

Sash stood awkwardly. "I did it. I did what you wanted!" he called, making an effort to be heard. His voice echoed across the Great Hall. The building's unique shape made it sound richer, more powerful.

Nobody said anything. At length, the Keeper moved towards the shelf with the box. The guards immediately assumed their positions at the exits, staring deadpan into space. The others in the Great Hall – the children scattering flowers, the men decorating the platform, the women in red – all dropped to their knees and bowed their heads. Noticing that Sash remained standing, the guard nearest to him raised his baton. Hastily, Sash copied the others, kneeling down and lowering his face.

Sash tried to watch the Keeper from the corner of his eye. The man was doing something to the box but Sash couldn't see what. His heart hammered. It was all he could hear in the silence of the hall. What if the Keeper found the tape? *What if*—

The Keeper took a step back. Sash could now see the shelf with the box. He noticed that the fabric covering had been tied together with red and black ribbons, beneath which no sign of the silvery plastic was visible. Tentatively, the women stood and approached the shelf. They carefully raised the box as the Keeper knelt before them. They lifted it over his caped head and tied the dangling ribbons beneath his chin. This took several minutes of fiddling, during which time nobody else moved. Eventually, the women stepped back. Fixed to the Keeper's head was a large, square headdress that trailed red and black ribbons down his back. Beneath the fabric of the headdress, Sash knew, was the tape player. He remembered the images of the Keeper that stonemasons had carved on the palace. One showed him in an odd hat…

Very slowly, the Keeper stood. He was already much

taller than the locals but the headdress added to his height. Towering in his floor-length robe, concealed behind a mask, he was like a giant, awesome bird. The look was electrifying.

He made his way to the centre of the hall. Carefully, he climbed onto the platform beneath the amber light.

Sash sighed deeply, rising to his feet. He'd delivered the batteries. The Keeper was going to let him go. He would go and find Verity, he would—

The Keeper made a sweeping gesture with his arm and guards encircled Sash, blocking his exit. At the same moment, people poured in through the seven doorways to the Great Hall. They entered quickly and sat cross-legged around the platform. They piled in until they spilled out into the corridors.

"We should take him to the dungeon," said one of the guards, leaning to another and glaring at Sash.

The other guard shook his head. "The Keeper is about to sing. There is not enough time. And how would we move him through all these people? Better we keep him close, and quiet."

Sash's heart sank. He scanned the crowds for Verity and Manah over the guards' shoulders. He did not see them, nor any of the Followers he had met in Aqarti.

People crammed into every available space on the circular floor, surrounding the Keeper. Some saw only his back, dark and menacing as a raven, with red ribbons dangling from his headdress like trickles of blood. The Keeper was swathed in cloth from head to foot. What could anyone really see of him?

The guards surrounding Sash also started to sit until he and the Keeper alone stood in the Great Hall, facing each other, separated by several rows of people. Sash had the sensation that the Keeper was staring at him. It was hard to be sure where he was looking beneath his mask. But a chill passed over Sash, a sense of dread.

"Sit!" hissed one of the guards, seizing Sash's arm and wrenching him to the floor.

The room fell silent. Specks of green light poured through the hole in the ceiling, mingling with the ambers and reds. Sash looked up and his jaw fell. Twinkling gems of colour circled above him.

The Keeper raised his hands in the air. His fingers ran over the headdress. He did this slowly, as though it was part of a ritual. Sash held his breath. The Keeper lowered his arms. For a few seconds there was silence as he seemed to clear his throat. Then he began to sing.

— The Joining of the Suns —

Verity led the Followers as they hurried in single file out of the dungeon. She stopped at the palace walls, gazing into the sky. Ribbons of silver and pink spun through a universe of violet and green. "It's so beautiful," she murmured.

"The joining of the suns," said Jonto. "The aruva will be here soon." He smiled for a moment. Then his face changed. "We need to find the archers. We have to stop them."

They tiptoed round the inside of the citadel, pausing to crouch behind its rocky foundations. Verity counted eleven archers dotted along the walls. She and Jonto divided the Followers into groups of three or four, each responsible for thwarting an archer.

"Break each and every arrow," said Jonto. "But be careful

of the poison tips. Do not hurt the archers. Remember that they are as much victims as we."

They sidled up to them stealthily. The archers were too busy watching the sky to see the Followers approaching.

Colours twisted above them. Verity looked towards the highlands. For a minute or two, nothing happened. Suddenly she saw them – the last remaining flock of aruva. At first they were just specks above the jungle. Soon they became clearer, nine birds flying in a diamond formation, swooping down towards the lowlands. The archers trained their bows above their heads. The Followers pounced, throwing them to the ground, seizing and breaking their arrows. But one of the archers had broken free. Fingers quivering, she pressed an arrow to her bow.

"Stop her!" cried Verity.

Beautiful music burst from the palace and with it the arrow shot into the sky.

The hall filled with the sound of string instruments, the trilling of flutes, the rumble of drums. The Keeper raised his arms and sang softly, with the voice of many.

Red flames of colour flushed across the domed ceiling of the Great Hall. Within this danced a kaleidoscope of greens, ambers and blues. The whole hall blazed from the rainbow that poured through the ceiling, playing across the faces of the Keeper's people, lighting the stone walls. Only the Keeper himself was untouched by the colours, lost beneath folds of black. He sang, this time with the voice of one man – a rich, deep, beautiful voice.

The people seated in the Great Hall watched wide-eyed. Seated among them, Sash felt the notes tugging at him, melting his resolve. Despite himself, his eyes prickled. Sitting so close to the islanders, sharing the colours and powerful music, he felt a part of something – something amazing. He knew that the Keeper was phoney; that the music came from a tape player hidden in the man's headdress. Yet a forbidden thought came to him: there was a power here, a power harnessed from the sky, from the joining of the suns.

Suddenly the music stopped. For a moment, the people in the hall sat in confused silence as the colours danced around them. The Keeper still stood before them on the platform, arms raised.

A new sound came from the tape player, not Pavarotti's tenor but Sash's urgent voice rising above a hiss of white noise: "People of Aqarti. You're here to praise the Keeper at the joining of the suns. But you're wrong about him. The Keeper isn't special. He's been pretending to have powers. But he's not a wizard or a magician. He's not anything. He's just a man!"

People gasped in astonishment. Hands covered gaping mouths. Standing on the platform, the Keeper shrank.

The voice from the tape player continued. "He wants to control you. That's why he's so scared of Followers – because they don't recognize his rule, because they won't bow down to him. In a moment he plans—"

The voice fell silent. The Keeper had grasped the head-dress with his fingertips and had managed to switch off the tape player. He straightened up, hands clasped together beneath black fabric.

"Can that be true?" cried one of the people in the crowded hall. "Is he really just a man?"

"He is!" shouted Sash. The euphoria he had felt on listen-ing to the "Keeper's voice" had vanished. In its wake, there was only self-disgust. He had allowed himself to be conned, even though he alone knew the truth. Shame surged through him, bubbling into anger. Leaping to his feet, Sash strug-gled between seated spectators to confront the Keeper. "I know who you are and I'm not scared of you!" he shouted. "I know why you sent me to that school! And I know why we moved to that stupid shop! You're sick!" He leapt at the Keeper and grabbed his mask. The man shrieked and pulled away, the headdress tumbling from his head to clatter against the floor. The mask tore off in Sash's hand.

Sash braced himself to see Max. But to his astonishment, he didn't recognize the pale, horrified face before him. The Keeper's cape had come down as the headdress fell. The head beneath it was balding.

"Who are you?" breathed Sash. The crowd watched, speechless. The colourful kaleidoscope still swirled around them but dark shadows crept between it. The ambers and pinks faded; the reds and blues deepened.

"What have you done?" choked the man, ashen.

307

"I thought..." Sash swallowed hard. A terrible wave of guilt soared through him. How could he have thought such a terrible thing? This man looked nothing like his father. And yet Sash had been positive that it was Max. Suddenly he remembered the words of Gertrude Trench, overheard on that Saturday in the shop: "Sometimes the mind plays tricks... Perhaps we see what we want to see."

The Keeper raised his hands to his cheeks. He ran his fingers over his own features, like a blind man exploring the contours of an unfamiliar face. "What have you done?" he repeated, shock turning to rage. He glared over his confused subjects. "I am still your leader!" he shouted. "Don't listen to this kid, this *traitor!* He's lying to you! It's all lies! I will cast a spell on any who believe him!" He raised his hands above his head, as though commanding dark forces. He spotted the group of guards who had previously surrounded Sash. "Seize the traitor! Take him to the dungeon!"

The guards glanced at each other uncertainly. One started towards Sash.

Sash dropped to his knees and scrambled for the head-dress. He could feel the tape player through the material. With a silent plea that the fall had not broken the machine, he hit the keys blindly. He heard the swirling sounds of the tape forwarding. He punched another key and Pavarotti's voice boomed out once more.

"You see!" cried Sash. "Watch his lips! They're not even moving! He isn't singing!"

More gasps from the spectators seated in the Great Hall.

The guard had reached Sash. His hand grasped his machete but he faltered. He looked around, at a loss. Pavarotti's rich tenor still rose from the fallen headdress, Italian words reaching mysteriously over the spectators.

The light faded. Beneath it, the Keeper's face shone a chilling blue. "You've ruined it!" he cried, pointing at Sash. He added, very quietly, "I'll kill you. I'll kill you..."

"He is no wizard!" said a young woman, rising. "All this time we have been bowing down to an imposter!"

"Did you hear how he speaks?" said someone else. "Both he and the boy... How strange they sound... How unusual they look."

"We followed his commands," said one guard to another. "We worshipped him, obeyed him without question. We helped him catch the Followers. He said they were evil, dangerous..."

The words echoed through the crowd. "Imposter ... nothing but a man..."

The twisting blues from the hole in the ceiling darkened into navy.

"You've ruined everything!" yelled the Keeper, leaping off the platform and throwing himself at Sash, who toppled backwards onto crowds of seated people. The Keeper landed heavily on top of him. The hall erupted into panic.

A thick hand covered in black cloth gripped Sash's throat. "How could you do this to me? I am a king! I am a *god*!"

he screamed in Sash's face. "Back in our world I was nothing! I was a caretaker once, years ago... Just a dogsbody to a load of selfish kids. I was nobody till I came here..."

Sash tried to twist out of the man's grip. "You're crazy," he wheezed. With a jolt of amazement, he realized this was the "careless caretaker" that James and Angus had spoken of. Maybe he had been listening to his tape player while working in the basement, and fallen with it into the Fleet. Struggling in the water, he must have tumbled through the portal. Somehow, the tape player survived – it was water-proof, suited for work in rainy weather. "East Heath College colours," Sash spluttered, realizing that the Keeper's use of red and black was no coincidence.

The Keeper screwed up his face and squeezed harder round Sash's throat. "They all treated me like dirt. Didn't I show them? I took their colours – I made them belong to *me*!"

Sash fought but no breath reached his lungs. His temples were thumping and pain throbbed behind his eyes. The Keeper was still shouting and small drops of spit gathered at the corners of his mouth. But his voice sounded distant. Sash's own lips moved soundlessly as his fingers tore at the Keeper's hands, desperately trying to release them.

"This is no wizard!" screamed a woman near by. "He is just a brute!"

"Get him off the boy, before he kills him!" yelled someone else.

"Take him to the dungeon! See how *he* likes it down there!"

The Keeper looked up in panic, forgetting Sash. He stumbled to his feet as Sash fell, gasping, against people sitting behind him. Gathering up his robe, the Keeper pushed through the crowd.

"Stop him!" cried a guard.

The sky fell black.

"Verity?" called Jonto.

"I'm just here!" she replied. "The archer..."

Jonto reached out and touched her shoulder. "She missed. The birds are still too far away."

Verity breathed a sigh of relief. "What's happening?" The sky was dark and starlit but no moon glowed above. Close by Followers talked anxiously among themselves and the archers sat against the walls, clutching their broken arrows in confusion.

"I do not understand... How can this be? It is the middle of the day! I have never heard of such a thing, I have never—" Jonto checked himself. "No, that is not quite right. It has happened before. It happened when the Keeper arrived in Aqarti. The sky blackened in the middle of the day."

"In the middle of the day?" repeated Verity. Yes, Manah had mentioned that. It was part of the reason that the people of the island had believed the Keeper to be special. "But it must be an eclipse," she said, without thinking. It hadn't occurred to her before.

"An 'eclipse'?" asked Jonto.

Verity nodded. "The moon is blocking the two suns. They're both in alignment because they're joining or whatever. We can't see them but they haven't disappeared, the moon's casting a shadow on Aqarti. That's why it's gone dark."

"But what can it mean?"

"It doesn't mean anything," said Verity. "It's just – well, it's just something that happens. It doesn't—" she broke off, remembering the riddle that had led her and Sash to Max Baranovski's trunk:

When earth and suns align, with moon betwixt
Until again the moon's dark intervention:
Hidden from the world a doorway opens

"Wait a minute," said Verity. "The portal opened during an eclipse ... that's how the Keeper got through." She was talking to herself. "I thought the reference to 'suns' was wrong when I first read it because ... because we only have one sun. But it wasn't a reference to our sun at all."

"I really do not understand what—"

"Oh no!" she shrieked, grasping what this meant. She reached out and gripped Jonto's arm. "It's like the riddle said: the portal opens on the first eclipse of the suns, and it shuts again on the second! The first eclipse happened when the Keeper arrived."

"When the Keeper arrived?"

312

"The first time that the sky went black in the middle of the day."

"And this is the second … the second 'eclipse' in Aqarti's history? Yes, I think that is true. But why—?"

"I need to find Sash! We have to get to Rising Beach!"

"Verity, what is it?" asked Jonto. "Is something wrong?"

Under the dim light of the stars, her pale eyes looked wild. "If we don't go now, we'll never get home! We'll be trapped here for ever!"

Mayhem descended on the Great Hall. Sash was shunted to one side as people hurried for the exits. They charged out of the palace beneath a dark sky, shouting for the capture of the Keeper. Struggling to his feet, Sash was jostled outside the palace walls. Although the suns had disappeared, there was enough starlight to see. Looking up to orient himself, Sash saw the Spiral Net blinking down at him but there was no sight of the moon at its centre.

"There he is!" cried a guard.

Sash rubbed his neck. He spotted a robed man hurrying through the citadel. Dressed in black, the Keeper was almost invisible, but starlight touched his balding head. The crowd stormed after him. Sash was drawn along with it, bewildered. He had never realized that his actions could have such a dramatic effect. Despite everything, he was alarmed at what was happening to the Keeper – scared at what the people of Aqarti would do to him now that they knew he was a fraud.

The Keeper bolted out of the citadel, beneath the entrance once guarded by the Bloodstone Bird. He wove between the high trees. Starlight barely made it through the gaps between the leaves, but the desperate Keeper lurched on blindly. With a jolt, Sash realized where the tyrant was going – he was making a break for the oval rocks, for the portal to the Fleet. He was escaping to London.

The Keeper struggled, tripping on his robe. Where the ground became sandy at the first palm tree, the crowds closed round him. Several guards stepped forward. Coming up behind them, Sash watched in horror.

"Your time has come!" spat a guard, approaching the Keeper with machete raised. "You shall terrorize this island no longer!"

"Stop!" A woman's voice rang over the din. "Stop at once! This is not our way!" She pushed through the baying throng. It was Zusa. Sash hadn't seen her since the Impossible Isles. Coming up behind her were Ren and Laars. "We are people of peace," Zusa went on breathlessly. "If we kill the Keeper – whoever he is – we shall be no better than he!"

"She is right!" someone agreed. "Let him go. His power is destroyed. His rule is over. It is not Great Aruva's way."

"Great Aruva's way..." echoed others, daring to utter the words publicly for the first time in years.

The guards surrounding the Keeper lowered their machetes, glancing back at the crowds. Their faces were silver. A blade of white light flashed beyond the moon.

As if possessed, the Keeper pushed between the guards, racing down to Rising Beach. The waters were slowly growing lighter from the reappearing suns. He splashed into the shallows, still covered in his floor-length robe. The people of Aqarti looked on. No one tried to stop him.

"The Keeper was an imposter! And now he is gone!" some whispered.

"Not Great Aruva's way…"

The Keeper swam through the placid water.

Sash watched from the beach. He could see the dark shapes of razor sharks floating at the edges of the reef. He tried to think what London would have been like in 1990, when the Football World Cup was hosted in Italy, when opera singer Luciano Pavarotti sang *Nessun Dorma* to throngs of eager football fans. Almost twenty years ago, an angry, bitter caretaker had fallen into the Fleet, beneath East Heath College, clutching his waterproof tape player. He had found himself in Aqarti. He had passed among sharks that didn't recognize his scent; he had been hailed a wizard.

But now, as the Keeper swam to the edges of the reef, the razor sharks shifted, nudging the coral impatiently. They sensed something familiar. A man who had lived on their island for years; no longer alien to their keen nostrils; no longer to be avoided. As the Keeper swam into open water, the sharks attacked. Feverishly, instantly, they fell upon the Keeper. The black robe sank without a sound. Bubbles broke on the surface of the water.

Rays of pink light shone beyond the moon, touching the tranquil sea. Plumes of blood drifted on the gentle current.

Sash shuddered. Some of the islanders were looking out to sea but others had turned away, distracted. Followers, who had escaped from the Keeper's dungeon, now walked among them in tearful reunion.

Sash heard laughter. "A new beginning," someone said.

"Sash? Is that you?"

For a moment, he thought it was Manah. He hardly recognized Verity with short hair. She moved as though to hug him but paused. Her face was golden beneath the emerging sun. "You're here…" She stood, smiling shyly at him.

"Of course I am." He didn't understand the change in her. The shyness seemed so unfamiliar, so inconsistent with the short hair and ruddy cheeks that gave her the look of a warrior.

"I thought you'd left … I thought you might have gone back to London," she said.

"I did. I had to get some batteries for the Keeper – he was just the school caretaker in the end. He needed batteries for a tape player. It's hard to explain…" Sash didn't know where to begin.

"So they let you return to London? Why did you come back?"

Sash shrugged. "Couldn't just leave you here, could I?"

Verity stared at him. "You came back for me?" she whispered.

Feeling embarrassed, Sash broke eye contact. He noticed a boy standing next to her.

"I am Jonto," said the boy. "Manah's brother. Have you seen her?"

Sash shook his head. "There are so many people..."

Shafts of violet escaped the moon, trailing over the lowlands and colouring the water.

Remembering, Verity cried: "It's an eclipse, and it's passing – I think the portal's closing! It's like the riddle, remember, 'the moon's dark intervention'!"

"Closing? Now?" said Sash. He scanned the oval rocks. No trace of the Keeper lingered. Even his blood had disappeared, had mingled with the ripples of the sea. Sash thought of London. Would anyone miss him if he never returned? He thought of a day like any other. Of school. Stuff the World. His father... He looked back over Aqarti. Beneath the kaleidoscope of colours, friends and family were embracing. The jungle rose behind them, alive with animals, buzzing with insects. Someone was stepping carefully between the palms. She was weighed down by a woven cage as she slipped over the fine sand.

"It's Manah!" said Sash.

Jonto spun round. "Manah?" He leapt up the sand to greet her, throwing his arms round her. The two of them joined Sash and Verity on the beach, flashing toothy grins. Jonto carried the cage. The aruva peeped out between the bars, green feathers flecked with red.

"The Keeper's reign is over. Could it be that we have you to thank for this?" asked Manah, raising her eyebrows.

Sash felt his cheeks redden. "We have to go, Manah. We have to go home." He glanced at Verity before continuing. "The truth is we're not from Trin. We—"

Manah raised a finger to her lips. She reached over to the cage and offered it to Sash and Verity. "Take the aruva," she said. "You want it... You came for it."

Verity gazed longingly at the bird.

Sash thought of the bright red feather in his father's study. How would Max react if Sash brought the bird back to him? Perhaps it would give him the fame he desired, the money and respect. No more shabby sofa; no more second-hand TV. No more standing on the outside look-ing in. And Max would be so happy, so grateful. Sash would be the golden boy, the son he always dreamed of. It could change everything...

Verity touched his arm.

Sash met her eye, cleared his throat. "It belongs here," he said.

Manah smiled. She didn't seem surprised.

Beams of colour burst beyond the moon. "The portal!" breathed Verity. She and Sash ran down to the shore.

"What are you doing? The razor sharks...!" Jonto shouted after them, haunted by the Keeper's gruesome death.

"We have no choice," Sash replied. "We have to hope for

the best. We have to risk it." He looked at Verity and she nodded.

Flying over the lowlands came the aruva. Their chiming voices stirred the air.

"The song of the sun!" cried Zusa, raising her hands.

The sky flooded with colour. Sash and Verity waded into the sea and swam towards the oval rocks. The razor sharks eyed them as they passed; they sniffed the water but kept their distance.

The islanders watched the birds, overcome with emotion. Standing next to Manah, Jonto lowered his eyes from the singing aruva. He spotted two figures swimming out beyond the reef. "Look!" he cried.

Others followed his gaze in time to see the figures disappear between the oval rocks. "Where did they go?" gasped Laars. "And how did they survive the sharks?"

"Magic," said Manah, catching Jonto's eye. She knelt beside the cage and pulled back the door.

For a moment, the bird hesitated, peering outside. Then it burst from the cage in a flutter of feathers, rising into the dazzling sky. Joining the chorus of chiming song. Meeting its flock beneath the light of two suns.

— Late for Latin —

At 6.02 a.m. on Friday morning, Sash arrived at the corner of Gully Lane. The street was dark, deserted.

He and Verity had only briefly passed through the River Fleet on their journey back to London. As they had swum through the portal, the light overhead had guided them to East Heath College. They had climbed through the uncovered manhole into the basement beneath the school. Sash had changed into his ill-fitting jeans, his sweater, parka and shabby trainers. He'd left Verity at her front drive, promising to return her suitcase. Then he began the long walk home to Kentish Town. He'd probably never talk to her again, not properly. He'd see her in class, of course, but that was different. In class they had never been friends. She had Camilla and the others. The portal to Aqarti was probably closed for ever. Why would she bother with him now?

Giddy with exhaustion, Sash wandered past the fried chicken shop. He stopped when he reached number 13. Above the door, the words "Stuff the World" were painted on a wooden board in old-fashioned lettering. He reached inside the pockets of his parka only to realize that he didn't have his key. That's right, he'd asked Gertrude Trench to lock up. His father wouldn't be home for another day. How would he get in?

Sash hardly had time to ponder this question. Someone shifted behind the security shutters. A moment later the front door clicked open. Hovering on the doorstep stood Max.

"Dad..." He didn't know what to say. Relief and shame coursed through him. How could he have imagined that Max was the Keeper? That thought seemed crazy now. Sash rubbed his tired eyes. Why was Max already home? Had he confused the days again? "I thought you were coming back tomorrow," he said sheepishly. He braced himself for his father's anger.

A streetlamp cast shadows around Max's eyes. "Gertrude called me at the hotel. She said you weren't staying with her. I was worried." His voice was surprisingly soft.

Sash bowed his head guiltily.

Max cleared his throat. "It scared me to think of you alone. I care about you, Sash. I know that I'm not good at showing it. When I thought that something might have happened to you..." His voice was hoarse.

Sash glanced up. His father's eyes were dewy. "I'm fine."

Max didn't seem to have heard him. "I met another taxidermist in Iceland. His daughter died of cancer last summer. We talked late into the night. He was so full of grief, and it reminded me of how I'd felt when your mother died. Perhaps I have pushed you away – I was scared of feeling such pain again. I realize now what madness that was. Because it means I have already lost you, and for nothing."

Self-consciously, Sash stared at his hands. "I'm still here, Dad."

"You have grown up and I hardly noticed. Soon you will be taller than me. And you were always so mature. Perhaps your childhood seemed briefer than those of others, less joyful... Perhaps that is my fault..."

"You shouldn't blame yourself. It must have been tough, after ... after Mum..." The word caught in Sash's throat. He never uttered it, not out loud. Because that was the past, and nobody talked about it, not normally. He swallowed and tried again: "You did the best you could."

"I should have tried harder. From now on, things will be different. There's still time. You're young, Sash. Your life is just beginning."

Sash nodded. But standing beneath the streetlamp on Gully Lane, he didn't feel young. He had seen more than many adults did in a lifetime – had travelled to the ends of the earth and back.

"Where were you last night?" Max asked.

Sash bit his lip. Could he tell his father about his journey to Aqarti? The bird of flames had been in his grasp, yet he had left it in its own world. How would Max react if he knew the degree of his son's deceit, if he realized that Sash had succeeded where he had failed? With a twinge of sadness he realized Max must never find out, that the world beyond the Fleet would be his alone – his and Verity's.

"A child should not have secrets."

"I'm not a child," said Sash, automatically, without thinking. As the words escaped his lips it struck him that this was an infantile complaint – a protest that only a child would make. He wanted to take it back, or to do something excessively childish: to shout, or laugh.

Max frowned, his dark eyebrows knitting over his eyes, and Sash wondered if his patience would finally snap. Then he sighed. "I can't blame you for having your secrets, can I? Not when I have mine. But things are going to change. I did a lot of thinking in Iceland. I've been wasting time. Wasting it on silly plans, on puzzles that cannot be solved. On foolish, pointless dreams... None of that matters now. No more secrets."

Sash blinked at his father. He searched his dark eyes. Could it be that Max knew he had ventured onto the Fleet? That he had found the portal? That he had seen the bird of flames?

"You're tired!" said Max suddenly. "Come, Sash. Come inside." He reached out his hand.

* * *

At seven o'clock on Monday morning, Sash swiped at his bleeping alarm. He rose and pulled back the curtains. It was still dark outside. For a moment, he thought of Aqarti, the land of two suns and endless light. He wondered what Manah was doing right now, reunited with her brother. He thought of the beautiful aruva and their chiming song.

As he walked towards the kitchen, he peered down the corridor to his father's study. The door was wide open.

"Dad?" Sash called.

Max appeared at the door, his face barely visible above armfuls of paper.

"What are you doing?"

"Time for a clear out." Max shoved the papers into a recycling bag. Sash could just see the top of the "Birds of the World" calendar popping out. "I wasn't really making good use of the space anyway," Max went on. "I thought this could be your room. You'll have a bit more privacy down the corridor. It's bigger too. We'll get rid of the old trunk and move your bed there. What do you think about that?"

Sash looked at his father. Could he be dreaming? Move his bed to where the trunk had been? He thought of sleeping above the underground river. It gave him a strange thrill. But what about Max's journeys on the Fleet? What about the hunt for the bird of flames? "That sounds…"

Max stood still, watching his son expectantly.

Sash smiled. "That sounds great."

Sash hurried into Hampstead and swung through the doors of East Heath College. As usual, he was late for class. Mr Mills would have something to say about it. Let him do his worst, thought Sash, heading towards the atrium. There was more to life than Latin – he knew that now.

He almost tripped in his haste. Glancing down he noticed that one of his shoelaces was untied. He lifted his eyes to see Verity standing by the double doors. She seemed different in school uniform. Her cropped hair had been styled. It gave her a cheeky look, like a pixie.

She beamed when she saw him but quickly rearranged her expression to one of disapproval. "Can't you be punctual for once in your life?" she scolded cheerfully.

"I guess not." Sash shrugged.

"Hopeless! Not like me. Dead punctual. Despite all the nonsense at home."

"How's it going? Did your parents get it sorted?"

"No, they did not!" she declared with mock indignation. "So much for 'friendship binds with song'. Dad's moving out. Some place in Marylebone. It's like you said, they do what they want." She glanced along the deserted corridor. Satisfied that they were alone, she dropped her guard. "To be honest, I'm gutted," Verity confided. Her eyes widened and Sash saw a vulnerability there that he hadn't noticed before. "I never thought this could happen to them... I'd do anything to keep them together." She threw him a sideways look. "Almost anything. But it's up to them, isn't it? It's their lives."

Sash nodded.

She smiled at him sadly. "And you were right. It's not the end of the world."

"Verity, I didn't mean..."

She shook her head. "It's true, Sash. I was a brat. And I was wrong about Manah. I thought she was just a schemer but she had better reasons than either of us. I'm not always the best judge of character."

Sash remembered how Verity had accused him of being like his father's stuffed animals, a spectator in his own life. Her words had stung, perhaps because there had been more than a little truth in them. Aqarti had changed him, made him stronger, and Verity had played a part in that. He reflected on his life in the days before Aqarti: alone at school, aloof at home. Another path was reaching out to him. A chance of a different life. *A better life.* "I don't know, you're not always wrong... And maybe the birds did something for us after all." His cheeks flushed red.

Seeing his discomfort, her tone was instantly light-hearted. "So that's that – my parents are happily married no longer." She wiped her hands together, grinning impishly. "I'm going to make them buy me a pony. Might as well guilt them a little, right?" She winked.

Sash shoved her playfully on the back. As they passed through the double doors into the atrium, he knelt to tie his shoelace. For a moment he thought he could hear something – a distant gush of water beneath the ground.

"Come *on!*" said Verity.

Shaking his head, Sash rose to his feet. They went into class together.

Lost and alone, a young cat called Mati seeks acceptance from a community of street cats at Cressida Lock. But Mati is no ordinary cat ... and Mithos, the mysterious assassin on his trail, knows it. To defeat his enemies, Mati must learn to harness an ancient feline power – a power so deadly that it threatens to destroy not only his friends but every cat on earth.

BY INBALI ISERLES

Rachel and Adam are sent to stay with their grandmother, following their parents' divorce. But the quiet English village where their mother was born is a sinister and unsettling place. Is there a genuinely dark heart beating beneath the thatched roofs of the picturesque village of Triskellion? Against a brooding background of very real danger, the two young outsiders follow an incredible trail on an archaeological adventure with a startling paranormal twist. In a community that has existed in the same place for centuries, many terrible secrets lie hidden, and the villagers of Triskellion have a great deal to protect...

By Will Peterson

When Will Lightfoot crashes his father's motorbike, he is catapulted to another world – one of knights, mages and talking creatures, where everything is familiar yet strange: the world of Story. Ages ago, the Perilous Realm fell under the shadow of the Night King and his desire to control all stories. Now, unwillingly caught up in the struggle against this ancient evil, Will must face a host of perils if he is ever to find the gateless gate that will take him home.

BY THOMAS WHARTON